Praise for *Kilts and Daggers*

"A classic story of disdain leading to love. Grace and Fagan make visiting the Highlands worth the trip."

—*Publishers Weekly*

"Roberts continues to craft fast-moving, well-written plots populated by real-life characters...a fascinating romance."

—*RT Book Reviews*

"Captivating...a delightful, exciting, and romantic Highland book."

—*Fresh Fiction*

Praise for *My Highland Spy*

"An exciting Highland tale of intrigue, betrayal, and love."

—Hannah Howell, *New York Times* bestselling author of *Highland Master*

"A master of Highland romance."

—Becky Condit of *USA Today*

"This book begs to be read and reread."

—*RT Book Reviews*

"Beautiful! This book has it all. A gorgeous English spy. A handsome Highland laird with a heart of gold."
—*Night Owl Reviews*, 4.5 Stars, Reviewer Top Pick

Praise for *Temptation in a Kilt*

"Filled with everything I love most about Highland romance."

—Melissa Mayhue, award-winning author of *Anywhere in Time*

"Full of intrigue and a sensual, believable romance, this book captivates the reader immediately."

—*RT Book Reviews*

"Everything a Scottish romance should be. Beautifully written, this story will captivate you from the very first page, bringing the Highlands to life right before your eyes."

—*Romance Junkies*

"An exciting Highland adventure with sensual and compelling romance."

—Amanda Forester, acclaimed author of *True Highland Spirit* and *A Midsummer Bride*

KILL *OR* BE KILT

VICTORIA ROBERTS

sourcebooks
casablanca

Published by Sourcebooks Casablanca, an imprint of Sourcebooks, Inc.
P.O. Box 4410, Naperville, Illinois 60567-4410
(630) 961-3900
Fax: (630) 961-2168
www.sourcebooks.com

Printed and bound in Canada
MBP 10 9 8 7 6 5 4 3 2 1

To Mary Grace, the woman who had the courage to gaze into the face of madness and encourage a dream. We are kindred spirits, you and I, and I'm so thankful fate allowed our paths to cross. Tha gaol agam ort!

Some books are lies frae end to end,
And some great lies were never penn'd...

—Robert Burns

One

Sutherland, Scottish Highlands, 1613

THIS WAS HIS LAST CHANCE TO TURN AROUND AND bolt from the gates as if his arse was afire. Against his better judgment, he kept his eyes forward, his hands steady, and he tried not to pay any heed to the warning voice that whispered in his head.

Laird Ian Munro wasn't aware of the death grip he held on the reins of his mount as he approached the portcullis. He'd sworn that he'd never again set foot on Sutherland lands as long as the four Walsingham sisters lived under the same roof as his friend. He was no coward, but between the troubles with the Gordon, Stewart, and the damn mercenaries, he'd made it a point to stay on his own lands.

Until now.

Laird Ruairi Sutherland's home was a fortified castle with round turrets, a square watchtower, and a curtain wall that was twenty feet thick at the widest point. Yet, to Ian's surprise, the stone structure wasn't strong enough to hold the wily Walsinghams at bay.

He passed the dangerous cliffs on the left, and to his right was a lush forest. He supposed he could always take a leap to the left if he found himself trapped within the walls with no means of escape.

As he reached the point of no return, his face clouded with uneasiness because the guards had already greeted him from the gatehouse. Ian continued through to the bailey and halted, hesitantly releasing the reins of his horse to the stable hand. Ruairi's captain greeted him with a brotherly slap on the back.

"Munro, how long has it been, my friend?" Fagan Murray's dark hair hung well below his shoulders, and he wore a kilt of green, black, blue, white, and orange—the Sutherland tartan.

"'Tis good to see ye, Fagan." Ian gazed around the courtyard, breathing a sigh of relief no Walsinghams were in sight.

"Then tell me. Why have we nae seen your face since Grace and I wed? Ye know it has been almost three years since we've last set eyes upon ye."

Ian raised his eyebrows and placed his hand over his heart. "Truly? Has it been that long?"

Fagan lowered his voice and playfully balled his fist into Ian's arm. "To be truthful, I ne'er thought of ye as a coward."

"I'm nay coward, but as I told ye before, keep your brood here because I sure as hell donna want them crossing the borders to my lands. I have enough troubles of my own."

Fagan chuckled. "Come. Ruairi's been expecting ye, and we'll have some food and drink to celebrate your return."

They entered the great hall, and Ian involuntarily burst into a smile. Tapestries remained on the walls that depicted swords, shields, and men in the throes of battle. He recalled the time when Fagan's wife, Grace, had insisted that Ruairi remove the wall hangings before her wedding day because she didn't favor them. Ian pursed his mouth in satisfaction when he realized Ruairi's bollocks were still in place, and he hadn't succumbed to the will of the women after all. Perhaps there was hope for his friend yet.

"Munro, I can nae believe ye're standing here in my great hall as I live and breathe." Ruairi's straight, long, chestnut hair had traces of red and fell to his shoulder blades. A plaid rested over his shoulder, and he sported the traditional Sutherland kilt. With a broadsword sheathed at his waist, his friend looked exactly as Ian had remembered him. "*Fàilte. Ciamar a tha thu?*" Ruairi asked warmly. *Welcome. How are you?*

"*Tha gu math.*" *I am fine.* Ian embraced the man who was like a brother to him. "'Tis good to see ye, Ruairi." Without warning, a hand clasped Ian's shoulder from behind, and he turned.

"I'm glad to see ye did nae live up to your promise. Ye did set foot on Da's lands again."

"Torquil?" With his reddish-brown hair and green eyes, Torquil was the picture of Ruairi. "Ye have grown. Soon I think there might be a need to fear ye on the battlefield. What age is upon ye now, lad?"

The man who was no longer a boy smiled from ear to ear. "I am fifteen."

A lovely lass stood beside Torquil, and she was poking him in the ribs with her finger. "Fifteen, perhaps, but he behaves more like he's ten." Blond locks framed her oval face. She had sparkling blue eyes and wore an emerald dress that hugged her young frame.

"Lady Katherine?" asked Ian.

"Yes, it's lovely to see you again, Laird Munro."

Ian shook his head as if he'd consumed too much ale. He couldn't believe so much had changed. The last time he'd seen the girl she was only nine. Ruairi's wife approached them, and her wealth of red hair dangled in loose tendrils that softened her face. She'd always looked elegant and graceful, and Ian was glad to see some things hadn't changed.

He kissed the top of her hand. "Lady Ravenna, ye're still as bonny as the day that I met ye."

"Thank you, Laird Munro. Although I don't know how much longer I'll appear this way." She lowered her hands and cradled her stomach in a gentle gesture. "Ruairi and I are expecting another child. We're hoping for a son to have a brother for Mary."

"*Another* bairn?" He forced a demure smile. "Please accept my condolen…er, congratulations to ye both."

Lady Katherine clapped her hands together. "I'm delighted that I'm going to be an aunt again. I do hope Ravenna has another girl."

Ian didn't know what to say in the presence of the women, but Torquil was the only man among them who found his voice.

"Kat, donna even jest about something like that. I think ye might put Da in an early grave."

Ruairi gave Ian a knowing look.

"If it wasn't for me and my sisters, this castle—and the men within it—would be running wild. You should be thankful you have us here to keep you all out of harm's way."

Torquil playfully wrapped his arm around Kat's neck and rubbed his knuckles over the top of her head. "I do like it when ye try."

Ian would be sure to pray long and hard that Ravenna carried a boy because the last Ruairi needed was another cunning female under his roof. If it wasn't bad enough that Ravenna was a "retired" English spy, her haughty sister, Grace, had even married Fagan. Oh, and that wasn't all the poor bastard was made to endure. After Ruairi had spoken his vows, he'd taken in all three of his wife's sisters.

As Ravenna took her leave from the hall, Kat wandered off with Torquil. The men took their seats at the long wooden table on the dais, and Ruairi poured them all a drink. He placed a tankard in front of Ian and smiled. "Here. Ye look like ye could use one—or many."

"Och, aye." He lifted the tankard to his lips and spotted something over the rim. Kat and Torquil sat on a bench...together, close. Ian briefly closed his eyes. The two of them used to run away from each other, avoiding the other like the plague. Now he wouldn't be shocked if he saw the two holding hands or making wooing gestures toward one another.

"Something in my gut told me that I should've just met all of ye in London," said Ian. When a growl escaped him and his mouth pulled into a sour grin, Ruairi waved him off.

"There's only so much Ravenna and her uncle can do to keep King James at bay. We've been fortunate that we have nae had to attend court in years. Besides, with the recent passing of Prince Henry, we should pay our respects to the king in order to stay in his good graces. I thought it would be good for us to travel to London at the same time. More to the point, ye know how much we enjoy the pleasure of your company. We always have such a damn good time when we're together, eh?" Ruairi held up his tankard in mock salute.

Ian lifted a brow. "Aye. I remember all the good times we've had with your father-in-law, the Stewart, Redshanks, and let's nae forget about the English spies ye shelter under your roof."

A young woman stepped in front of the dais and cleared her throat. She had reddish-brown hair that hung in loose waves down her back. Her figure was slender and regal, and Ian could have easily drowned in her emerald eyes. But what captured his attention the most was the way the lass carried herself—confident, yet seemingly unaware of her true beauty.

She wore a black gown with hanging sleeves, and the embroidered petticoat under her skirts was lined in gray. With the added reticella lace collar and cuffs dyed with yellow starch, she looked as though she should have been at the English court rather than in the Scottish Highlands.

"Pardon me, Ruairi. Ravenna wanted me to tell you that we're taking little Mary to the beach. We won't be long. We'll be in the garden until the mounts are readied, if you need us."

When the woman's eyes met Ian's, something clicked in his mind. His face burned as he remembered.

He shifted in the seat and pulled his tunic away from his chest. Why was the room suddenly hot? He felt like he was suffocating in the middle of the Sutherland great hall.

God help him.

This was the same young chit who had pined after him, following him around the castle and nipping at his heels like Angus, Ruairi's black wolf. But like everything else that had transformed around here, so had she. She was no longer a girl but had become an enchantress—still young, but beautiful nevertheless. His musings were interrupted by a male voice.

"Munro, ye do remember Lady Elizabeth, eh?"

How could he forget the reason why he'd avoided Sutherland lands for the past three years?

❧

Laird Ian Munro was as daunting—and handsome—as Elizabeth remembered him. His long, red hair fell down to his elbows in complete disarray. His broad shoulders looked bigger than she'd recalled, and wisps of light hair curled against the V of his open shirt. He had a strong, chiseled jaw and green eyes that would make any woman swoon.

For goodness' sake, she thought—prayed—she was over this foolish fancy she'd had for him. After all, she'd been only fifteen at the time. Her brother-in-law often jested that women were terrified of Ian's wild appearance. The man even had a reputation for frightening men on the battlefield by his fierce looks alone. She supposed that's why her family was shocked when she'd shown an interest in him. But there was something about Ian that always drew her like a magnet.

Elizabeth willed herself to speak only to Ruairi and was proud that she didn't nervously stammer her words in front of the men. She had no idea how she'd managed to avoid Ian's gaze for that long. But when Ruairi asked if Laird Munro remembered her, she made a grave error in judgment.

She looked into Ian's eyes.

There was tingling in the pit of her stomach, and she found herself extremely conscious of his virile appeal. His nearness was overwhelming. Her pulse pounded, and she couldn't breathe as memories of the past flooded her with emotion.

Irked by her response to him, Elizabeth was determined to show the laird she wasn't the same young, stupid, senseless girl he'd known years ago. She'd changed, grown. And she needed to let him know that his presence no longer affected her the way it had in the past.

"Laird Munro, what a pleasure to see you again. You look well," she said with as much indifference as she could muster. She gazed back at Ruairi. "Ravenna and Grace are waiting for me in the garden. Pray excuse me."

Elizabeth resisted the urge to bolt out of the hall and not look back. She slowed her pace as much as she could so as not to look as though she was trying to flee. She was a Walsingham, and her family never ran from anything or anyone.

Kat followed Elizabeth out of the great hall, and Elizabeth said a silent prayer of thanks when she made it to the safety of the gardens. The scent of flowers wafted through the air, and blooms lined the garden path. This was the time of year she favored. They made their way toward a stone wall about waist high. Stretching her neck, Elizabeth leaned forward and glanced over the structure.

The blue waves of the ocean crashed onto the rocky shore below. She closed her eyes, and the sound was so peaceful, soothing. She enjoyed the sea wholeheartedly and found her calm demeanor was finally returning.

"The mounts will be ready soon." Ravenna was holding her daughter in her arms. She brushed her hand over Mary's tiny head, smoothing the girl's red curls.

As Grace approached, she lifted her arms into the air. "Time to give her up, Sister. Come to your Auntie Grace, Mary."

"I wonder who your new baby will resemble the most," said Kat.

The sisters all laughed in response when they'd realized what Kat meant. Ravenna had red hair, Kat had beautiful blond locks, Grace's hair was a warm-colored brown with golden strands, and Elizabeth's was more of a reddish-brown. Their mother and Uncle Walter didn't look like brother and sister either. Mother had pale skin, and Uncle Walter's was much darker. Everyone said the man looked like a pirate with his dark looks and cool demeanor. He always had an air of command about him, as if he were the captain of a ship on a stormy sea. At least, that's what Grace always said.

"I almost forgot to ask you, Elizabeth," said Grace.

Elizabeth schooled her expression to one of innocence because she knew what was coming next. "How do you feel seeing Laird Munro again?"

Grace was dying to ask that bloody question, and Elizabeth knew it. As she'd expected, her sisters waited for a response. In order to avoid prying eyes, Elizabeth waved her hand in a dismissive gesture. "I was only fifteen. That passing fancy has long since fled." For added measure, she gave a look of disgust in the event her sisters hadn't believed her words.

"I'm pleased to hear that you've finally come to your senses. It certainly took you long enough." Grace always knew what not to say. As Elizabeth was about to give her sister a piece of her mind, Kat grabbed Grace's arm.

"Did I hear you correctly? Elizabeth had a fancy for Laird Munro?" Kat's head whipped back to Elizabeth. "Did you?" Elizabeth shrugged, and Kat's expression bordered on mockery. "What could you possibly see in that man? Not only is he very large, but I don't think he's very attractive with all that unruly red hair."

Elizabeth briefly closed her eyes, her patience wearing thin. "'Good Lord Boyet, my beauty, though but mean, needs not the painted flourish of your praise: Beauty is bought by judgment of the eye, not uttered by base sale of chapmen's tongues.'"

"Pardon?"

"Shakespeare, Kat. Perhaps you should be taking your studies more seriously if you've never heard of *Love's Labour's Lost*."

"Don't pay her any heed," said Grace. "She always quotes literary works when she's in a foul mood."

As they walked through the gardens waiting for the horses to be readied, Elizabeth felt more and more irritable, not that Grace helped matters. Her sister had no right to lecture anyone, especially since she'd never even followed her own advice. There had been a time when Grace despised Scotland and the captain of Ruairi's guard, but now, here she was living in the Highlands and married to Fagan.

Joy bubbled in Ravenna's laugh. Elizabeth wasn't a jealous person, but she was envious of the love her sister found with Ruairi. Even more so since the two had now started a family of their own. The more Elizabeth pondered the matter, the worse she felt. Ravenna had Ruairi, Grace had Fagan, Kat and Torquil were inseparable, and Elizabeth had no one but Angus to confide in. But lately, even the black wolf had parted from her company. She could only find the animal either with the men or out stalking small game in the woods.

When they entered the bailey, the horses were already saddled. The stable hand had just brought Elizabeth's chestnut mare over to the mounting block when a rider came through the gates with Angus trailing on his heels.

"I have a message for Laird Sutherland."

"I'll find him, Ravenna." Elizabeth lifted her skirts and walked with hurried purpose into the great hall. She wasn't a bit surprised when she found the men in the same place she'd left them with tankards in hand. All eyes were upon her as she made her way toward the dais.

"I thought ye were going to the beach. Is something amiss?" asked Ruairi.

"There's a messenger waiting for you in the bailey."
Ruairi stood, and Elizabeth didn't wait around to see
who followed.

When Ruairi entered the courtyard, he talked
briefly with the messenger and then broke the seal
of a letter that was handed to him. Although her
brother-in-law always had an air of authority and the
appearance of one who demanded instant obedience,
his face was bleak. He dismissed the man and stood
as still as a statue. She'd known him long enough to
recognize when something was troubling him, and
this was clearly one of those times.

"What is it, Ruairi? What has happened?" asked
Ravenna.

Fagan, Torquil, and Ian came into the bailey at the
same time Ruairi approached Ravenna, giving her a
compassionate smile. But when he reached his wife,
he hesitated, gazing down at the letter as if he was
having second thoughts.

Elizabeth had never seen the man so unsettled,
and that frightened her. Ruairi was always a rock,
confident with his every move. After several moments,
he handed Ravenna the missive. As her sister read the
contents, a glazed look of despair washed over her
face. When she burst into tears, Elizabeth's spirits sank
even lower.

Ruairi pulled Ravenna into the circle of his arms
and kissed the top of her head. "I'm sorry, Wife. I'm
truly sorry." He pulled back and wiped her tears with
his thumbs. "But ye can nae allow yourself to be so
distraught and must consider your health and that of
our bairn."

"What has happened?" asked Grace.

Ravenna turned and faced her sisters. The pain in her eyes was unbearable. "Uncle Walter is dead."

Elizabeth gulped hard, hot tears falling down her cheeks. She could feel her throat close up and started to tremble. As her family embraced each other, she stood alone with only her misery to accompany her.

Uncle Walter was dead.

He was not coming back. She would never see him again for as long as she lived and breathed. The pain was insufferable, and she felt an acute sense of loss. When a large hand gently wrapped around her midriff, Elizabeth gasped. Green eyes studied her intently, and she lowered her gaze.

Ian pressed his body tightly to hers, and his arms encircled her. "Lass, let me offer ye comfort," he whispered, his breath hot against her ear. "I'm sorry for the loss of your uncle. Mildmay was a good man. He'll be sorely missed."

At first she tried to resist being held in Ian's arms, but then she buried her face against the corded muscles of his chest and yielded to the compulsive sobs that shook her. Her feelings toward him at this instant had no significance whatsoever because this was the second time she'd lost a father in her lifetime.

And that was the moment Elizabeth realized her life would never be the same again.

Two

IF IT WEREN'T FOR GRACE'S ENDLESS PRATTLE, Elizabeth would've closed her eyes in the carriage long ago. Her sister's words grated on her nerves, sticking to her like wet blades of grass. Just when Elizabeth allowed herself to believe that she would never be rescued from this torment, she heard the voice of an angel.

"It's been *three* hours since we've taken our leave. Will you please do us all a favor and close your mouth?" asked Ravenna. She shifted her weight on the seat and let out a heavy sigh.

"Here, let me help you." Elizabeth sat forward and moved the pillow out from behind Ravenna's back, plumping it.

Grace spoke in a whisper. "You should be thanking me that Mary is asleep in my arms. I think the sound of my voice lulls her."

"If only all of us could be as fortunate," replied Ravenna. As Elizabeth replaced the pillow at Ravenna's back, her sister smiled her thanks. Lowering her hands, she cradled her stomach. "My body isn't even showing that I'm with child yet, and already I'm uncomfortable."

When Kat reined in her horse beside the carriage, waved, and then rode off, Elizabeth laughed. "I believe our sister might ride that mount the entire way to England with the men if they'd let her. One would think her bottom would be sore by now."

"Mmm… No doubt she follows Torquil. Have you taken notice of the two of them lately? Do you want to know what I think?" asked Grace.

"No!" said Elizabeth and Ravenna at the same time.

When Mary cried, Grace snarled at them as she tried to soothe her niece. "You've both gone and done it now."

Ravenna pounded on the roof of the coach as it slowed to a halt. "Just as well. I need to feed her." Ravenna's eyes met Elizabeth's. "Besides, I think we could all use a rest."

Elizabeth didn't wait for the driver's hand and stepped down from the coach into the glade. She walked with hurried purpose, and branches cracked under her feet as she made a mad dash through the brush. It wasn't long before a bunch of thistles attacked the hem of her skirts, and she was pulling and tugging to free her dress. As she stepped behind a bush to see to her personal needs, she yelped in pain.

She should've known better than to lower herself too far to the ground. Something pricked her bare bottom. Closing her eyes, she stood. She glanced over her shoulder, and the unyielding patch of nettles appeared as though they mocked her for being so careless. After reaching behind her and determining no unwanted remnants of the dreaded plant remained, she dropped her skirts and wandered deeper into the forest.

Although the summer solstice would soon be upon them, spring had bloomed in the Highlands like a sigh of relief after the long, dark months of winter. Leaves were green, blossoming flowers blanketed the fields, and the sun was shining. If she weren't so distraught over Uncle Walter's death or irritated by her sister, this would have been a perfect day.

Elizabeth jumped when something snapped behind her.

"'Tis only me," said Laird Munro. "I did nae mean to startle ye. Are ye hurt? I heard ye cry out." He gazed into the forest and, as if he was expecting something to appear, uncertainty crept into his expression.

Rays of sunlight through the pine trees cast his face in contorted shadows. His long, red hair was ruffled by the wind. He looked powerful standing there in his kilt and tunic, not to mention the hand that rested on the hilt of a very large broadsword strapped to his waist. There were age lines around his mouth and eyes, but she'd barely noticed. After all these years, Ian still had a commanding way about him, but she certainly wasn't going to answer him with the truth—well, at least not all of it.

"Nettles pricked me."

He closed the distance between them. "Do ye want me to have a look? Ye donna want to leave any nettles beneath the skin."

"Thank you, but there's no need. I'm certain nothing remains." An unwelcome blush crept into her cheeks as he held up a large flask.

"If ye pour water over it, the pain will lessen. Where did the wee bastards pierce your skin?"

She felt her face turn to crimson. "I don't think I need the water, but thank you just the same."

"If ye change your mind, lass, let me know." Ian secured the flask on his belt. "We're resting the horses, but ye should nae be wandering this far into the trees. Let me escort ye back."

Elizabeth wasn't about to defy his order. As she walked beside the laird, she silently cursed when the memory of being held in his arms in the bailey came to mind. But as quickly as the thought emerged out of nowhere, the feeling passed. She girded herself with resolve, refusing to relive the humiliation of the past.

Silence lengthened between them, making her uncomfortable. She was helpless to halt her embarrassment, not only for the nettles, but for so brazenly stalking—*pining*—after the man when she was younger. To her amazement, her mood became buoyant when they reached the clearing.

Ravenna's hand was on the small of her aching back. Grace's fingers were pressed on her temple as she held a screaming Mary, and Kat was rubbing her sore bottom. Only hours from home, and her sisters were weary from their travels. They wouldn't reach London for weeks and had a long ride ahead, even more so with Grace pestering everyone in the same carriage. Perhaps their youngest sister had the right idea after all. Then again, Elizabeth quickly curtailed the thought. She'd rather be uncomfortable in the carriage with her sisters than face a gamut of emotions riding next to Ian.

She glanced to her right, and he was no longer by her side. Her eyes searched around the glade until she found him. As he was patting his horse on the neck, she realized that he and the animal looked as though they were made for each other—both massive in size. When Ian caught her staring, she lowered her gaze to the ground and gave herself a firm reminder that she was no longer fifteen.

∽

God was punishing him. There was no other reason. They'd only been riding for a few hours before they had to stop, and Ian already had to round up one lass who'd wandered from the group. At least the women rode in the carriage. If he had to listen to their incessant pecking the entire way to England, he might've run himself through with his sword before it was too late and he had to suffer another moment in their presence. Even though Lady Katherine rode with the men, he was thankful she only conversed with Torquil.

Ian approached one of the carriages and was untying the reins of two packhorses when Ruairi, Fagan, and three Sutherland guards returned from watering their mounts. "Ye might want to have a wee chat with your women," he called out.

Fagan chuckled as he tethered his horse to a tree. "What did my wife do now, Munro?"

"For once your wife is nae the problem. I found Lady Elizabeth wandering around the forest alone. Did ye nae tell them to stay close?"

"Och, aye, but I'll talk to them again," said Ruairi. "I usually have to have words with them three or four times before they listen."

Ian glanced at the women, and his eyes met Elizabeth's. He forced his tight expression into a smile, but she dropped her gaze to the ground before she saw it.

He led the mounts to the stream, pondering the affections Elizabeth had held for him when she was but a mere child. Not that she was that much older now, but she'd become a lovely young woman. In fact, the regal curves under her blue dress reminded him of that. For one absurd moment, he contemplated what it would be like to have the lass by his side.

When the realization washed over him of the price he would pay for being involved with a Walsingham, his priorities were once again set to path. Becoming entangled with one sister meant you got them all— willing or not—and he was not as daft as his best friends to take on such challenges. Furthermore, it wasn't as if Elizabeth still wanted anything to do with him. The lass could barely stand to be held in his arms when he'd offered her comfort for the loss of her uncle, and as a result, she still couldn't look him in the eye.

"These are the last two." Fagan dropped the reins of the mounts as the animals drank from the stream. He pulled out his flask and handed it to Ian.

The fiery liquid burned Ian's throat. He paused, and then took another drink. "*Mòran taing.*" *Thank you very much.* He gave the flask back to Fagan and lifted a brow when his friend took an even longer swig.

"I think this is going to be a long journey." Fagan glanced around, lowering his voice. "The women—"

"I dare you to finish that sentence, Husband."

Grace stood there with her oval face pointed daintily in the air. Her brownish-gold hair was pulled up on the top of her head, and she wore a green traveling dress. Although all the Walsingham sisters were beautiful, this particular temptress had a bite that could bring a man to his knees. She was nothing but trouble.

Fagan's eyes widened. "I was only going to say if nae for the women accompanying us, the trip to London would nae be as pleasurable."

When the lass folded her arms over her chest and cast a look of death upon her husband, Ian led the horses away and murmured, "Good luck, my friend."

"Coward," said Fagan with a scowl.

Ian fled the scene of the battle before it had even begun. He was far from a coward, but there was no way in hell he was going to stick around for that confrontation. There were several reasons why he was not wed. And right now, he savored every one.

৵৽

Elizabeth settled back into the seat of the carriage as Mary rested her little head on her chest. She was so soft, warm, and tiny. Elizabeth covered her niece with a blanket and kissed the top of her curls. Mary's breathing was slow, and she was now in a peaceful slumber like her mother, who sat across from them.

As Elizabeth brushed her finger gently over her niece's cheek, she was filled with a sense of longing. She wanted to be a mother some day and thought she might be a good one. But that couldn't happen without a husband first, and her options were quite limited in the Scottish Highlands.

"You're so good with her," said Ravenna.

"I thought you were sleeping."

Ravenna sat up and stretched her back. "You'll learn there's no such thing when you have a child of your own." She reached out and patted Elizabeth on the knee. "I don't think we're going to make it to the inn this eve. We should be stopping soon." She nudged Grace in the arm. "I know I shouldn't ask, but why are you so quiet?"

"I've been thinking about Uncle Walter. He's always been so good to us. And poor Aunt Mary... I wish we could've been there for the funeral."

"I do too, but they couldn't hold his body for weeks until our arriv—"

Grace held up her hand. "You don't need to explain."

"I'm certain Aunt Mary will be all right. She knew when we moved to the Highlands that we would be far from home—England," said Elizabeth. "But I can't help thinking about Uncle Walter too. We're all we have left."

Grace placed her hand over Elizabeth's. "We'll always be a family, and now we have Fagan, Ruairi, and Torquil too."

She understood that her sister was trying to make her feel better for once, but Grace's words only made Elizabeth think about the future even more. Of course, no one lived forever, but Uncle Walter had been a strong man. She was reminded that life could be stripped away without reason or warning.

As the carriage slowed, a part of her was thankful they didn't make it to the inn. Although a soft bed would've been welcome, she needed to breathe fresh air after being confined all day. The last time she'd slept under the stars was when she'd moved to the Highlands with her sisters.

Kat was helping Torquil secure a post in the ground, and Ravenna and Grace were seeing to Mary. As the men were setting up tents and taking care of the horses, Elizabeth was becoming restless. She needed to occupy herself. Spotting one of Ruairi's guards, she closed the distance between them. She held out her hand for the reins he had just untied.

"Let me help you with that. I'll water them. I don't mind."

He hesitated, looking at her as though she had three heads. "This is nay task for a lady. Why are ye nae over there with the women?" He abruptly flinched and took a step back, a strange look flashing in his eyes.

She whipped her head around at the same time the reins were shoved into her hand. Ian towered over the guard and was giving him a steely gaze as if he'd run the poor man through right where he stood. From the look of apprehension on the guard's face, Elizabeth felt sorry for him, especially when he didn't linger.

"Laird Munro, did you threaten him?"

Ian released the stern gaze he cast upon the fleeing guard, and his expression softened. "I did nae say a word. If ye want to water the horses, have at it, lass." He lowered his head and spoke in a whisper. "Speak in truth. Is Lady Grace driving ye mad?"

The corners of her lips lifted into a smile. "You have no idea." She couldn't believe Ian read her thoughts, but her sister's candid behavior wasn't exactly a secret.

When his eyes widened, Elizabeth's cheeks flushed

when she discovered her hand resting on his arm. She quickly removed her fingers from Ian's solid body. Not only was she embarrassed for her brazenness, but the man felt like a rock beneath her touch.

⤫

Ian volunteered with one of Ruairi's guards to take first watch. It wasn't as if he could sleep now anyway. In a few weeks, he would set foot on English soil, something that took a piece of his soul every time he made the journey. At least Ravenna had been able to stay their yearly trips to England for a few years. Who would've thought knowing a retired spy for the Crown could have its advantages?

He leaned his head against a tree trunk and watched the flickering flames dance well into the night. Everything was silent except for the occasional popping sounds of the wood in the fire.

Something moved out of the corner of his eye.

Elizabeth smoothed down her skirts and walked quietly into the brush. When she returned to the glade, she stood on the other side of the fire, gazing into the glowing embers as if they told a secret. He didn't think she saw him sitting there until she stepped around the flames and approached him.

"Isn't one of the guards supposed to relieve you? You've been keeping watch for hours."

"I did nae want to wake them. Besides, I'm nae able to sleep. What are ye doing up and about?" When she gestured to the trees, he added, "Why can ye nae sleep? Is the ground too uncomfortable for your liking?" He had a difficult time keeping the sarcasm from his voice because he knew the women were disappointed they didn't make it to the inn this eve. Heaven forbid the lasses had to sleep in the open air.

"No. If you must know, I was thinking about Uncle Walter," she replied in a clipped tone.

"Why donna ye sit?" he asked in a gentle voice. He didn't mean to cause her more pain. When she hesitated and couldn't meet his eyes again, he decided he wasn't giving her the opportunity to retreat. Leaning slightly forward, Ian lengthened his plaid from the back of his kilt and spread it on the ground beside him. "I may bark, but I give ye my word that I will nae bite ye. If ye can nae sleep, sit." He patted his hand on the plaid.

"Thank you, Laird Munro." Elizabeth lowered herself to the ground and fixed her skirts.

"My apologies ye're distraught this eve. As I told ye before, Mildmay was a good man."

She turned her head to the side, using her hand to shield her eyes from him. He had a feeling she was guarding her tears, especially when her voice became unsteady. "One would think I'd be able to cope with death by now—Mother, Father, Uncle Walter."

"'Tis foolish to think anyone can prepare for losing someone, especially when 'tis unexpected. But if I were ye, I'd be more distraught over having to ride with Lady Grace the entire way to England."

A laugh escaped her. "Are you attempting to make me feel better?"

Ian shrugged. "I donna know. Is it working?"

"Perhaps."

The firelight cast Elizabeth in an angelic glow, and her smile warmed him in the cool night air.

"It's so peaceful and quiet out here at night."

"Ye have noticed Lady Grace is sleeping, eh?"

"There is truth to that." She hesitated. "It will be good to be home again, even under unpleasant circumstances."

"Ye donna favor living in the Highlands?"

"I didn't mean to offend you. Scotland is beautiful, and I enjoy Ruairi's home very much."

He lifted a brow. "'Tis your home too."

"Of course."

⁓

Elizabeth wasn't about to tell Ian that her brother-in-law's castle never quite felt like home. There was only one location where she'd spent countless hours with her mother and father under the same roof, and that was where she grew up. That was the place that was truly home. She hadn't intended for the conversation to become awkward and decided to change the subject.

"May I ask you something?"

"Aye."

"Why isn't the captain of your guard traveling with us…with you?"

He chuckled in response. "He stays behind with my men to guard Munro lands in my absence. I can nae leave my clan and lands unprotected."

"I understand, but what about your safety?"

"Now lass, ye would nae be questioning my prowess on the battlefield, would ye?" When she took a sharp intake of breath, he smiled, and she realized he was jesting. "Many men will nae approach or engage me because of my looks. Ye witnessed that nae long ago with the Sutherland guard. Sometimes being nae fair of face has its advantages."

"I believe true beauty comes from within, and I don't think men stay away from you because you *think* you are not a comely man. I'm certain their behavior has more to do with the fact that you're the size of a mountain." Brushing her skirts, Elizabeth wiped off imaginary dirt. "How many days will you be staying with us before you and my brothers-in-law attend court?"

"I donna know. It depends on when we arrive, a few days mayhap."

"Have you been to court before?"

"Aye, more times than I care to count." There was strong censure in his tone.

"I've never had the chance. Grace attended a few times, and then we moved to Scotland."

"Ye're nae missing anything. In truth, 'tis nay place for a young lass."

"Then I guess I'm in luck because I'm eighteen now." When a questioning expression crossed his face, she quickly rose. She wasn't certain what provoked her sudden flare of temper, but between Uncle Walter, Grace, and the unexplained emotions raging within her about Ian, her voice became laced with sarcasm. "It's getting late and past the bedtime for a young lass."

Ian flew to his feet. For such a large man, he moved faster than she would've expected. He loomed over her and grabbed her arm to stay her. "Wait. That's nae what I meant."

There was a heavy silence.

"Then what did you mean?" When he didn't respond and released his grip, she met his gaze. "Have a pleasant evening, Laird Munro." She turned on her heel and did not look back. As she walked away, she almost laughed at the irony. That's what she should've done years ago. At least now she was determined to leave the past where it belonged.

She was traveling home to England, and that's where her future lie.

Three

ELIZABETH SAT IN LONELY SILENCE IN THE CARRIAGE across from Fagan and Grace. Her brother-in-law rubbed his thumb back and forth over her sister's fingers, and neither one spoke. Elizabeth hadn't even realized they'd arrived at the manor house until Fagan stepped down from the coach. He extended his hand for Grace, but she hesitated and gazed at Elizabeth.

"You haven't said a word since we left Uncle Walter's grave. Are you all right?"

"I'm fine," said Elizabeth in a solemn tone. "Your husband is waiting."

"Fagan can wait. You know that you can talk to me about anything. We're sisters." Grace continued to study her. "I do recognize that seeing Uncle Walter's grave wasn't easy for any of us, but it's not good to keep your feelings locked away. We're here for you. We're all here for each other. That's what family is for."

Elizabeth made no attempt to mask her foul mood

when a pain squeezed her heart at the mention of Uncle Walter. In truth, she didn't want to talk because her sense of loss was now beyond tears. She felt numb, inside and out. Since her sister wasn't moving her buttocks from the seat, Elizabeth leaned forward and grasped Fagan's hand. When she stepped out of the carriage, she smiled her thanks and walked to the front door without them.

Scadbury Manor was a pleasing sight with its drawbridge, gatehouse, walled gardens, and cobblestone courtyard. The Walsinghams had occupied the moated residence since 1424—at least until Ravenna had moved the remaining family to Scotland. Located on the eastern edge of Chislehurst, the manor had eight bedchambers that overlooked the valley of the River Cray, and Elizabeth welcomed the change of venue. Furthermore, even though there were no armed guards walking the walls as she'd been used to, she felt safe being back at home.

She opened the heavy, wooden door of the house she grew up in. A similar feeling had washed over her yesterday when she'd reached for the same latch, once again returning to her childhood residence. She felt as if whatever was missing from her life was instantly filled with a sense of peace and familiarity.

Ravenna, Ruairi, Kat, Torquil, and Ian sat in the great hall as Elizabeth gave pause at the entry. She could only imagine what her mother and father would've said about all the kilted men sitting around the family table waiting to sup. And God only knew what her parents would've thought about two of their daughters marrying these burly Highlanders.

Ravenna stood and approached Elizabeth. "How are you?"

"I'm weary." Elizabeth smiled blandly. "Pray excuse me. I think I'll just retire to my chamber early." She started to turn away when her sister stayed her.

"I will hear nothing of it. Mary is the only one who is napping. You'll come and take your place at the table with the rest of the family. We need each other now more than ever."

Grace and Fagan made their way into the hall, and Grace stopped in her tracks. "Is there something wrong?"

Ravenna's eyes narrowed. "No. Elizabeth was just taking her seat."

With no voice in the matter, Elizabeth approached the table and stood behind the only seat left, which was next to Ian. Her fingers wrapped around the top of the chair, and she didn't move. Though she implored silent help from Ravenna, her sister didn't pay her any heed and started talking with Ruairi.

Ian stood. "My apologies. I should've pulled out the chair for ye. Thank ye for reminding me of my manners, Lady Elizabeth."

For God's sake, she didn't want the man to pull out her bloody chair. She wanted him to leave enough distance between them so he didn't muddy her thoughts. Against her better judgment, she sat at the table when she wanted nothing more than to stop the incessant chatter around her. Was it too much to ask to be left alone?

Ravenna held a wine goblet in the air as the servants stood back with trays of food in hand. "I'd like for us to reflect and give pause to remember two great men who graced our lives, Lord Francis Walsingham and Lord Walter Mildmay. May our father and our uncle, who was a second father to us, be gazing down at us now with our dear mother with smiles on their faces and love in their hearts…for they are all sorely missed."

Everyone held up their drinks and took a sip in response, except for the men, who finished the contents of what was left in their goblets in a single swallow. As one servant replenished the empty drinks, two others placed platters of meats, breads, and cheeses on the table. Ruairi grabbed a piece of bread and placed it on Ravenna's plate.

"Nay time is ever good when we lose one of our own, but we're glad to have ye lasses along on the long journey," said Ruairi.

Elizabeth thought she heard Ian grunt beside her, but she dared not look in the man's direction.

"Since we'll be staying with Aunt Mary for a few weeks at Apethorpe Hall, when you're finished at court, you should come and see Uncle Walter's lands," said Ravenna. "They're magnificent, and the estate is one of the finest in Northamptonshire. Queen Elizabeth owned Apethorpe Hall at one time, and Uncle Walter and Aunt Mary have been known to entertain King James there on occasion."

Elizabeth felt her empty goblet being gently removed from her fingers and was startled when Ian poured something into it from a flask.

"What are you doing?" she whispered.

He returned the goblet without a word. She stared at the contents for a moment and then studied him intently. His face was a mask of stone, and he was paying attention to the conversation at the table. As she was about to look away, he met her eyes and scowled. Leaning back in his chair, he gazed at her as though she'd had the nerve to question his manhood.

❧

Ian tapped his finger on the table in front of Elizabeth's goblet. "I want ye to drink that." When she gave him a look as though he'd gone mad, he slid his chair closer and lowered his voice. "I know how ye feel. Drink."

"But what is that?"

He lifted a brow and was taken aback that a woman wouldn't immediately heed his command. "Do ye always question everything? And they wondered why I stayed on Munro lands and ne'er crossed the border for as long as I had."

"Pardon?"

"God's teeth, lass. Drink up." She picked up the goblet and swirled the contents like he'd asked her to swallow muddied water. She took a small sip and crinkled her nose. "Och, aye. I should've known ye'd drink like an English lass."

She huffed. "Well, how am I supposed to drink—whatever this is—if no one has ever shown me how?" When he grabbed her goblet and downed the contents in one swig, her mouth dropped opened.

"Now that is how ye're supposed to drink, lass."

"That's not wine. What is that?"

"*Uisge beatha.*"

"And that's Gaelic for…?"

"Water of life." He pulled out his flask and filled

her goblet again. "Would ye like to try again? But I have to warn ye, ye'll need to drink like a Scot this time. Good *uisge beatha* is nae to be wasted on the bloody English." When he said the words in his best English accent, Elizabeth's mouth trembled with the need to smile.

"But you do remember that I am English, Laird Munro."

"Aye, how could I forget?"

To his amazement, Elizabeth lifted the drink to her lips and tossed back the contents in a single swig. Her eyes were squeezed shut, and for an instant she was frozen. She placed her fingers to her mouth, facing him with a pained expression.

"I'm afraid that's simply dreadful."

"'Tis an acquired taste."

"Why, pray tell, did you want me to drink that?"

He softened his voice. "If ye donna release the pain ye suffer for the loss of your uncle—well, let me just say nay good will come of it. I've lost some of my closest friends and kin in battle and had more than enough experience with death. If ye donna want to talk, then let *uisge beatha* ease your pain."

"And how is that supposed to help, exactly?"

"The drink will dull the pain ye feel, and if it does nae, ye can always count on it to put hair on your chest." He smiled when she glanced down at her bosom.

Elizabeth pushed the goblet in front of him. "I'm afraid you don't have nearly enough 'water of life' in your flask to ease my pain, Laird Munro, but you may pour me another if you're so inclined."

Ian had no intention of encouraging or rekindling the ridiculous fancy that Elizabeth had held for him in the past, but he couldn't sit and watch her suffer from the affliction of losing her uncle any longer. As he poured the fiery liquid, he noticed Ruairi watching him from the other end of the table.

"*Mòran taing.*" *Thank you very much.* Ruairi mouthed the words without actually speaking, and Ian returned a quick nod.

Elizabeth grabbed the goblet and swallowed the contents, tapping her fingers on the table. "I thought it would be better going down the second time, but I assure you that it wasn't."

"Usually after the fourth, ye donna notice the burn anymore."

He was about to pour her another when she placed her hand over the top of the rim. "Oh, I'm afraid there will not be a fourth time."

Ian chuckled. "Aye, but ye did nae say anything about a third."

Her gentle laugh tinkled through the air as she studied her hands. "I truly must thank you for a much needed distraction. And I never thanked you for offering me comfort when the messenger came about Uncle Walter's passing."

"'Twas my pleasure, lass." Ian meant his words.

She reached out and touched his arm and then pulled back as if her hand was aflame. "Laird Munro, I don't want there to be awkwardness between us. Please accept my apologies for the past. I was only fifteen. I—"

"Lady Elizabeth, all is forgotten. There is nay need

for apologies. Now that ye're older, wiser, I'm certain your opinion has changed. Now ye can take your place among the other lasses and run at the sight of me."

&

And therein lay the problem. Elizabeth wasn't certain her feelings toward the man had changed at all, especially because she felt a warm tingling all over her body. Ian drove her completely mad when he said words like that. Granted, he was a brawny man, but he was always kind. Any woman who ran away from him because of his daunting appearance was a fool. Laird Ian Munro was a great man. She'd always believed that and hadn't altered her views now.

She gazed down to see that part of his kilt had separated, exposing his thigh. Her eyes boldly roamed over his body, and she had a strong urge to reach out and touch him again. He was hard, firm. She also remembered that from being crushed in his embrace. Oh, yes. His body was solid as a rock. She closed her eyes for a moment. What was wrong with her? She felt as if she'd lost her mind.

Elizabeth stood, pausing when she became lightheaded. "Pray excuse me, everyone. I'll be retiring now." She felt Ravenna's eyes studying her, passing judgment, but Elizabeth wasn't about to sit next to Ian any longer without having any wits about her. As she made her way out of the great hall, unsteady on her feet, Ruairi grunted.

"Ye've gone and done it now, Munro. I do believe my sister-in-law is in her cups."

Elizabeth knew better than to acknowledge

the truth of that matter. She made her way to the study when she more than likely should've gone to bed. As she closed the door behind her, she took a deep breath.

The room smelled of leather and wood, reminding her of her father. She smiled when the bright sunlight came through the window and reflected from the blades of his eight daggers that hung on the wall. She took that as a sign that her father was still watching over her. As she ran the tips of her fingers along the spine of the leather-bound journals on the shelf, she realized his influence was the reason that she could be found in the library more often than not.

His desk sat in front of a large window, and she rubbed her hand over the smooth, wooden surface. She sat in his chair, wondering how many times her father and Uncle Walter had met within these walls. A memory came to mind of being scolded with her sisters in this very room. In those days, Grace and Ravenna had been in trouble most of the time. Fortunately for Elizabeth and Kat, they had been too young to get into the kind of mischief that their sisters had. Then again, Grace was always causing enough trouble for them all.

Ian was right. His "water of life" had dulled her senses. The pain she felt hadn't entirely disappeared, but it was bearable. She laid her head back on the chair, trying to clear the haze. She'd close her eyes if only for a brief time.

"Wake up!"

Elizabeth was jolted awake and placed her hand over her racing heart. "What is it?" She rubbed her hands over her face. "For heaven's sake, what's the matter with you?"

"What's the matter with *me*?" Grace placed her hands on her hips. "You've been in here for most of the night. Time to seek your bed, Sister."

"Do ye want me to carry her?" asked Fagan.

Elizabeth hadn't noticed her brother-in-law, and she stood. "There's no need to carry me, Fagan. I'm perfectly capable of walking on my own accord."

"Are ye sure about that, lass?"

"I assume you do remember how to find your chamber," said Grace in a clipped tone.

Elizabeth stumbled to the door. "I only grew up in this house," she said under her breath.

She climbed the darkened stairs. Even though she wasn't sure of the time of night, she supposed everyone else had sought their beds. Making her way down the hall to her bedchamber, she passed the family portraits that hung on the wall. She could feel her father's gaze upon her and briefly pondered what he would've thought about all the Highlanders sleeping under his roof.

Hearing the soft click of a latch, she stopped. A door opened, and Ian emerged from his chamber. The way the candle was flickering from his room made him look ethereal, unreal in the dim light. His long, red hair was tangled, and his tunic was half pulled out of his kilt. His feet were bare, and she almost chuckled at his disheveled appearance.

"I thought I heard someone out here. Ye did nae get into too much trouble, did ye?"

"If you consider trouble as sleeping in my father's

chair in the study, then yes, I'm afraid that I've been badly behaved."

His smile brought an immediate softening to his features. "Everyone knows that I got ye into your cups this eve. Your sisters would've had my head if something had befallen ye. At least ye're here and did nae wake up in a strange place like the barn."

She regarded him with a speculative gaze. "Speaking from experience, Laird Munro?"

"Och, aye. Although I've ended up in more dire situations than a barn, I'm afraid. *Oidhche mhath*, Lady Elizabeth."

"Good night, Laird Munro."

She continued down the hall to her chamber and gently closed the door behind her. For a moment, she glanced around her room and then donned her nightrail, climbed into bed, and blew out the candle.

A loud sigh escaped her. She couldn't believe how wonderful she felt laying in her own bed. If she were being honest with herself, she'd have to say that she was at ease being home again under the same roof where her father and mother had raised her. Although it was difficult, she remembered a time when there were no tartans, no men in kilts, no brawny Highland lairds, and no Scotland. Life was so much simpler then.

Elizabeth had spent weeks thinking about her future, realizing perhaps it was time to go back to the place where her life had begun. She closed her eyes, needing to rest, because on the morrow, her sisters weren't going to like what she had to say.

At least some of Ian's worries were over because the women would not be underfoot. The lasses were taking their leave to Apethorpe Hall for at least a fortnight, and he would be traveling with the men to court. The sooner he paid homage to his liege, the faster he'd be back on Munro lands—free of the English.

He descended the stairs to break his fast, wondering how Walsingham had managed to live in this manor house with a wife and four daughters. Although Ian had never met the man, he held a great degree of respect for him. Any man who could survive in close quarters with five lasses under the same roof was a brave soul. When he entered the great hall, Kat, Torquil, Fagan, and Grace sat quietly at the table. The smell of oatmeal invaded Ian's senses, and he pulled out a chair.

"*Madainn mhath*," said Fagan. *Good morning*.

"Aye." Ian had just placed his arse in the seat when Grace spoke.

"I know you were only trying to help Elizabeth last night, but—"

"Grace…" Fagan warned.

Ian scowled. "'Tis too early in the morn to hear the cackling hens." When Grace huffed, he looked at Fagan and shrugged. "Ye need to rein in your woman."

"Now you listen to me you big—"

"What did you do for Elizabeth?" asked Kat.

Torquil tapped Kat on the hand. "This does nae concern ye. Break your fast."

"I heard my name. Is everything all right?" Elizabeth pulled out a chair across from Ian and beside Grace.

"How are you feeling this morning? I was

worried about you," said Grace, placing her hand on Elizabeth's shoulder.

"I'm fine." Elizabeth waved her sister off. "If you're talking about finding me in father's study, it was nothing. Are Ruairi and Ravenna with Mary this morn?"

"Yes. We'll need to start packing soon. Ravenna wants to leave for Apethorpe Hall on the morrow after we break our fast," said Grace.

"I'm not coming with you."

Ian raised his eyes from his oatmeal and studied Elizabeth. Perhaps he should pick up his meal and run while he still had a chance to eat in peace. Fagan's wife had a venomous tongue on a good day. He hoped to hell Elizabeth knew what she was getting herself into.

"What do you mean you're not coming with us?"

"I'm going to court. Father and Uncle Walter made certain you and Ravenna both had the privilege. Now it's my turn. I'm eighteen. You can't deny me that. I've lived in Scotland for the past three years. I've done as you've asked. Ruairi will be my chaperone. I've had the entire journey to England to think about it."

Fagan leaned his arm on the table. "Elizabeth, court is nay place for a lady. There are dangers that—"

"And that's why I'll have you along to protect me." Elizabeth met Grace's eyes without flinching. "You and Ravenna chose to live in Scotland, but I'm not sure living in the Scottish Highlands or on Sutherland lands for the rest of my days should be my fate. While we're in England, I want to mingle with peers of the realm. Perhaps I'll even find a suitor. How can you deny me a chance when you met Lord Casterbrook at court? If anyone would understand, I thought it would be you."

Ian exchanged a knowing look with Fagan.
Casterbrook was dead, but Elizabeth knew nothing of
her family's history or their secrets of spy craft. What
the lass was asking was nothing more than a foolish
endeavor. He reminded himself that she was only
eighteen and didn't know any better. But Fagan was
right. Court was no place for Elizabeth. He'd tried to
tell her that before.

As Ian waited for Grace to put an end to her sister's
madness, he dropped his spoon onto the table when
he heard Grace's surprising words.

"I don't necessarily agree, but yes, you should go
to court."

Four

ELIZABETH WASN'T PROUD TO ADMIT IT, BUT SHE'D taken the coward's way out and successfully avoided her family, lingering in the parlor for a few hours. When she grew tired of that, she ambled along the paths in the gardens. Of course, she'd counted on Grace telling Ravenna about the little declaration she'd made at the morning meal, but Elizabeth wasn't ready to confront both her sisters so soon. She'd learned long ago that Ravenna and Grace were easier to address each individually.

But now, Elizabeth was trapped.

She sat behind the closed doors of her father's study, but this time she wasn't sleeping in his chair and didn't have Ian's "water of life" to dull her senses. To her dismay, she was facing Ravenna and was flanked by Grace. When the feeling that she was a small girl getting scolded in her father's study washed over her, she reminded herself that she was no longer a child. She was a woman, and she had every right to speak her mind to her sisters, who also never minded their own tongues.

Ravenna leaned back in the chair behind the desk and picked an imaginary piece of lint from her purple day dress. But when she cast Elizabeth the kind of smile that was surely to be the calm before the raging storm, Elizabeth knew better than to think she was safe from her sister's wrath. Ravenna always had a way of showing her disapproval without even speaking a single word.

"I know why I'm here. Can you stop delaying the inevitable and say what you need to say?"

"This decision was rather sudden. Wouldn't you agree?" asked Ravenna.

"I've thought about it the entire journey home."

"Court can be a very dangerous place for a girl who knows nothing about it."

"And that's why I'll have your husband along as my chaperone."

Grace cleared her throat. "Fagan and Laird Munro will also be accompanying her, Ravenna. Fagan would never let anything happen to our sister because he knows he'd have to deal with me. Furthermore, you've seen Laird Munro. The beastly man would frighten away anyone who'd even think about causing her harm, not that she'd be hurt with so many people in attendance. Why would you deny Elizabeth a chance to go to court, especially with Ruairi as her chaperone?"

Ravenna's eyes flashed a gentle but firm warning. "You know why."

Elizabeth studied her sisters back and forth. "Are you two ever going to tell me the truth about what happened with Daniel? I know you're withholding something. You can tell me. I'm not a child anymore."

"She's not, Ravenna. Elizabeth and Kat have been living in the Highlands. When you wed Ruairi, the girls didn't have a choice but to come to Scotland. Granted, I wed Fagan and made my decision, but I still had an option to stay in England or to reside in Scotland. Don't you think Elizabeth should be given the same opportunity? What if her future husband is here in England? I know our parents would've been delighted if one of their daughters married a peer of the realm, as they'd intended for all of us to do."

Elizabeth touched her sister's arm. "Grace, thank you, but I'm capable of speaking for myself." She turned to Ravenna. "You've done so much for us, and I appreciate all that you've sacrificed to keep our family together. You've been more of a mother to Kat and me since our parents died all those years ago. But now you have Ruairi, Mary, and a family of your own."

Ravenna leaned forward. "You are my family."

"I know, Sister, but I'm not sure that I want to remain on Scottish soil for the rest of my days."

"Is that what this is about? Ruairi and I have no intention of arranging a marriage for you now. When you're ready, I'll—"

Elizabeth shook her head. "No, this isn't about arranging a marriage for me at all. Please don't misunderstand me. I love Scotland, but I love England too. I miss our old home and want to be around girls my own age for a change. I know my decision to go to court was rather abrupt, but I'm tired of seeing bloody tartans everywhere. If you haven't noticed, that's why I've been wearing our English dress. Now that we're back in England, I want to attend the theatre and do everything that I've not been able to do in Scotland."

When a laugh escaped Grace, Elizabeth's temper flared. She should've known the luck she'd had with her sister had run out.

"And what do you find so comical?" asked Ravenna.

Grace smiled from ear to ear. "I have more in common with Elizabeth than I'd thought."

Ravenna sighed and squeezed her fingers over the bridge of her nose. "God help me."

❧

"What did ye say?" Ian ran his hand through his hair and then pulled out his flask and took a swig. He kept his drink on Walsingham's desk, needing to keep it in plain sight for easy reach, or to beat Ruairi over the head.

"Ye heard me."

"Why the hell would ye agree to take her to court?"

Ruairi shrugged. "The women and Torquil will take their leave to Apethorpe Hall for a fortnight, and in the meantime, there is nay reason why we can nae escort Elizabeth. We have to attend, and she wants to come along. Ye donna have to do anything. The lass will be in my charge. Besides, ye should be grateful 'tis Elizabeth and nae Grace who will be accompanying us."

"I know that I should be offended," said Fagan. "But I suppose ye both know my wife well enough to say those words." He paused. "I did try to deter Elizabeth, but—"

"Ye did nae try hard enough. The English court is nay place for a lass, especially one as young as Elizabeth," said Ian.

Fagan slapped Ian on the shoulder with an expression of pained tolerance. "Mayhap ye have nae taken notice, Munro, but Elizabeth is eighteen now. Most lasses are wed at her age."

"And most lasses donna have family who are…er, were spies for the Crown."

Ruairi took a swig from Ian's flask. "Howbeit Elizabeth is part of the English aristocracy. 'Tis her birthright to experience such madness for herself. More to the point, nay one would dare come near her with ye standing by her side, Munro."

Ian wagged his finger at Ruairi. "Wait a moment. I heard ye with my own ears. I donna have to do a damn thing, and I'm holding ye to that." He grabbed the flask back and then pointed it at Ruairi. "And I hope ye brought more *uisge beatha* with ye because we're going to need it. I will nae drink that watery piss at court that these English let pass for ale. I require a man's drink."

Ruairi chuckled. "We had to journey from the Highlands to London with four English women and a wee lassie. I brought more than enough. And Elizabeth will nae be any trouble. We'll only need to keep the wolves at bay."

"So says the man who let an English spy into his home."

"Ye know Ravenna has retired from service," said Fagan.

"So says the man whose wife brought mercenaries onto our lands."

Ruairi held up his hands in defense. "Need I remind ye that Mildmay and my wife, being in favor with the king, are the reason ye did nae have to attend court for years?"

"Aye, but I'm here now."

Fagan scowled. "Ye're in a foul mood, Ian. How long has it been since ye've tupped a woman, eh? Mayhap a courtly harlot is what ye need to improve your miserable demeanor."

"Bastard."

"Aye."

Needing to find air that his friends did not breathe, Ian made his way out into the garden with his flask in hand. He sat on a bench and was brooding beside a rosebush when Elizabeth stumbled upon him from the garden path.

"Laird Munro, I didn't see you there. Where are Ruairi and Fagan?" When she noticed the displeased expression on his face, she added, "Oh, I'm afraid I've seen that look before. Are my sisters driving you mad, or Ruairi and Fagan?"

He chuckled and took a swig. "How verra observant of ye, lass."

She approached him and gestured to the bench. "May I?"

"Aye."

"Do you want to tell me what's troubling you?" When he took too long to respond, she spoke again, changing the subject. "What do you think of our Scadbury Manor? I know our home is much smaller than your own."

"Ye have a fine home and should be proud, Lady Elizabeth. And donna mind my foul mood. I find myself brooding every time I cross the English border."

He also could have added "Sutherland border," but knew it was best to keep that thought silent.

She returned a smile. "Come now, Laird Munro. Do you truly find our company so dreadful?" When he didn't respond to another one of her questions, she stood. "I'd like to show you something."

All he wanted to do was stay on the bench with his drink to accompany him, but at the last moment, he reluctantly agreed to follow Elizabeth through the garden. They continued over the drawbridge and turned right onto a dirt path in the woods. "Where are we going, lass?"

"Do ye always question everything?" When she spoke the words in a Scottish accent, he laughed.

"Ye best keep to your King's English, Lady Elizabeth."

"Was I that terrible?" she asked over her shoulder.

"Aye."

As they followed the trail through the trees, the forest closed in around them. Ian rested his hand on the hilt of his sword, knowing better than to lower his guard. His eyes darted back and forth through the thicket as Elizabeth slowed her pace beside him. He couldn't stay the nagging feeling that someone or something was watching them from the shadows of the trees. His instincts were usually right, especially when the little hairs were sticking up on the back of his neck.

A shrill scream pierced the air.

❧

A fallow deer jumped onto the path, and Ian withdrew his sword.

Elizabeth covered her mouth, but it was too late. When she spotted the animal, a laugh escaped her. "Are you still hungry, Laird Munro? I could always ask the cook to prepare more food for you."

He sheathed his weapon. "Your screams did nae help matters. Ye may think ye're comical, lass, but let me assure ye that ye're nae."

"The deer startled me. Please accept my apologies." She turned her head away to hide her smile.

They walked into a clearing and followed the dirt path up a hill. When they reached the top, she gestured to the view before her. "Isn't it beautiful? This was what I wanted to show you."

The open lands that encircled the pond were covered with grasses and other soft, green plants. As a hawk glided fluidly through the air, she stole a glance at Ian. He stood tall, unwavering, and his expression remained impassive.

"I know the water is nothing in comparison to your Scottish lochs, but I thought you'd enjoy the view nevertheless."

He finally graced her with a smile. "Thank ye, Lady Elizabeth. Your thoughtfulness means a great deal to me. Did ye come here as a child? I mean to say, before ye came to Scotland."

"Yes, I often came here with my sisters and have many fond memories of this very spot. Not that you'd be interested, but wildflowers grow in the valley below during the late summer solstice. We used to pick them for my mother's table."

"Why did ye come all this way and nae pick the blooms from your mother's own garden?"

"I think my mother enjoyed when my sisters and I were away from the house at times. She would ask us to do tasks around my father's lands, often coming up with ideas to keep us occupied so we wouldn't be causing mischief, especially Grace and Ravenna." Elizabeth gave him a knowing look. "But I'm not certain her efforts worked because one of us was usually in trouble."

There was a heavy silence.

"Would nae ye rather travel with your sisters to pay your respects to your aunt on the morrow? I'm certain she'd want to visit with ye after Mildmay... 'Tis nae too late to change your mind." As if he was guarding a secret, his expression was closed.

"Why, Laird Munro? Do you want me to change my mind?"

He shrugged, casually resting his hand on the hilt of his sword. "I know ye are nae going to favor court, lass. Men and women are there for a purpose. They seek the king's favor and will nae think twice about stabbing anyone in the back to get it."

She leaned toward him and spoke in a low tone, as if she was telling him a secret of her own. "Truth be told, I'm not worried. What could possibly go wrong? I'll have three Highland warriors there to protect me from the vultures and to see that no one stabs me in the back. Besides, I'm not going to seek His Majesty's favor." She met his eyes and smiled. "I'm going to dance."

He chuckled.

"Do you dance, Laird Munro?"

"Nae even under the threat of death. We'd better return before darkness falls."

As Elizabeth walked back to the manor house with Ian by her side, she felt as though she was in a wonderful dream and didn't want to wake up. Her eyes wandered from his handsome face down his massive frame. She'd spent endless nights picturing times like these in her mind. That's another reason why she wanted to attend court. She needed to move forward with her life and couldn't keep dwelling on something that could never be.

They continued silently on the dirt path. No sooner did they cross the drawbridge when Ravenna approached.

"Elizabeth, may I speak with you for a moment?"

"Yes, of course. Pray excuse me, Laird Munro."

"Aye."

They had taken a few steps away from Ian when Ravenna asked, "Where did you go with Laird Munro?" Her sister had a curious expression on her face.

"He was brooding in the garden so I decided to take him to the pond. He doesn't favor being in England, as if we didn't know that already. But I thought seeing the water might remind him of his home."

"Laird Munro is a grown man. You do not have to entertain him. He may not favor being in England, but he has to perform many duties as a Scottish laird that I'm sure he doesn't like to do."

Elizabeth changed the subject, not wanting to hear another one of her sister's lectures. "What did you want to speak with me about?" When they entered the house and climbed the steps to the bedchambers, Elizabeth felt slight relief that she wasn't being escorted to her father's study to face another inquisition.

"It shouldn't take long for our trunks to be secured in the morn. Are you certain you don't want to travel to Apethorpe Hall with us? I'm sure Aunt Mary would love to see you again."

Elizabeth stared at her sister with rounded eyes. "Have you been speaking with Laird Munro?"

"Why do you ask?"

"Because he said something similar to me at the pond."

"I have never doubted Laird Munro is a wise man," said Ravenna under her breath, but loud enough for Elizabeth to hear.

"Pardon?"

Her sister wisely didn't respond. They entered Ravenna's bedchamber, and their mother's portrait hung above the mantel of the stone fireplace. Ruairi's plaid and Mary's blanket were resting on a chair in the sitting area, and the sight warmed Elizabeth's heart. She was reminded that the strong Highland laird had a softer side that he didn't want many people to know about.

"I have something for you," said Ravenna.

Elizabeth approached the bed that had tall, carved corner posts and counterpanes of gold cloth. The color was the reason she'd almost missed the dress. A beautiful golden gown was adorned with a laced bodice and had long, tight sleeves, armbands, a ribbon waistband, and a wheel farthingale.

"The dress is lovely."

"I was hoping you'd like it because we don't have time to buy you a new wardrobe." Ravenna paused. "Well, don't just stand there. Try on the gown."

Her sister didn't need to ask twice. Elizabeth removed

her day dress, and Ravenna assisted her to don the garment. "You look beautiful. I wore the same gown when I attended court years ago. Come over here and see yourself in the looking glass." Ravenna piled Elizabeth's hair on the top of her head. "You look elegant—beautiful."

"Thank you." Elizabeth turned from side to side. "I feel as though I'm a princess and belong at court. Perhaps I'll meet my prince."

"I'm not sure the kind of man you desire will be found at court, but I do have a few other dresses that I'll give you to take along." Ravenna let Elizabeth's tresses fall and smoothed Elizabeth's hair away from her shoulders.

"I know you don't want me to go to court, but thank you for understanding…and for the dresses."

"You're quite welcome, but there is something else that I wish to discuss before you go."

"You're not going to change my mind."

"That's not my intention." Ravenna sat on the bed and patted her hand on the feather mattress. "As my husband would say, ye and I need to have a wee chat."

Elizabeth sat on the bed.

"When you arrive at court, please make certain you're accompanied by Ruairi, Fagan, or Laird Munro at all times. Never wander anywhere alone. Give me your word."

"Ravenna…"

"Please hear me out. For instance, if a man asks you to walk with him in the gardens, especially at night, politely decline. You never want to place yourself in a situation that you cannot immediately walk away from. Men, especially men at court, will say anything to get a woman alone. Perhaps they only desire to steal a kiss, but sometimes they want far more from a woman than she's willing to give. Men should never take anything from a woman that is not offered, even a kiss. Do you understand?"

Elizabeth forced a demure smile to appease her protective sister.

"And there's something else." Ravenna approached her trunk and lifted the lid. She pulled out a cloth and returned to the bed. Unfolding the material on the mattress, she uncovered a shiny dagger. She handed the blade to Elizabeth, hilt first.

"What is this?" When a puzzled look crossed her sister's face, Elizabeth added, "I know what this is, but why are you giving it to me?"

Ravenna slowly lifted her skirts and gestured down to her leg. A matching blade was strapped to her thigh. "Grace and I both carry a dagger, and now is the time for you to have one too."

"I've seen you and Grace throwing blades at mock targets, but why do you both carry daggers underneath your skirts?"

"Father taught me how to defend myself years ago. He insisted that I carried a blade, especially if I was attending court. In turn, I taught Grace how to protect herself, and now she carries one too."

"You do know that our sister's aim is terrible."

"I didn't say she was perfect." Ravenna stood and walked again in front of the looking glass. "Come over here for a moment." When Elizabeth reached her sister, Ravenna pulled her dagger from under her skirts. "We leave on the morrow, and unfortunately, I don't have ample time to teach you. But let me show you something that may save your life."

"If the men are my escort, why would I ever need to draw a blade?"

"Because if there is ever any trouble that cannot be avoided, the last any man would expect is for you to be hiding a weapon under your dress. But the *only* time you are to unsheathe that dagger is when your life is in peril. Do you understand?"

"Yes."

"Good. And when you pull out the blade, you do not hesitate. You aim for the heart." Ravenna pointed her blade at Elizabeth's chest. "Here…"

"Ravenna, I am not going to stab anyone in the heart. I don't think I could."

There was a flicker of awareness in Ravenna's eyes. "You'd be astonished what you can do when your life is threatened, but there is a quicker way to bring a man to his knees."

"Other than stabbing him through the heart, you mean?" Elizabeth couldn't stay the sarcasm that escaped her mouth.

"Yes."

"And what is that?"

"Grab him by the bollocks and don't let go."

Five

As Elizabeth walked down the hall from her bedchamber, she thought back to the conversation she'd had last eve with Ravenna. To say that her sister's words had troubled her wouldn't begin to describe the uncertainty Elizabeth felt. She was supposed to be a lady and didn't think many women of title wielded a dagger, let alone concealed one under their gown strapped to their thigh.

But she could be wrong.

Ravenna had shown Elizabeth how to fasten the blade so that she'd be able to secure it by herself at court, and her sister had done the task fluently. Perhaps times were changing, and women were becoming more self-sufficient, not needing a man to protect them. A male voice startled her from behind as she descended the stairs.

"Good morn, Lady Elizabeth."

She stopped, glancing over her shoulder. "And the same to you, Laird Munro. Did you sleep well?"

"As well as can be expected." When they reached the bottom of the stairs, he faced her. "Did ye have a chance to think about my words?" When she gave him a confused look, he added, "Will ye be traveling with your sisters to see your aunt this morn?"

She gave him a patient smile and tapped her fingers on his arm. "Not this day, Laird Munro. Not this day." She stepped around him and walked into the great hall where everyone, except Ian, was seated to break their fast. "Good morn."

"So it's true. You're not coming with us to see Aunt Mary," said Kat.

Elizabeth pulled out her chair as Ian sat across from her. "Yes, I will be traveling with the men to court." She didn't miss it when Ian stiffened at the table.

"Will I have to go to court, too? Not now, but I mean to say in a few years."

"Katherine, you're only twelve. You will not be attending anytime soon," said Ravenna in a clipped tone.

"Why would ye even think about going there, lass? I'm sure those English lads are nae as enjoyable as me," said Torquil, poking Kat in the ribs with his elbow.

"All right, all right. I've heard enough talk about court. I think that's all I can bear," said Ravenna. She turned to Ruairi. "Are you certain you're not willing to take all of them with you? Perhaps I can change your mind. Will you accept a bribe? You only need to name your price."

He chuckled. "I'm nae that foolish, lass."

"Ravenna told me she gave you a few of her gowns to take along," said Grace. "I'm sure you'll look beautiful. Ruairi will more than likely have to keep all your suitors at bay—well, the unsavory sorts anyway."

Elizabeth swallowed her oatmeal. "I'm not sure

about that, but the dresses are beautiful." She thought about bringing up the subject of the dagger but then decided against it. This was probably not the time or the place to discuss such matters, and besides, Ruairi and Fagan already knew what lay under their wives' skirts. But being that Kat was only twelve, Elizabeth was pretty certain she wasn't aware of their older sisters' peculiar dress habits.

"I do hope, Elizabeth, that ye did nae pack as much as my wife," said Fagan. "We need another coachman just to carry her trunks."

Grace playfully slapped her husband on the arm. "How can you speak such lies about me? You know perfectly well that we need another coachman just to carry the whisky for the men."

Fagan shrugged. "There may be some truth to that."

After everyone finished their meals, Elizabeth stood in the front hall holding her niece as the men brought heavy trunks down the stairs to pack onto the carriages for the journey to Aunt Mary's. When little Mary squealed with delight, Elizabeth glanced down. She couldn't believe how fast her niece was growing. In a few months, Mary would be taking her first steps.

"I'm hoping Fagan and I will have a child of our own soon—although, the man doesn't seem to be in any hurry to be a father. I think all the women under the Sutherland roof dissuade him. He doesn't want to tempt fate," said Grace.

"Fagan loves you. I'm certain he'd love your child no matter what the gender."

"I know you're right."

"I haven't had the chance to thank you, Grace."

A puzzled expression crossed her sister's face. "For what may I ask?"

"For helping me talk Ravenna into letting me attend court. I don't know why you did what you did for me, but I do appreciate your words."

Grace led Elizabeth gently by the arm over to the far wall and then lowered her voice. "No one understands better than I do how you feel. I was fascinated when I first attended court, but I'm happier now with Fagan by my side. Ravenna and I had a chance to decide for ourselves which path we wanted to take. I want the same for you and Kat. Whatever you choose, England or Scotland, I will always support you. Don't forget that."

Elizabeth smiled with sincerity. "Thank you."

"If you would've given us notice, we could've had new gowns made for you. But you're going to look beautiful in Ravenna's dresses." Grace glanced around and then spoke in a conspiratorial whisper. "I know our sister spoke with you about the daggers."

"Yes."

"Promise me that you'll heed Ravenna's advice. Wear the blade at all times. The men will watch over you, but remember that you can't be placing yourself in situations that you cannot remove yourself from."

"Ravenna said the same to me last night."

"Our sister is wise. Be cautious, Elizabeth. I can't stress that enough."

The way Ravenna and Grace kept telling her to be safe and not to be foolish made Elizabeth wonder if there was something more to their odd behavior, or if this was simply her sisters being too protective. Grace's voice broke her woolgathering.

"I'm sure you're going to have a grand time. I hope that you'll find a handsome suitor, one who sweeps you off your feet in a dance, and one who makes you forget all about Laird Munro."

Elizabeth gasped. "I don't—"

"Your words do not fool me." Grace leaned in close. "The man does not return your interest; therefore, he does not deserve your love. There are men who are far younger and much more pleasing to the eye than that hardened Scotsman. You'll discover that at court."

Elizabeth stood in awe as her sister walked out the front door.

❧

Ian breathed a sigh of relief when the last coach rode over the drawbridge with the Sutherland guards in tow. At least three women and a wee lass were no longer underfoot. But now the worst part of his trip to England was about to begin, and he wasn't looking forward to it in the least. Who the hell would want to travel to the English court and appear before the king? That had to be a fate worse than death. He also wasn't in favor of being among so many English. At least Ruairi and Fagan were along to share in the misery.

Fagan and Ian mounted their horses as they waited for Ruairi and Elizabeth. Hampton Court Palace was a day's ride from Scadbury Manor. Of course, they'd have to stay at court since the palace was too far to travel from the manor house. Ian gave pause, thinking perhaps he should've journeyed with the women and Torquil to see Aunt Mary too.

Elizabeth lingered by the front door of the house, and he hoped she was having second thoughts about coming along. But to his dismay, Ruairi escorted her to the waiting coach.

"Is everything all right?" asked Ruairi.

"Yes, I just wanted to be certain that I didn't forget anything."

"Lass, this is the last time I'm going to ask ye."

Elizabeth stepped around him. "For heaven's sake, yes, I'm certain that I want to go." She climbed into the coach and closed the door in Ruairi's face.

"I donna think there's anything we can say or do to change her mind," said Fagan, as Ruairi was approaching them.

Ruairi grabbed the reins of his mount. "We're wed to Walsinghams. Have ye ever been able to change their minds about anything?" When Fagan took a moment to think about his friend's words, Ruairi added, "I did nae think so."

Ian laughed. "And that's why I'll ne'er be wed. I did warn both of ye besotted fools."

They followed the carriage over the drawbridge and out the gates. To the right was the dirt path where he had walked the evening before with Elizabeth. He was amazed the lass had thought of him and wanted to show him more of her father's lands. Although it wasn't too difficult to see how much he missed his own lands, his home—Scotland. He felt as if he was caught in a nightmare and couldn't wake up. Then again, he always felt that way when he traveled to England.

"Was your wife able to pull her favor with the king and grant us an earlier audience? Mayhap he'll see us on the morrow, and we'll be able to take our leave with haste," said Ian.

Aloofness showed in Ruairi's face. "Ye know verra well how the king enjoys watching the Highland lairds suffer. He'll keep us waiting for as long as possible, only to torture us. 'Tis his way of trying to get us to heel like dogs. Best ye get used to that now."

"Damn."

"Mayhap ye can take that opportunity to seek out a willing lass or two, Munro," said Fagan. "Then again, it may take ye that long to find just one."

"Bastard."

Fagan chuckled. "Aye. Dinna fash. We brought plenty of whisky, and we'll be back in Scotland before ye know it."

No sooner did Ian open his mouth to tell Fagan that he didn't believe a word he said when the coach stopped. Elizabeth opened the door and stepped down from the carriage.

"I need to search my trunk," she called to them. "I think I forgot my silk slippers."

What Ian wouldn't give to be home again.

❦

The men certainly weren't pleased with her, but they were not that far from Scadbury Manor. They could have easily turned around if Elizabeth had forgotten the slippers that Ravenna had given her to match her gown. Fortunately, they did not need to return.

Ruairi and Fagan returned the trunk to the carriage

and secured the bindings as Ian continued to scowl at her. The man could be irritated with her all he wanted. She'd be making her first appearance at court. Her clothes needed to be in perfect order, and she refused to be the one who tarnished the Walsingham family name. She wanted to make her sisters, uncle, and her mother and father proud.

It wasn't long before she once again sat in the coach and nestled into the seat. With the sound of hoofbeats and the gentle, rhythmic movement, she should've been able to fall asleep, but she couldn't. She was wide awake and eager to experience all that court had to offer.

The hours dragged, and one mile faded into the next. Being confined in the carriage was suffocating enough, especially when she had no one to talk with to pass the time. They'd stopped along the way to rest the horses, but every waking moment managed to feel eternal.

Elizabeth's mood turned buoyant when they finally arrived at London Bridge, roughly the middle between Scadbury Manor and Hampton Court Palace. At least they were getting closer. Large buildings sat on top almost the entire length of the magnificent structure. She stared in awe, resolving never to undervalue the skills of a mason.

When they reached the end of the bridge, a gasp escaped her, and her body stiffened in shock. She closed her eyes, trying to banish the image of the two heads impaled on long spikes as a warning to all those who conspired against the realm. She supposed there was a reason the end of the bridge was named Traitors' Gate.

Her fingers tensed on her lap, and her mind was consumed with doubts and fears. Although she was eager to attend court, she ought to remember that men and women of great power and influence would also be in attendance.

Ravenna and Grace were right.

Elizabeth needed to be careful, praying her head wouldn't be joining the other two on the road they'd just passed.

The sun was starting to set. They'd traveled the entire day, and the gates of the palace still weren't in sight. She gazed out of the carriage for the hundredth time, watching pieces of wood floating in the strong currents of the River Thames. Ironically, she could relate to the sight before her. She was being swept toward a future that was unclear and unknown.

When the coach abruptly stopped, she sat up. Ruairi, Fagan, and Ian rode to the front of the carriage, and a wave of apprehension swept through her. She was both thrilled and frightened.

Finally, she'd arrived at Hampton Court Palace.

After a few restless moments, the coach rolled forward. They continued through the first courtyard and stopped at the second inner gatehouse. The carriage door opened, and Elizabeth stepped down.

A large astronomical clock made for Henry VIII hung over the gatehouse. The piece showed the date, time of day, phases of the moon, and the water level at the London Bridge.

She gave herself a pinch because she couldn't believe she was standing on the grounds of royal history. King James was the son of Mary, Queen of Scots, and the great-grandson of Henry VIII, but now here she was, Lady Elizabeth Walsingham, attending court. She'd soon be walking through the same halls as kings and queens of past and present.

Ruairi, Fagan, and Ian were talking with two men as she approached, and Ruairi's voice was irritated. "I suppose we donna have a choice." When he turned around, Fagan and Ian grabbed their mounts.

Uncertainty made Elizabeth's voice harsh and demanding. "What has happened?"

"I'm sorry, lass. There are one thousand people attending court, and the palace only has forty-four bedchambers. There is nae enough room for everyone. Ravenna was able to send word ahead, and even though there is a bedchamber readied for ye, there is nae room for all of us," said Ruairi. "Lodging has been made for us in the city. We best make haste before darkness falls."

When he started to lead his mount away, she called after him. "Where are you going?"

A puzzled look crossed his face. "I told ye."

She closed the distance between them. "But aren't you going to see me to my chamber before you leave?"

Ian rubbed his hand over his face. "Lass, ye're coming with us."

"I don't understand."

Ruairi placed his hand on her shoulder. "We can nae leave ye unattended."

"You're not leaving me unattended. You're returning in the morn."

"If ye think we're going to take our leave without

ye, ye're nae thinking verra clearly. Ye can nae stay in the castle alone," said Ian.

She folded her arms across her chest and lifted her chin. "I'm not alone. You said there were one thousand people attending court. What could possibly happen between now and the morning?"

"Elizabeth, ye are nae staying here alone. 'Twas your decision to suddenly come along. Be thankful ye're able to attend court. Now get back in the carriage," said Ruairi in a commanding tone.

All pleasure left her body, and she tried to keep the whine out of her voice. "I understand." She didn't.

Fagan placed his hand on her shoulder. "I know ye're disappointed, lass, but ye'll still be able to dance and mingle with your own kind. We just won't be sleeping here."

"Thank God for small favors," said Ian.

Between the disappointment she'd felt about not being able to stay at the palace, and now Fagan and Ian's words, Elizabeth's blood started to boil. "The last I want to do is scold the two of you like children, but I have to say, whether you realize your words or not, I am English. Need I remind you there is nothing I can do to change that?"

She glowered at Fagan. "Thank you for telling me that I'll still be able to mingle with my 'own kind.'" She whipped her head to Ian. "And thank you, Laird Munro, for reminding me how much you despise my countrymen. Although I've lived in Scotland for years and have appreciated all that Ruairi has done for us, I am greatly insulted by your rudeness. And frankly, you two should know better."

Elizabeth spun on her heel and approached the waiting carriage, leaving the men standing with their mouths agape.

∾

"Now why did ye have to go and do that, Munro? Ye've fired Elizabeth's ire," said Fagan with a smile. "And if she's anything like Grace, she won't let ye forget that anytime soon."

"Bastard."

"Aye."

Ruairi lowered his voice. "*Tha thu mi-mhodhail.*" *You're badly behaved.* "I've learned that even if ye feel the way that ye do, 'tis nae always best to tell the lasses what ye are thinking. Now let's get the hell out of here. I can nae stand being this close to the English." He gave them an amused look. "And notice ye did nae hear me say that in front of Elizabeth...or her kind."

Ian mounted his horse and said a silent prayer of thanks as they traveled out the gatehouse and into the city. At least they wouldn't have to sleep under the same roof as all those English. Even though he wasn't fond of the Walsingham sisters, he hadn't meant to insult Elizabeth. After all, the lass had taken the time to talk with him on several occasions, a task most lasses would've avoided. He'd be sure to mind his words in the future; he owed her that much.

As the men followed the carriage through the narrow, barely lit streets of London, Ian cringed. A pungent odor filled the air from all the rubbish that lay on the dirty roads, and he willed himself not to gag.

Feeling a sense of compassion for his horse, he patted the animal on the neck. "*Tha mi duilich.*" *I am sorry.*

They arrived at a nearby inn, and as Ruairi secured their rooms, Ian paid the stable master more coin than what was required to see that their horses were well cared for. He certainly hoped his own accommodations would be more welcoming than the streets of London.

Elizabeth approached Ruairi as he came out of the inn. "There are enough rooms for us all. The innkeeper will have your trunks brought up to your room, lass. Why donna we have something to eat before we retire?"

"That sounds delightful."

Ruairi held open the door for Elizabeth, and the men followed her into the inn. Bawdy laughter filled the small dining hall, and the lass hesitated at the entrance. There were roughly two women and ten Englishmen who sat at the tables with tankards of ale in hand. Large, wooden beams stretched overhead, and lanterns were lit on the walls.

Fagan gestured to a table in the corner. "Over there, lass." He pulled out her chair, and she smiled her thanks.

"This has been a long day." She sat and straightened her back. "I'm weary. I can only imagine what you must be feeling."

"I didn't know we allowed their kind in here," said one of the men who sat at the next table.

Ruairi, Fagan, and Ian exchanged carefully guarded looks, but none of them paid the English curs any heed because of Elizabeth. Ian walked around the table and pulled out his chair. His gaze rested on one of the men.

The whelp had blond, curly locks and barely looked old enough to be weaned from his mother's breast.

Ian removed his scabbard. He smiled at the young man, and then sat in the chair, resting his weapon against the table. Ruairi and Fagan followed suit, but they didn't look at the bastard. If Elizabeth heard the comments of her countrymen, she didn't say.

"I'm sure you're all famished," said Elizabeth.

"I could always eat," said Fagan.

Ruairi chuckled. "Aye, we know."

A small lass brought over three tankards of ale for the men and wine for Elizabeth. The woman was a few years older than Elizabeth and had brown hair pulled into a tight bun. As the lass returned to the kitchen, the blond whelp from the other table grabbed her arm and pulled her close.

"Tell me. Did you serve wine to all the women over there? I'd be amazed if any of them drank ale." His comrades laughed in response, and the man slapped the woman on the bottom before he let her go. "They must be here for court. I hear the king makes them crawl out from under their rocks in the north to come to London once a year."

"And I heard they're nothing but a bunch of barbarians. Have you heard them speak? One can barely understand their words," said another arse at the table.

Elizabeth leaned forward. Lowering her voice, she asked, "Pardon, but are those men talking about you?"

Ruairi patted her hand. "Donna pay them any heed."

"That's very bold and isn't right. You know how my sisters and I become cross with you when you speak about England the way you do, but those men have no right to say such horrible words either. They don't even know you, and I find their manners sorely lacking."

"I donna think they worry overmuch about manners, but Ruairi is right. Pay them no heed," said Fagan.

There was a heavy silence around the table when the woman returned with their meals. "Here you are." She placed the food in front of them and wiped her hands on her apron. "I'll bring you some bread with your meal. Is there anything else I can bring you?"

"No, thank you. This looks delicious," said Elizabeth.

"My pleasure, m'lady. I made the stew myself."

"Then I'm certain it's very good."

No sooner had the woman turned away from the table when they all ate like they hadn't eaten in days. A few moments later, the lass returned with the bread. Ian chuckled as they all reached for a piece at the same time. He broke off a chunk and handed it to Elizabeth.

"Thank you, Laird Munro." She turned to Ruairi. "When do you want to leave for the palace on the morrow?"

He wiped the crumbs from his lips. "Right after we break our fast."

"And you don't know how long we'll remain?" asked Elizabeth.

"Nay. Our names will be put on a long list for the king. When he is ready, he will grant us an audience. Until then, we wait."

One voice could be heard above all others in the hall.

"I think they call them kilts, but I could never wear one of those skirts. If I did, I think my betrothed might question my preferences."

Ruairi, Fagan, and Ian had known each other for years, so much that they knew the thoughts of one another without a spoken word between them. And this was one of those times. If the English bastard didn't shut his mouth, the man was going to find himself in a heap of trouble with three Highlanders who were tired and worn.

When a worried expression crossed Elizabeth's face, Ruairi said, "The men are young and foolish. Finish your meal." She looked down at her empty bowl.

"I'm afraid that I can no longer keep my eyes open. I saw my trunks being carried up to my room. Are you ready to retire, or will you be staying for a while longer?"

Ruairi stood. "I'll escort ye to your room." With a tip of his head, he gestured toward his drink. "And then I'll be back to finish my ale."

Elizabeth stood and brushed down her skirts. She placed her hand on Fagan's shoulder. "Good night. I'll see you on the morrow."

When her eyes met Ian's, his heart jumped in response. He wasn't sure what the hell that was about, especially because he couldn't tear his eyes away from her until she was out of sight.

"Damn. I'd like to give that chit a good tupping. I wonder if she's chaste. She looks soft and ripe for the picking if you ask me."

Ian glanced sharply around, his eyes blazing. He flew to his feet and closed the distance between him and the blond whelp. The man's eyes widened when Ian pulled him roughly to his feet. When the arse raised his hands in defense, the other men stepped away from the table. Ian was amused when the man's "friends" no longer wanted to have any part of him.

"I was only jesting! I'm a sot who has had too many!" The man hesitated, and the corners of his lips slowly lifted into a smile. "Tell me. Have you already bedded her then?"

Ian rammed his fist into the man's face. When the whelp fell onto the table with a thud, Ian patted the idiot on the head. "Now there's a good laddie." His eyes darkened, and he glared at the men who remained standing. "Anyone else have something to say, or mayhap ye donna understand my words, eh?"

The men paled, shaking their heads nervously.

Ian walked back to the table and grabbed his scabbard. On his way out of the hall with Fagan, he paused, handing the woman from the kitchen a coin. "The stew was delicious, and I apologize for the mess."

Six

ELIZABETH OPENED HER EYES AND ROLLED ONTO HER back. Her entire body protested. Still weary from traveling, she wasn't ready to throw back the blankets and start a new day. Even her less than desirable room didn't provide her with enough encouragement to put one foot on the floor.

Other than the bed, there was a chest of drawers with a looking glass and a small sitting area with a table and two chairs. Her disappointment returned when she knew her accommodations at the palace would have been on a much grander scale. But she felt guilty thinking that way. She was only considering herself, and her poor traveling companions hadn't wanted to be here in the least.

When memories returned of the abhorrent behavior of her countrymen in the dining hall last night, she fought a war of emotions. Those men were quick to judge someone and something they knew nothing about. Frankly, they were ignorant, and she had no tolerance for stupidity.

There was a knock at the door.

"Elizabeth, are ye awake?" asked Ruairi from the other side.

"Yes, but I'm not yet dressed."

"We're going below stairs to break our fast. Throw something on and come with us. Ye can always return to change your clothes before court if ye wish. I'll wait for ye."

Elizabeth grudgingly rose from the bed. After seeing to her personal needs, she donned a simple day dress and her silk slippers. She approached the washbowl, and the looking glass that hung above the chest of drawers returned a vision of red, tired eyes and unruly hair. Wetting a cloth, she wiped her face with cool water. If that didn't wake her up then nothing else would. She patted her skin with a drying cloth and smoothed her long locks with her hand. That would have to do for now. At least she was present-able. When she opened the door, Ruairi was leaning against the wall.

"I'm sorry to keep you waiting."

"Dinna fash, lass. Fagan and Ian are below stairs. Did ye sleep well?"

"As soon as my head touched the pillow. I didn't move all night." She closed the door behind her, and he chuckled.

"I'm glad to hear it."

"And you?"

"The same."

Elizabeth knew her brother-in-law probably slept with one eye open, but he'd never admit it. They descended the stairs and entered the dining room where Fagan and Ian stood upon her approach. Only a handful of men sat at the other tables, none of whom were the obnoxious ones from last night.

"Good morn, lass," said Fagan.

Ian gave her a brief nod. "*Madainn mhath.*"

"Good morning to you both."

"Och, aye. Ye're definitely going to stop a few hearts at court. Ye look verra bonny in that dress," said Fagan.

She stilled. "I'm not even dressed for court, and you've seen me wear this many times before."

He lowered his voice. "My apologies, but I gave Grace my word that I'd remember to tell ye that ye look bonny before court. She said that's important for a lass to hear."

In the years she'd lived with Ruairi and Fagan under the same roof, the men had never taken notice of a new dress. The only time they'd ever said anything was when the cook made a new meal and placed it in front of them. Fagan's explanation shouldn't have surprised her.

They took their seats as the serving woman approached the table with a tray in hand. Her hair was the same as last eve, pulled back in a tight bun, and a long apron covered her brown dress. She gave them all an easy smile.

"Good morn. I hope you like what I've made for you."

"If the meal is as good as the stew last eve, then I think we're in for a treat," said Elizabeth.

The woman's face turned scarlet. "Thank you, m'lady."

"We're going to be here for a while as we're

attending court. I'm Lady Elizabeth." Elizabeth gestured around the table. "This is Laird Munro, Laird Sutherland, and Mister Murray, the captain of the Sutherland guard."

"I'm Mistress Betts. It's a pleasure to make your acquaintance."

The woman lifted a trencher from the tray and placed it in front of Elizabeth. There was an egg, oatmeal, and biscuits, and flavorful smells wafted through the air. When Ian lifted his hands to assist the woman with the food, his knuckles were red and bloodied.

"Laird Munro, whatever happened to your hand?" asked Elizabeth.

Mistress Betts placed the remaining food in front of Ruairi and Fagan. "Please accept my apologies for last evening, but the innkeeper told those men they are no longer welcome here. They had to find another place to stay."

As Mistress Betts walked away, Ruairi became interested in his trencher, and Ian picked up a biscuit.

"Laird Munro?" asked Elizabeth again.

Fagan cleared his throat at the same time Ruairi spoke for Ian. "'Twas naught."

"Aye, he hit his hand on the wall," added Fagan.

Ian shook his head. Ruairi and Fagan's reactions seemed to amuse him. "I hit my hand on the...*what*?"

"Munro," Ruairi warned.

"Don't listen to Ruairi and Fagan. My sisters and I rarely do. Tell me, Laird Munro. What happened to your hand?"

"God's teeth, lass. A man's face came into contact

with my fist. Is that what ye wanted to know?" Ian returned to his meal.

"I can only assume you struck one of those men from last eve." When he didn't respond, she added, "They were clearly in the wrong, but I don't think violence is ever an answer to anything. The innkeeper tossed them out, and they won't be returning. Do you think that was truly necessary?"

Ian scowled at Fagan and then glared at Ruairi. "I am giving ye fair warning to rein—"

"Elizabeth, finish your meal. I will have the horses readied while ye dress," said Ruairi.

She ate the rest of her meal in silence and listened to the men talk about much of nothing. No matter how many times she'd heard the same conversations about tending to the fields and crops, she was never interested in the subject. She supposed the men felt the same way when she and her sisters discussed literature or the latest fashions. Although, fashion wasn't a subject that often came up in the Highlands because there was only one type—plaid.

Mistress Betts walked over to the table, and Elizabeth welcomed the interruption. "Do you need anything else?"

"No, thank you."

While the men were still conversing among themselves, Mistress Betts stooped down next to Elizabeth. The woman lowered her voice. "I hope that I'm not being too forward, my lady, but I noticed you don't have a lady's maid with you. If you need my assistance with your clothes or hair for court, please let me know. I've done hair for all my sisters, and I don't often get a chance to leave the kitchen. It would be my pleasure, and I'd be delighted to help you."

"How many sisters do you have?"

"Five."

Ian coughed, and Elizabeth gave him a scolding look. She didn't think the men were listening to their conversation. Even though she didn't need a lady's maid to assist her, the woman was eager to help. And Elizabeth understood the need to escape a mundane life and try something new.

"I'd be delighted to have you as my lady's maid while I'm here, Mistress Betts."

The woman straightened. "Thank you, Lady Elizabeth. You won't be disappointed."

Elizabeth pushed back the chair and stood. "I'll be ready within the hour." She turned to Ian. "I do hope you manage to stay out of trouble until then, Laird Munro."

"Elizabeth," Ruairi warned.

Her scolding was quickly forgotten as soon as she entered her chamber and Mistress Betts closed the door. Elizabeth pulled out one of the gowns from her trunk and held it up to her frame. The blue dress with sky-colored reticella collar and cuffs was adorned with a scrolling, embroidered gold design inlaid into the gown, petticoat, and linen jacket.

"I think that I'll wear this one."

"A wise choice, my lady. The gown is beautiful."

Elizabeth removed her day dress and stood in her chemise. "Are you certain they won't miss you in the kitchen?"

"My assistant will handle my duties until I return.

Don't you worry about that. The boy will do as I tell him." Mistress Betts placed the dress over Elizabeth's head.

"I don't know that I'll look as beautiful as my sister did in this gown, but I'll try." As soon as the dress slid over her shoulders and fell to the floor, Mistress Betts sighed.

"I'd bet coin that you look as beautiful, if not more so, than your sister. It seems as though this gown was made for you."

"My sister and I are about the same height."

"Come in front of the looking glass. I'll straighten your dress and fix your hair." Elizabeth stood near the foot of the bed and gazed at her reflection. "May I ask why you didn't travel with a lady's maid?" As the woman bent to adjust Elizabeth's skirts, Elizabeth wasn't certain how to answer because she'd never really thought about the question.

"The women in my family never had ladies' maids. We fended for ourselves. My sisters and I have always done each other's hair or helped the other dress. I'm not sure why. It's been that way for as long as I can remember." She paused. "Now that I think on the matter, I don't recall my father having a valet either. We've had the same servants in our employ for many, many years."

Mistress Betts stood and smoothed the material on Elizabeth's shoulders.

"I must apologize. This is my first time at court. I'm nervous, and I know that I'm babbling."

"There's no reason for you to apologize. That's part of the reason why I asked you the question, to get your mind thinking about something else." Mistress Betts pulled over a chair. "Here you are. Why don't you sit, and I'll do your hair now?" As she ran a comb through Elizabeth's tresses, she asked, "Could you please hand me those pins?"

"Do you think we'll be finished within the hour? I don't want the men waiting for me. I'll never hear the end of it."

"You'll be done in a few moments. Remember that I have five sisters, and if we didn't work fast, nothing would've ever been completed."

As the kind woman pinned up Elizabeth's hair, Elizabeth fingered the material of her gown. She wondered if Ravenna felt the same way when she'd worn the dress. When the last pin was in place, Mistress Betts tapped Elizabeth's shoulders.

"There. You're all finished."

Elizabeth stood and was amazed when she saw herself in the looking glass. She turned her head from side to side. "I must say that you've done wonderfully."

"Thank you, m'lady."

Elizabeth approached her trunk and pulled out the matching silk slippers. She placed them on her feet and then smoothed her skirts. "What do you think?"

"I think you look beautiful."

"I'd better get below stairs before the men come looking for me or they find themselves in trouble again." When Elizabeth opened the door, she realized she'd forgotten to secure her blade underneath her skirts, and she did give her word to her sisters that she would. She was about to make her excuses to Mistress Betts when a hand reached over and held the door partially closed.

Mistress Betts cleared her throat. "I wouldn't be too harsh toward Laird Munro."

Elizabeth was taken aback by the woman's words. "What do you mean?"

"If you don't mind me speaking freely, those men got what they deserved." When a soft gasp escaped Elizabeth, Mistress Betts added, "Laird Munro's actions were just, my lady. He was defending your honor."

❧

Ian glanced down at his swollen knuckles and smiled. The whelp deserved a blackened eye and a sore face, and he was happy to have provided both. But he couldn't believe Elizabeth's words in the dining hall. She didn't think violence was ever the answer? That was another example of her youth and inexperience in the world.

After the men dressed for court, they waited at the bottom of the steps for Elizabeth. Ian pulled at his open-necked doublet. He still wore his kilt and plaid, but he tried to dress more formally. After all, he was a Highland laird. Although he was aware that he wasn't fair of face, the king didn't need to think all Highlanders were barbarians.

A slow, steady smile of happiness crossed Ruairi's face. "That's the gown Ravenna wore the day I asked Mildmay for her hand in marriage."

Ian turned around, and his expression stilled as Elizabeth descended the stairs. From her long locks that were pinned on top of her bonny head, to her blue gown and matching silk slippers on her feet, everything was perfect. Hell, *she* was perfect. She looked like an angel sent from the heavens above. For a moment, he had to remind himself the lass was Elizabeth. He was even more unsettled when he caught himself giving her body a raking gaze.

As she reached the last step, Ruairi grasped her hand. "I find myself at a loss for words."

"I hope you mean that in a favorable way, Laird Sutherland," she said in a jesting manner.

"Aye, I do."

"Thank you, Ruairi. That's kind of you to say. And you look very handsome in your courtly attire."

Fagan smiled and inclined his head. "How I wish Grace could see ye." He lowered his voice. "I think she'd want me to say this now. Ye look lovely, lass."

"Thank you. Is the carriage waiting?"

Ruairi gestured to the door, but Ian reached out to stay her. His muscles tensed, and he cleared his throat. He thought he should say something and follow suit from his friends. "Ye're a verra fine young lass, Lady Elizabeth."

Her glowing, youthful happiness abruptly faded, and she looked as though his words had insulted her. She cast her eyes downward. "Thank you, Laird Munro." She brushed past him, walked out the door, and stepped into the coach.

The men mounted their horses and followed the carriage at a snail's pace through the narrow, crowded streets of London. Ian had barely noticed the merchants shouting and selling their wares along the busy streets because something in the back of his mind refused to be stilled. He had tried to be kind to Elizabeth back at the inn, but he couldn't stay the feeling that she was cross with him.

"Fagan, did ye hear my words to Lady Elizabeth?"

A puzzled expression crossed his friend's face. "When?"

"Before we took our leave from the inn. After ye and Ruairi told her how bonny she was, I said she was a fine young lass. 'Twas if she was angry with me. What did I say?"

Fagan laughed. "Ye're asking me? I ne'er understand the lasses. I can nae comprehend why I fire my own wife's ire at times, let alone her sisters'. But I will tell ye this… Having lived under the same roof as all the Walsingham sisters, more often than nae, they're angry with us men most of the time. If ye think Elizabeth is cross with ye, offer her an apology."

"And what the hell do I apologize for?"

Fagan shrugged. "I donna know. Mayhap being a man, being born. I'd start with one of those."

They arrived at Hampton Court Palace and rode through the courtyard to the second inner gatehouse. Even in the light of day, Ian didn't favor the structure. A gaudy astronomical clock hung over the gatehouse, and he couldn't imagine having such a monstrosity on Munro lands. From the elaborate detail of the brick chimneys to the blending of old and new styles, the palace looked as though it belonged in Rome.

As the stable hands secured their mounts, Ruairi escorted Elizabeth from the carriage. Her head whipped from left to right, and the smile never left her face. She was clearly enamored with the sights before her, and Ian was disappointed that she couldn't see Hampton Court Palace for what it truly was—a structure built to impress the gentry and flaunt the wealth of the Crown.

"I donna need to ask what ye think, lass. I can see ye are pleased," said Ruairi.

"Yes, I am thrilled to finally be here, and I can't wait to explore."

Ruairi tapped Elizabeth's hand. "I'll be happy to escort ye wherever ye'd like to go."

They entered the main hall, and Ian frowned unapprovingly at the audacity. The inside of the palace was more elaborate than the outside, the same as he'd remembered it. There were marble statues in every nook, and circular, decorated windows as far as the eye could see. Men and women flooded the hall dressed in their finery.

"I'm going to find the king's secretary with Fagan to put our names on the list for an audience. Will ye stay with Elizabeth?" asked Ruairi.

"Aye," Ian answered. He knew his friends hated the English court as much as he did. The sooner they met with the king, the faster they could be home.

Elizabeth walked at a leisurely pace beside him. He studied her, but she paid him no heed. He stepped around men and women in the crowded hall and then escorted her by the elbow to an unoccupied wall.

"Laird Munro, what are you doing?"

"I'm offering ye an apology."

"For what, may I ask?"

"Umm… I said something that offended ye at the inn." He wasn't about to ask what.

"Yes, well, I wanted to talk to you too." She rested her hand on his arm, and there was some unidentifiable emotion that crossed her face. "Mistress Betts told me that you defended my honor. I can't tell you how grateful I am that you thought that much about me to come to my defense."

He felt her thumb brush his arm, and she was watching him intently. A knot formed in Ian's throat. It was important that Elizabeth thought highly of him. "'Tis naught I would nae have done for any other lass."

Once again an expression of hurt crossed her face, and he was to blame.

Seven

Elizabeth was brooding at the tennis court when a large shadow loomed overhead. She didn't need to look to know that Laird Munro stood by her side. His feelings toward her were clear. She'd never be any different from all the other women. From now on, she resolved to let her trip to Hampton Court Palace restore her senses. No longer would she allow herself to think of the man as "Ian" because he'd never be anything more than the steely Highland laird that everyone knew. Although she was one of the few who had seen kindness within him, his walls were formidable, and they'd never be penetrable.

"I believe the tennis court was built for King Henry VIII," said Laird Munro.

She kept her eyes forward. "It was actually built for Cardinal Wolsey, but yes, King Henry loved to play. Many say tennis is the sport of kings."

"Swordplay is all the sport I need." He chuckled, and she regarded him with impassive coldness.

"And I believe that *is* all you need, Laird Munro."

He was staring at her, speechless, when Ruairi and Fagan approached them.

"Our names are on the list. Now we wait," said Ruairi.

"Thinking about playing a wee bit of tennis, Munro?" asked Fagan.

"Nae in my lifetime."

A loud commotion came from behind them as guards clamored into the palace with swords drawn. Men were shouting, but Elizabeth couldn't make out their words. Ruairi moved in front of her, his arm keeping her in place. She tried to gaze around the mountain that was her brother-in-law.

"What is happening?"

"I donna know. We'll stay here until we know what is afoot," said Ruairi.

Laird Munro placed his hand on the hilt of his sword. "I'll find out and meet ye back here."

As he walked away, Elizabeth jerked Ruairi's arm. "Do you think that's wise? Perhaps Laird Munro should wait here with us as you said. Wouldn't it be easier for us to take our leave if we had to? I don't think he should go in there."

Ruairi turned around and rested his hands on her shoulders, as if he were comforting a child. "Munro could walk into the middle of a sword fight and come out unscathed. There is nay cause for ye to worry. Where did ye wander in the palace when we were seeking the king's secretary?"

Her eyes narrowed. "Trying to distract me?"

"Is it working?"

"No."

"Do ye know that ye and Kat are becoming more like Ravenna and Grace every day?" asked Fagan.

Satisfaction pursed her mouth. "Thank you."

Long, red hair and a massive frame walked toward them at a hastened pace. Laird Munro's face was a mask of stone, and she couldn't tell if he brought good news or bad. When he started to speak to her brothers-in-law in Gaelic, she became instantly irritated.

"Would someone please tell me what is happening—in English?"

"A member of the king's Privy Council was found. He is nay longer of this world," said Ruairi.

"The poor man. That's simply tragic. Do they know how he died?" When a strange look passed between the men, she lifted a brow. Having lived under the same roof as Ruairi and Fagan, she was getting pretty good at recognizing when they were trying to keep something from her sisters.

"Nae yet," said Fagan. "Dinna fash yourself." He glanced at Ruairi. "Why donna we show Elizabeth the gardens?"

Why were all the men in her life masters at diversion?

✎

When Ian discovered a man of the king's Privy Council had been killed, his senses were heightened. Mildmay had also been a member of the king's inner circle, and Ian didn't believe in coincidences. Granted, there were differences between their deaths. Elizabeth's uncle was crushed under the wheel of a carriage when the horses were startled—an accident—whereas this latest man had his throat slashed. But Ian didn't miss the spark in Ruairi and Fagan's eyes. They thought the same. Perhaps Mildmay's death was not by chance at all. Ian's doubts certainly weren't something he was going to express at this moment in front of Elizabeth.

The lass wandered aimlessly through the gardens. Her reddish-brown hair lifted into the wind, and tiny curls escaped the heavy, silken mass. She stopped to study the roses, some kind of purple flowers, and other types of orange blossoms. He wondered if every woman paid attention to such frivolous detail. Thistles and stinging nettles were all the plants he'd ever concerned himself with in the Highlands, only because he tried to avoid them.

A blond-haired man several years older than Elizabeth approached her on the stone path. He wore tan breeches and a linen shirt with deep cuffs, and a black capotain crowned his head. He closed the distance between them, removed his hat, and gave her a low bow.

"My lady, I do not believe we've been formally introduced." He lifted her hand. "I am the Earl of Kinghorne." He brushed a brief kiss on the top of her knuckles, and his eyes never left Elizabeth's.

Ian didn't like him at all.

When she gave the man a brief curtsy, Ian glanced at Ruairi and then at Fagan. Instantly, his friends looked elsewhere and appeared interested in the blooms. What a picture the two made as fierce Scottish warriors smelling the dainty flowers. For an instant, he wasn't sure if they were English fops or Scottish fools. What were they thinking? They had no idea who this man was or what he wanted from Elizabeth. He knew one thing for certain. If Ruairi and Fagan weren't going to intervene, he would. He couldn't stand there and do nothing.

"My lord, it's a pleasure to make your acquaintance. I am—"

"Lady Elizabeth, is everything all right?" Ian stood to his full height and gazed down at the earl as if he were a mere insect that Ian could crush under his heel. As the man took a step back, looking like a cornered animal with no means of escape, Ian smiled. This wasn't the first time he used his mountainous size to his advantage. The earl looked terrified, and he was pleased at the thought.

"Laird Munro, allow me to introduce you to Lord Kinghorne."

Ian placed his hand on the hilt of his sword. He didn't care if the man was an earl. In truth, he wasn't thrilled with the idea of any man approaching Elizabeth. He'd have time to figure that out later because as of this moment, all he wanted was for Kinghorne to move along.

"*Ciamar a tha sibh? Mar sin leat.*"

The earl studied Ian from head to toe. "Pardon?"

"Laird Munro!" Elizabeth chided him and then turned back to the earl. "Please accept my apologies. He asks how you are and seems to have forgotten that not everyone in this world understands Gaelic." She cast Ian a look of disdain. "We are in England after all."

"No apologies are necessary, Lady Elizabeth. If you'll excuse me, I gave my word to my mother that we'd take a leisurely walk in the garden, and I'm afraid that I've neglected her too long. She's resting over there on a bench. Too much sitting isn't good for mother's circulation." He gestured to his left, and Ian spotted the elderly woman through the branches of a tree.

"Of course. I hope to see you again, my lord."

"We'll meet again soon."

When the earl gave Ian a stern look, Ian lifted a brow, and a chuckle almost escaped him. The man minced away to his waiting mother when Elizabeth whirled around to face Ian. Glowering with rage, she poked him in the chest with her finger.

"How dare you! Your behavior was rude, and you humiliated me in front of the earl. Not only did you ask the earl how he was in Gaelic, but you told him good-bye. You're lucky Lord Kinghorne didn't understand your words."

Fagan slapped Ian on the shoulder. "Ye've done it again, Munro. I think the lass is angry with ye."

Elizabeth's response held a note of impatience. "And what gave me away?"

Ian folded his arms over his chest. "Ye're supposed to be her chaperone, Sutherland."

Ruairi laughed as if he was sincerely amused. "Fagan and I were watching. The man only made an introduction. I did nae think he needed to face the end of my sword for that."

"For goodness' sake, we only arrived yesterday. We're not able to stay at the palace because none of you will leave me alone for a single moment, one of us has already been in a heated brawl, a man has died, and now, Laird Munro frightens off the first person who begs an introduction. We're off to a fine start, gentle-men. Need I remind you that *Ruairi* is my chaperone? The three of you had been no more than a stone's throw away the entire time. What could have possibly happened to me in the garden in the light of day with three Highlanders hovering about?" When no one responded, she added, "That's what I thought," and bristled off without them.

"Ye know the lass gets that tenacity from your wife," said Ruairi.

Fagan chuckled. "I was thinking the same of yours."

"How many names are on the king's list before ours?" asked Ian.

❧

Elizabeth had to step away from the men before she strangled them. If they—rather, Laird Munro—thought he would be hovering over her shoulder at every turn, he was in for a surprise.

Even though she never really fathomed why Ravenna and Uncle Walter had always kept her sheltered from the London aristocracy, she was pleased that she'd already met Lord Kinghorne, a bloody earl. Perhaps her luck was changing. But if Laird Munro's careless actions ruined any chance she'd had to make the acquaintance of an earl, she'd make certain the laird's head joined the others at Traitors' Gate on their return home.

As she entered the palace, she disappeared quickly into the crowd with her Scottish guard dogs nipping at her heels. She turned down the hall, slowing her pace, and there was a room on the left that had pomegranates carved into the corners of the arch of the door. When she walked into the great hall by mistake, she paused.

A carved hammer-beam roof hung overhead, and she stood in awe. The ornate architecture on the ceiling was a magnificent sight. At least fifteen colored glass windows were throughout the hall. There were many tables and benches on the floor, but her eyes were drawn to the dais. That's where King James and the royalty before him dined.

Ruairi flanked her. "What do ye think?"

"I find myself at a loss for words."

"I've ne'er known any Walsingham sister to be at a loss for words, but they say there is a first time for everything."

Her eyes darted around the hall. "Have you ever seen anything so grand?"

"Aye. Every time I look into Ravenna and Mary's eyes."

Seeing how much love her brother-in-law held for her sister and her niece brought an instant smile to Elizabeth's face. As Fagan and Laird Munro prowled around the great hall, she approached the empty dais with Ruairi.

"Can you imagine the number of kings and queens who have dined here with their loyal subjects? Do you think King Henry would have sat here at this very table with his many queens, even Anne Boleyn perhaps?"

"I donna know about that, but we'll be dining here this eve—well, nae on the dais. Mayhap King James will grace ye with his presence."

She didn't realize her voice raised a notch, and she

slapped her hands together. "I would be happy beyond measure. And to think Uncle Walter was part of the king's Privy Council. I should have begged my uncle for an introduction a few years ago."

"I have nay doubt he wanted to keep ye from the madness of court, lass. After a time, the view and the people become stale." Ruairi leaned in close and lowered his voice. "Even the king."

"You're probably right, but until then, I'm going to enjoy every moment. Do you think we can find the chapel?"

"Aye, I think we can find it well enough."

They walked through the halls of the palace and through the seas of people. Elizabeth was perfectly aware she must look like a small child on market day. Her head whipped from left to right, her gaze scanning from the ceiling to the floor, not wanting to miss anything of importance. She smiled in greeting to everyone she passed, loving the spark of excitement.

"The chapel is this way," said Ruairi.

They entered through the carved wooden doors. Not only was the timber and plaster ceiling of the chapel breathtaking, but the altar was framed by a massive oak reredos. Opposite the altar on the first floor was the royal pew where King James and his family attended services. When she realized this was probably the place where Queen Catherine Howard had pleaded for King Henry to spare her life, a shiver ran down Elizabeth's spine. She was so deep in thought that she jumped when a warm, male voice spoke from behind her.

"Are ye cold?" asked Laird Munro.

"No. I was thinking about ghosts. I assume you don't believe in them."

He glanced up at the colored glass windows. "I worry more about the living, but I would ne'er tempt fate." His gaze met hers. "Ruairi and Fagan are waiting for ye at the entrance when ye're ready."

Laird Munro stopped in his tracks, and her attention was drawn to the chapel doors where Lord Kinghorne was escorting his elderly mother inside. Laird Munro hesitated as if he was deciding to stay, but then he walked out the chapel door. She was thankful he remembered the verbal thrashing that she'd given him for his earlier unnecessary intervention.

Lord Kinghorne assisted his mother into a pew and then approached Elizabeth. He gave her a bow, and she curtsied. "Lady Elizabeth, how wonderful it is to see you again so soon."

"I was thinking the same of you, my lord."

He gestured to the pew. "Mother enjoys coming to the chapel a few times a day. She claims prayer soothes her soul."

Elizabeth smiled. "Your mother speaks the truth."

"Be that as it may, after she is done here, I'll be taking her back to her room to rest. She needs to lie down or her ankles swell."

"You're staying at the palace, my lord?"

For a moment, he stared at her. "You're not?"

"No." She had many words that came to mind about her chaperones but thought it in her best interest to keep her mouth closed.

Lord Kinghorne glanced over his shoulder. "Yes,

well, if you don't mind me asking, why are you accompanied by those three men?"

"They're my chaperones." When he gave her a puzzled gaze, she added, "My sisters are wed to two of them."

"I see." His eyes rested on his mother. "If you'll please excuse me, I don't like to keep mother waiting."

"Of course not."

"Will you be dining here this eve, Lady Elizabeth?"

"Yes, my lord."

He smiled with an air of pleasure. "Good. Mother prefers to dine early, but perhaps I'll see you in the hall."

"That would be lovely."

Lord Kinghorne sat beside his mother in the pew, and the sight warmed Elizabeth's heart. The man cared for the woman, and Elizabeth took his actions as a positive sign of character.

The men were still lingering out in the hall, and she didn't want to torture them too much on their first day at court, but she couldn't resist one last look around the chapel. Furthermore, they deserved to wait for not permitting her to stay in a grand bedchamber at the palace.

Heavy footsteps approached her from behind.

"We'll be attending court for some time, lass," Ruairi said. "I can always escort ye here anytime ye wish."

"Thank you."

When she realized her brother-in-law came to fetch her, she stole a quick glance out in the hall. She could've sworn Laird Munro was actually scowling at her. Whether the laird was irritated with her, Lord Kinghorne, or court, she couldn't discern. And frankly, she didn't care. She made up her mind to stay the course.

The man did not return her interest; therefore, he did not deserve her love. Grace said the words herself.

❧

Ian gritted his teeth, knowing his vexation was evident. He was resentful of the entire situation—court, Elizabeth, and this English lord that Ruairi and Fagan didn't seem worried about. Ian wasn't an idiot. The lass would one day wed. He knew that, but was it too much to ask that he did not have to bear witness to men who sought Elizabeth's attention?

Something clicked in his mind, and an unaccustomed pain formed in his chest. When he thought about another man sharing the lass's company, companionship that she'd freely shared with him, his mouth felt dry and dusty.

As the men escorted Elizabeth back through the halls, far too many English crowded court for Ian's tastes, but then a smile crossed his face. Laird Ross, Laird Fraser, and Laird MacKay stood huddled against a far wall. Ruairi and Fagan saw them too. All the lairds stood over six feet, and each wore their clan tartan plaids and badges proudly.

"Munro, Sutherland, I see ye've come to share in the misery of the English court," said the Fraser.

"Aye. There's naught like a Highland gathering to be held in the middle of the English," said Ian.

"'Tis good to see ye. Ye remember the captain of my guard," said Ruairi.

Laird Ross extended his hand to Fagan. "Murray, *ciamar a tha thu?*" *How are you?*

Fagan shrugged. "*Tha gu math.*" *I am fine.*

The MacKay cast a puzzled gaze at Elizabeth. "And *dè an t-ainm a th'oirbh?*" *What is your name?*

"This lovely lass is Lady Elizabeth. She is my sister-by-marriage," said Ruairi. "Lady Elizabeth, these are Lairds Ross, Fraser, and MacKay."

She placed a fallen lock of hair behind her ear. "My pleasure, gentlemen. Have you just arrived at court?"

"We came three days ago and tried to get our names on the list before the others to nay avail," said Laird Fraser.

A glazed expression crossed Elizabeth's face. She was growing weary of hearing men complain about court.

"Are ye staying in the palace?" asked Ian.

"Nay, thank God," said Laird MacKay. "There was nay room for us, even three days ago. We're staying in the city. I think most of the lairds came to pay their yearly homage to the king. I saw the Grant, the MacLeod, and the MacKenzie wandering around. None were verra pleased."

A scowl crossed Ian's face. "Mmm… If ye arrived three days before us, it could be some time before we are called before the king."

Elizabeth let out a heavy sigh.

"Were ye here when the guards were running awry over the death of another member of the king's Privy Council?" asked Laird Ross.

"Och, aye. We were at the tennis court," said Ruairi.

"They're saying the man's neck was sliced from ear to ear. Now we can look forward to having a cut-throat among us at the palace," said Laird Fraser.

Elizabeth cleared her throat. "Pray excuse me, Laird Fraser, but did you say the man was killed?"

"Come to think of it, I believe this is the second member of the king's circle who died within the month." Laird Fraser didn't notice the color drain from Elizabeth's face. Otherwise, he would have known to keep his mouth shut.

"Fraser," Ian warned.

Ruairi placed his hand on her shoulder. "Now, lass, there is nay cause for ye—"

"I can nae remember. What was that man's name?" asked Laird Fraser.

Elizabeth spoke through gritted teeth. "Mildmay. His name was Lord Mildmay. He was my uncle."

Eight

ELIZABETH SAT IN THE CROWDED GREAT HALL DRINKING her third goblet of wine and was almost foolish enough to ask Ian—Laird Munro—if she could have a sip of his whisky. It had been a long day. She was mentally exhausted. And just as luck would have it, King James did not sup in the great hall this eve.

With so many warm bodies packed in the hall, the heat was unbearable. Sweat dripped from her brow and in other places no lady should ever mention. To add to her enjoyment was the fact that she could barely hear herself think with the incessant chatter all around her. As she gazed at the tables, she wondered if the other women in attendance felt as miserable. A male voice spoke from beside her.

"So tell me, Lady Elizabeth. Is court everything ye thought it would be?" asked Laird Munro with a knowing grin.

She cleared her throat. "Yes, even more than I'd hoped for." She took another sip from her goblet, not about to admit to the man she'd been ready to take her leave well over an hour ago. The thought of removing her gown, donning her nightrail, and climbing into a soft bed was delightful.

A devilish look came into his eyes. "Och, aye. I can see how much ye're enjoying yourself at this verra moment."

"Is my discomfort that apparent?"

Laird Munro leaned in close. Too bloody close. She silently cursed her heart that turned over in response.

"'Tis written all over your face, lass."

Elizabeth instantly wondered if everything she felt was written all over her face. She averted her eyes and when she did, there was a man staring at her. He was handsome with dark eyes and a secret expression. When he smiled, his teeth, even and white, agreed pleasingly with his dark, tanned skin. His wavy, black hair flowed from his face like a crest to his shoulders, and drops of moisture clung to his damp forehead. There was an exotic look about him that captured her attention.

He sat very still, and his eyes hadn't left hers. She instantly became aware of another kind of excitement, one that didn't involve Laird Munro. The dark-haired man looked away from her, and she watched him as he rose to his feet. He stood there as if he prided himself on his good looks. Her eyes froze on his long, lean form, and his eyes once again met hers. He inclined his head in a deep gesture and with that, he spun and was gone.

Perhaps fate had granted her a boon after all.

❧

Under a dusk sky, Ian, Ruairi, and Fagan followed Elizabeth's carriage through the streets of London.

Ian's patience was wearing thin. He'd had enough of the English court and was pleased they were finally returning to the inn. Although he'd rather be on Munro lands and sleeping in his own bed, for now, the accommodations would have to do.

"What an exciting first day among the English, eh?" asked Ruairi.

Ian kept his eyes ahead as his mount whinnied, almost as if the animal had responded to Ruairi's question. "Aye. One hell of a day. I've been meaning to ask something of the both of ye."

Fagan chuckled. "Munro, have ye nae learned anything from me? I told ye to offer Elizabeth an apology. Beg for her forgiveness." He gestured to Ruairi. "Tell him that I speak the truth."

"I donna know about that. Ravenna is becoming the wiser when I offer her any type of apology. Now she asks what I'm apologizing for, and I donna always have an answer."

"My question has naught to do with Lady Elizabeth. I want to know your thoughts on Mildmay."

Both men were silent, their expressions guarded.

"Sutherland," Ian warned. "I've known ye forever. Your attempts at subtlety donna fool me nor do they suit ye."

Ruairi hesitated. "I've had my doubts, but I ne'er mentioned my views to Ravenna."

"Nor I to Grace," said Fagan.

Ruairi glanced around, reining in his mount next to Ian. "Even before this man was killed at court, I had a difficult time believing a man as skilled as Mildmay died in a carriage accident because of startled horses."

"Did your wife suspect anything untoward?" asked Ian.

"If she had, she ne'er would've let me bring Elizabeth to court. And I think Ravenna was too distraught over her uncle's death to even ponder the question. Besides, she's again with child. The spy craft should be left with the spies. I will nay longer allow her to place herself and our bairns in danger."

"And what of Lady Elizabeth?"

"We are nae staying at court, and she has three Highland warriors as chaperones." A smile crossed Ruairi's face. "Why do ye ask? Do ye question your prowess?"

"Nay. I was questioning yours. If I'm nae mistaken, the Gordon is dead, the Stewart is imprisoned, and there have been nay mercenaries as of late to challenge your skill with a blade." Ian's expression held a note of mockery. "Ye have nae grown soft in my absence, have ye?"

"Ye donna need to worry about that, Munro," said Fagan. "My laird is wed to Ravenna. I'm certain the lass does nae favor her husband growing *soft*. And being that she's again with child, evidently she's making Ruairi practice his swordplay quite often."

Ruairi leaned over and punched Fagan in the arm. "Bastard."

"Aye."

They arrived at the inn, securing the horses and carriage with the stable hands. When Elizabeth stepped down from the coach, she looked tired, worn. She lifted her skirts and walked into the inn as Ian trailed behind her once again today. Mistress Betts greeted them at the entrance with a smile.

"How was your first day at court, my lady?" The woman wiped her hands on her apron.

"Lovely, thank you. I'm weary and think that I'll just retire to my room for the rest of the night."

"Do you need anything to eat or drink?"

Elizabeth returned a tired smile. "No, we dined at court."

"Give me a moment to clean up a bit, and then I'll be up to help you with your dress."

"Thank you, Mistress Betts." Elizabeth turned to Ruairi and Fagan. "Did you want to leave on the morrow after we break our fast?"

"Aye, but we donna need to make haste. I'm afraid ye've worn out Munro from the tour of the palace. He'll need plenty of rest before he returns to court on the morrow," said Ruairi.

Ian placed his hand over his heart. "I'm afraid 'tis true, Lady Elizabeth. My feet nay longer want to carry me."

"And I'm certain your feet have nothing to do with the fact that you men will be getting into your cups this eve."

"Ye know me too well," said Ian.

Elizabeth's face turned scarlet, and she looked away from him. "I'll be bidding you all a good night, gentlemen."

"*Oidhche mhath*," said Ian. *Good night*. He watched the lass as she climbed the stairs to her chamber. Once she was out of sight, he elbowed Ruairi in the arm. "I need a drink."

"I think we could all use many," said Ruairi.

They found an unoccupied table in the corner of

the dining hall and pulled out their flasks. A young lad with light-brown hair approached the table from the kitchen and placed three tankards of ale on the table. He wrung his hands in front of him in a nervous gesture.

"For God's sake, lad. We donna bite," said Ian.

"Pardon?"

Ruairi chuckled. "Donna let the Munro frighten ye lad. He was born that way."

"I'm not frightened." The boy looked terrified. "Is there anything I can bring you?"

"What do ye have left from this eve's sup? I could always eat," said Fagan.

Ruairi pulled out his flask and took a swig of whisky. "Aye, we know."

"There are some biscuits and gravy left."

"Aye, my friends and I will take a few of those," said Fagan.

"Would you like me to bring you more ale too?"

The men laughed in response, and Ruairi held up his flask. "Nay. We have all that we need."

When the boy walked away, Ian shook his head. "Do ye think there will ever be a time when I donna frighten the wee lads?"

Teasing laughter answered him, and Ruairi handed Ian the flask. "Have another drink, Munro."

"It feels so damn good to sit here with a man's drink in hand. Did ye see the watery piss they were drinking at court?" He took another swig and then glanced around at the handful of men and women in the hall. Lowering his voice, he added, "The English would nae know something good if it bit them in the arse."

"Och, aye. I saw the Fraser empty the contents of his goblet on the floor and pour his own drink into it. The Highland lairds know to bring their own *uisge beatha* by now," said Ruairi.

The lad returned with Fagan's food, and as soon as the boy left the table, Fagan tossed a biscuit to Ian, which he didn't even attempt to catch.

"Are ye going to leave it on the table?" asked Fagan.

"I donna want to eat. I want to drink myself into a stupor. I think I've earned it for spending all this time with the English."

Ruairi gave a mock salute, and Ian took another swig. He'd seek his bed when his senses were dulled. And at the rate he was going, it wouldn't be long.

❧

Elizabeth removed her gown, donned her nightrail, and washed her face. She didn't think Mistress Betts had noticed the dagger strapped to her thigh and hidden under her chemise. If the woman had seen anything, she didn't say, and Elizabeth didn't take the time to explain. After a while, she'd even forgotten the blade was there. But all she wanted to do now was crawl under the blankets and embrace the darkness.

As soon as Mistress Betts departed, Elizabeth didn't waste any time. She climbed into bed and blew out the candle. Wiping the hair away from her face, she rolled onto her side, placing her hands under the pillow. She felt empty and drained. Her last thought before she drifted to sleep was of an exotic stranger who cast a furtive smile from across the table.

The next she knew, her eyes flew open. The latch

was rattling on her door. She sat up abruptly, pulling the blankets up to her chin. For an instant, she dared not breathe. The sound she heard wasn't her imagination since it happened again. Elizabeth fumbled to light the candle, and once the room was illuminated, she thought she'd feel more secure.

But she didn't.

Heaven help her. Someone was trying to come into her room. Perhaps if she waited silently, one of the men would come to her rescue. When she heard a curse outside the door, she flew out of the bed, thinking she recognized a Scottish accent. How she prayed that voice belonged to Ruairi, Fagan, or Ian, who were coming to her aid. Placing her ear to the door, Elizabeth waited.

When she didn't hear anything, she whispered, "Is anyone there?"

Receiving no response, she donned her robe that rested on the chair. Once again, she paused at the door. God only knew what was on the other side. Slowly, she lifted the latch and stole a peek into the hall.

Laird Munro sat on the floor with his back resting against the wall. His head was bent forward, and his body was hunched over. What was he doing? She found it difficult to believe the intruder at the door had been strong enough to knock the Highland laird from his feet.

Elizabeth glanced down the hall. Even though there were two candles lit on the wall, she didn't see anyone else. She walked out of her room and knelt beside him. When he didn't move, she gave him a firm shake.

"Laird Munro."

The man jumped to his feet. She lost her balance, falling on her rump in the middle of the hall. She had evidently startled him because when he lifted his arm on the way up, he'd barely missed her face. He gazed around, unsteady on his feet. After a moment, he glanced down and looked at her twice, as if he needed to make certain she was there.

"Lady Elizabeth, what are ye doing on the floor in front of my room?"

She could hardly make out his words. The sweet smell of whisky was on his breath. He extended his hand and pulled her up, but then she had to steady his quaking body in return.

"Your room? I'm afraid this is my chamber, Laird Munro." Something clicked in her mind. "Was that you grabbing the latch of my door? I thought someone was trying to… You startled me."

His words were slurred. "Nay one would dare enter your room with me here, unless they had a wish for death."

"Yes, well, let's get you to the right door, shall we? Where are Ruairi and Fagan?"

"Bed. They gave up on their drinking hours ago."

"And from the look of you—"

He waved her off. "Donna tell me that I should've given up too. I can handle my drink."

She laughed. "I can see that. Try to keep your voice down. Everyone is abed."

Elizabeth wrapped her arm around Laird Munro's waist, and he was so close that she could have rested her head on the man's broad chest. He was only able to take a few tottering steps at a time, but at least he was moving in the right direction.

When they reached his room, she lifted the latch and pushed open the door. Darkness greeted them. Even the dim flicker of candlelight from the hall didn't provide much help to see inside.

"You didn't think to leave a candle lit?"

"I donna need to see. I'm going to fall into bed anyway."

She sighed in exasperation. "And you're going to kill yourself getting there. Did you leave the candle by the bed?"

There was a heavy silence.

"Laird Munro!"

"Aye. Aye."

The man could barely finish his words, and it took all Elizabeth's strength not to leave him where he stood. Then again, perhaps she should wake up her brothers-in-law to handle the mess this eve that was Laird Munro. She was certain they wouldn't be pleased. "Wait here by the door and I'll light the bloody candle."

"Are ye cross with me again, Lady Elizabeth?"

"Am I... Laird Munro, please do us both a favor. Stand here by the door, and keep your mouth closed. Please."

"Why do I feel like I'm being scolded by my mother?"

"If you wouldn't act like a child, I'm sure you wouldn't feel that way." She fumbled to light the candle and was pleased when it finally lit. "There."

She turned, and he closed the door behind him, barely able to stand on his own two feet. As he approached her, she steadied him. He stood at the side of the bed and was gazing down at her when she heard herself swallow.

"Lady Elizabeth." Raising his hand, he placed it gently on her cheek.

She closed her eyes and leaned into his palm. She couldn't help herself. When she opened her eyes, he was looking at her so intensely. His long, red hair fell into his face, and he was so alluring. He had no idea how handsome she thought he was.

What was she thinking? The man was in a drunken stupor. But that certainly didn't stop her impure thoughts. She glanced at his full lips, and all sense of reason deserted her.

"Lady Elizabeth, ye better seek your bed. Ye're in my chamber." He gave her body a raking gaze. "And barely dressed." He pulled her closer and slowly bent his head forward.

There was no denying that he was going to kiss her. She'd been waiting for this moment. No man had ever touched her, and how appropriate the first would be Ian. The walls could fall around her, but she was determined to make this happen. She closed her eyes, knowing one touch of his lips would change her life forever.

Elizabeth waited, and nothing happened. When she opened her eyes, he was shaking his head and pulling away from her.

"I can nae. Ruairi and Fagan are my brothers. They trust me. And ye're far too young, bonny, and sensible for the likes of me."

She stiffened as though he had struck her. "I'm

eighteen, and you're thirty-three. I don't think you're too *old* for me. I'm a woman now, and yet, you don't see that. All you see is that foolish girl from years ago." Tears welled in her eyes. "You drive me completely mad. Everyone warned me that you're nothing more than a brooding laird, but I've seen your kindness and compassion. I've seen how you defend your closest friends and always stand up to the enemy. If I can see that in you, why can't you see that in yourself? You say no woman would ever want you because of your looks, but you never give yourself or anyone else a chance. Why do you always push me away when I'm the only one who—"

Her last words were smothered beneath his lips.

⌘

Ian knew he had to kiss Elizabeth when he saw that fire in her eyes and heard the passion in her voice. He pulled her against him, and his kiss was urgent, like that of a hungry lover. Licking her lip, he forced her to open her mouth, and she did not resist. How he wanted to devour her softness, her innocence.

"Och, Elizabeth."

He clutched her as if he could not get enough. His lips left her mouth, trailing down her neck to her collarbone. She moaned at each touch, her mewling sounds firing his passion even more. Trying to maintain some sense of reason, he pulled back, giving her the opportunity to deny him. But she only looked at him with glazed passion.

Ian molded her to him, his arms wrapping around her like a vise. Her breasts flattened against his chest, and he shuddered with desire. She gently pulled away from him, breathless.

"Laird Munro…" She placed her hands on his arms, and a chuckle escaped him.

"I would think after that kiss, ye'd call me Ian." Rather than releasing her as he should, he pulled her close. "We will cease, but let me simply hold ye."

Rubbing his hands over her back, he felt her hands on his chest. What the hell was he thinking? He'd almost lost control with Elizabeth. God's teeth! If the lass would have permitted him, he would've taken her standing here. That wasn't necessarily true. He still had some sense of chivalry left within him. He would have at least thrown her on the bed.

Reluctantly, he pulled away from her. "Come. I will escort ye back to your room."

She couldn't look him in the eye. "That's not necessary. It's late. No one will be in the hall."

He placed his hand at the small of her back. "I insist."

Neither spoke as he escorted her to her chamber. He did not know what to say. Besides, he was trying too hard not to fall over his own two feet. Opening her door, he waited as she entered her room. She turned around and gave him a tender smile.

"Ian…" She spoke softly, and her eyes never left his. "I don't understand what just happened between us, but I don't want to be hurt anymore."

His eyebrows shot up. "What do ye mean? I donna understand all of this either, but I assure ye, my intentions are nae to cause ye pain." At least he spoke the truth because he wasn't sure what his purpose was in kissing her.

"I don't want you to push me away. My heart couldn't bear it because I've loved you from the first time I saw you."

Elizabeth slowly closed the door in his face, and Ian paled.

Nine

WHEN ELIZABETH ROSE IN THE MORNING, SHE HAD TO pinch herself to make certain last night wasn't a dream. She brought her fingers to her lips and smiled. No, Ian had definitely kissed her. She was certain of that. As she dressed to break her fast, she pondered if he'd altered his opinion of her. After the beautiful kiss they shared, his feelings toward her must have changed for the better. Furthermore, she wasn't about to let him change his mind.

As she entered the dining room, only Ruairi and Fagan were seated at the table. The way Ian could barely stand last night made Elizabeth think he didn't have enough energy to pull himself from bed. Ironically, Ian was a pillar of strength, and she was amazed at the effects whisky had on a grown man.

Ruairi pulled out her chair. "*Madainn mhath*, Elizabeth."

"Good morning to you. Did you both sleep well?"

Fagan laughed. "Aye. I slept like the dead."

"Do I dare ask if either of you have seen Laird Munro this morn?"

Mistress Betts approached the table and gave Elizabeth a bowl of oatmeal. "Here you are, my lady."

"Thank you."

Ruairi took a drink from his cup. "Nay. I'll see to him soon to make sure he's nae dead. When we last saw him, he was well into his cups."

She thought about mentioning that she'd found Ian at her door last night but then decided against it. The last she wanted to do was get him into trouble with Ruairi and Fagan. Not to mention Ian might kill her if she opened her mouth. After all, the men were her brothers-in-law and Ian's best friends.

"Are ye ready to return to court, lass, or mayhap ye've had enough, eh?" asked Fagan.

"Oh, I'm afraid I don't frighten off that easily."

Fagan turned to Ruairi as if he was giving up in battle. "Ye can nae say that I did nae try."

Elizabeth cleared her throat. "If we could, I'd love to explore more of the palace and the grounds."

"Just what we all need, lass, more walking. Did ye nae do enough of that yesterday?" asked Fagan.

"You're very comical. I'm certain that's why my sister married you."

"Hmm… For some reason, I donna think that was the reason Grace wed me."

When he looked like he was deep in thought, Elizabeth laughed. "I wouldn't ponder over that too much if I were you. I do hope everyone is having a wonderful time at Aunt Mary's and Apethorpe Hall. The poor woman could use some cheering up after Uncle Walter's passing. I know she always loved entertaining a houseful of people. I'm sure my sisters, Torquil, and my cousins are keeping her occupied."

"Aye, but let's hope Torquil and Kat are being helpful and nae driving the poor woman mad," said Ruairi.

"I'm sure they're not, and you know Aunt Mary would scold them if they were."

"I also pray that your aunt makes Ravenna rest. Your sister is a stubborn lass and seldom admits she needs to lie down. Ye remember how weary she was when she carried Mary. And speaking of the wee one, I hope she's nae causing too much grief."

"Half of your daughter's blood is Walsingham, you know. It's bound to happen at some time or another."

"Och, aye. Ye donna need to remind me of that. At least the lassie has nae yet taken her first steps. I can only imagine the trouble waiting to happen once she does."

"And I have no doubt her father will be there to save the day. There is a natural bond between a mother and daughter, but I think fathers are very protective of their daughters."

"I can nae deny it." Ruairi lifted his cup to his lips and froze, an amused smile crossing his face. "Munro has certainly seen better days."

Ian walked toward the table at a leisurely pace. His hair was more unruly than usual, and his kilt and tunic were in complete disarray. If he had told her that he'd slept in the streets of London last night with no protection from the elements, she would've believed him.

Fagan laughed as Ian pulled out a chair. "Did ye sleep in the stable last eve with the horses? It would nae have been the first time."

Although he had not even glanced at her, Elizabeth noted that Ian's eyes were red. "I awoke in my bed this morn. But I can nae be certain that I did nae pay a visit to my mount in the barn some time during the night."

"Are you feeling better, Laird Munro?" asked Elizabeth.

"Aye." He briefly met her eyes and then started talking with Ruairi.

When they finished their meal, Ruairi and Fagan excused themselves from the table, and Ian flew to his feet. She was surprised that he didn't want to stay and talk with her but didn't think too much of his actions.

Elizabeth followed the men up the stairs, and when they reached the hall to their rooms, she gave a few tugs on the back of Ian's tunic. Looking over his shoulder, he gave her a puzzled gaze.

"Could I speak with you for a moment?" she asked.

Ruairi and Fagan entered their rooms, and Ian returned a blank stare. When the doors closed, he asked, "What did ye want to speak with me about?" His flat, unspeaking eyes prolonged the moment.

"What did I want to speak with you about? I want to talk about last night."

He sighed, and then gave a resigned shrug. "Aye, I may have been in my cups a wee bit more than I should have, but Ruairi and Fagan watched over ye. I know they did."

Elizabeth hesitated, confused by his odd behavior. "I don't understand what you're talking about. I wanted to speak with you about the kiss."

Ian folded his arms across his chest, an irritated expression crossing his face. "What are *ye* talking about, lass?"

"The kiss we shared in your chamber last night." She felt the screams of frustration at the back of her throat as he rubbed his hands over his face.

"Lady Elizabeth, there was nay kiss in my room. My only bed partner last eve was the *uisge beatha*. I think that I would remember if a kiss was shared, especially with my best friends' sister-by-marriage. And besides, ye sought your bed quite some time before Ruairi and Fagan found theirs. I thought we discussed this at Scadbury Manor. Ye said ye were young and foolish when ye fancied me. Why are ye bringing this up again? We were getting along so well."

Heaviness centered in her chest, and there was sourness in the pit of her stomach. She'd given the man her heart, and he might as well have impaled it on her dagger. A hot tear rolled down her cheek, and she wiped it away. "No, of course you don't remember." His eyes remained icy and unresponsive. "I don't know much about your whisky. I don't even understand how it's possible that you can't recall last night. But I do know that if you're lying only because you don't want to address what happened between us, you're not the man I thought you to be."

A muscle ticked at his jaw, and his gaze was unwavering. "Lady Elizabeth, I donna remember ye being in my room last eve, and I certainly donna recall sharing a kiss with ye. If any of that happened, I offer ye my sincere apologies for my lack of—"

Her voice raised a notch. "*If* any of that happened?" She brushed past him, opened the door to her room, and shut it in his face.

Ian leaned back against the wall, squeezing the bridge of his nose with his fingers. His memories of Elizabeth last night were pure and clear, but his mind had been confounded ever since. Now added to his misery was the expression she'd held on her face only a moment ago. How would he ever forget the look she had given him when he pretended not to remember holding her in his arms? What troubled him even more was the fact that he had one hell of a time denying how wonderful she felt there.

But he believed the best recourse for them both was to deny everything. After all, Elizabeth's declaration last eve had made him realize how innocent she still was.

Love.

The lass had no clue what she was talking about. He'd certainly bedded his share of women before, but every tupping had the same result. None of the women had stayed around long enough or even held any fondness for him for more than a fortnight afterward. He'd never have the companionship of a woman or a wife, a truth he'd come to terms with long ago.

Elizabeth had no idea how hard he'd pondered the subject. He couldn't even sleep last night. But no matter how many times his brain hammered him with possibilities, there was only one truth he knew beyond a shadow of doubt. Somewhere out there was a better man for the lass.

She was young, beautiful, and had her whole life ahead of her. Furthermore, he was almost sixteen years older than Elizabeth. He was nothing more than a battle-hardened Highland laird who had nothing to offer a woman, not even a handsome visage. The idea of Elizabeth taking pity on him, something he had always thought she'd done, drove him mad. He refused to have a woman marry him out of sympathy for his looks or lack thereof.

Mistress Betts cleared her throat. "Laird Munro, I was coming to assist Lady Elizabeth with her gown. Were you waiting to see her? I could tell her you're wait—"

"Nay, I was just taking my leave."

After making himself presentable for court, Ian met Ruairi and Fagan below stairs. To keep his mind occupied from his earlier encounter with Elizabeth, Ian stepped out to the barn and had the horses and carriage readied while they waited for the lass to dress. As soon as he set foot back in the inn, his jaw dropped at the sight before him.

Elizabeth's gown barely covered the parts of a lass that should always be concealed, at least on a lady. Her dress was black with a low, rounded bodice. The swells of her breasts were perched high like they were being offered on a trencher for a meal. His eyes discovered the only item covering her rounded globes was the jewelry that hung on a black, silk string around her neck. A belt encircling her waist displayed its smallness, and he remembered the softness of her milky skin. He was even more annoyed when something moved below his waist on its own accord.

Fagan elbowed Ian in the arm and whispered, "Lift your fallen jaw, Munro. Ye look like Angus awaiting a meal."

"I think we'll be fending off many a suitor this day," said Ruairi.

"Ye're nae going to let her wear that, are ye?" Ian didn't realize the edge in his voice until Ruairi's gaze sharpened.

"'Tis how most English women dress at court. Ye've seen them. Who am I to tell the lass what to wear? I am nae her father nor her husband."

Ian gazed at his friend as if the man had lost his wits. "Ye're her brother-by-marriage, her chaperone. As long as she lives under your roof, she'll do as ye say."

"Ye do remember that she is Ravenna and Grace's sister, eh?" Ruairi returned a look as though his words explained everything.

"Is there anything the matter?" asked Elizabeth, lifting her skirts and walking toward them.

Fagan chuckled. "Munro thinks ye should change your gown before we take our leave for court."

"And Laird Munro has no right to tell me how to dress. I'll be waiting for you in the carriage when you're ready." The lass lifted her head in a defiant gesture and walked haughtily out the door.

Fagan slapped Ian on the shoulder. "Munro, when will ye ever learn? Start this day like ye did the last. Offer the lass an apology for thinking like a man."

❧

Although Elizabeth had the entire ride to court to calm her fury, as soon as she stepped out of the carriage and saw Laird Munro, that spark of anger that still remained kindled into a raging fire. She was furious at her vulnerability toward the man. She'd dreamed of the moment when Ian would finally take her in his arms and kiss her, but all she was left with now was the reality that he'd never want her. Who in her right mind would've pined after someone for three long years? What a fool she'd been.

When she entered the hall of the palace, a hand reached out to stay her, and her eyes lit up. Lord Kinghorne inclined his blond head and gave her a slight bow. If that wasn't a sign that she needed to move forward with her life, she didn't know what was.

"Lady Elizabeth, how wonderful to see you again." He glanced over her shoulder. "Gentlemen…" When his eyes returned to hers, he smiled. "I was just going to take a walk in the gardens. Would you care to join me?"

"I'd love to." She turned, speaking only to Ruairi. "May I meet you back here in an hour's time? I promise that I won't wander off anywhere else, except the gardens with Lord Kinghorne."

A male voice spoke from behind her. "You can be assured that Lady Elizabeth will be in good hands. I have to meet my mother within the hour, so I'll be sure to bring Lady Elizabeth back on time."

She saw a slight hesitation in Ruairi's hawk-like eyes, and just when she thought he wouldn't give his consent, his words pleased her. "Go on, lass." He gazed over her shoulder and rested his hand on the hilt of his sword, as if Lord Kinghorne needed any warning to behave.

Elizabeth took the earl's extended arm and walked along beside him. When they reached the gardens, she took a deep breath. She tried to enjoy the view, wanting nothing more than to banish a certain laird from her mind. The scent of flowers wafted through the air as several men and women ambled along the garden paths.

"Have you seen this lovely orange blossom?" Lord Kinghorne lifted the bloom from its stem. "It's quite beautiful."

"Yes, the palace gardens are extraordinary."

"My mother has a lovely garden," he said, moving closer to study a rose. "Her blooms aren't as magnificent as the palace flowers, but they're beautiful nevertheless." He placed his finger to his lips. "Shhh… Don't tell her that I told you that. She'd be cross with me."

Elizabeth laughed. "I won't. And is your mother enjoying court, my lord?"

"Indeed. My father passed a few years ago, and mother has accompanied me ever since. She says it keeps her young. And what of you, Lady Elizabeth? Why aren't your sisters accompanying you?"

She placed a fallen lock of hair behind her ear. "My sisters are visiting my aunt at Apethorpe Hall."

"My word, was Lord Mildmay your uncle?"

She gazed down at the grass and couldn't meet his eyes. "Yes."

"Please accept my condolences for your loss." He handed her a long-stemmed flower. "Roses are Mother's favorite, and I hope you enjoy them too. Be sure not to tell anyone that I picked the bloom from the palace grounds. The king—and my mother—would have my head."

"Your secret is safe with me, my lord."

"I only knew your uncle in passing, but I know he was favored by the king."

"He'll be sorely missed."

Seeing the expression of sadness that crossed her face, the earl placed her hand on his arm and they continued to walk along the garden paths. "The musicians will be playing after supper this evening. Will you stay to dance?"

"Yes, I should hope so. I'll have to speak with Laird Sutherland first, but I'd like that."

Elizabeth knew there was a gleam in her eye. Her first dance in England would be with a peer of the realm at the king's court. This was what she'd been waiting for. But a sour expression crossed her face when she realized she'd already had her first kiss with a Scot. That was something she could never take back.

"Mother loves to dance. She wouldn't miss it."

Elizabeth wondered if the man meant to dance this evening with her or his mother.

❧

Ian didn't know what the hell he was doing. He was a Highland laird and used to making decisions for the clan. But when Elizabeth had taken the English peacock's arm, a feeling washed over him that he couldn't explain. For the first time in his life, he doubted his own judgment. And that frightened him more than anything.

"I'm surprised ye let the lass go alone," said Fagan.

"I think Kinghorne will be the least of our worries. Be thankful ye have an hour to yourself and donna have to follow the lass around," said Ruairi.

Laird Fraser and Laird MacKay approached them with wry grins. "I see ye've had nay such luck in seeing the king either," said Laird Fraser.

"Did ye think we'd be granted a boon so soon?" asked Ian. "Where is the Ross?"

"He's taking advantage of the liberties offered at court." Laird MacKay gestured down the hall to a group of buxom women. Several "ladies" were running their hands all over Laird Ross, and he looked as though he was enjoying every moment.

When an elbow poked Ian in the back, he knew that little shove had come from Fagan. He didn't need his friend encouraging him to sate his needs with some English harlot. Frankly, he wouldn't have been irked at an idea like that in the past, but the thought of bedding another woman after he'd held Elizabeth in his arms instantly killed his ardor.

Giddy laughter came from the blond lass who led Laird Ross away, as another one of the women turned and gave Ian what she thought to be a luring gaze. She placed her forefinger into her mouth, sucking, and licking it. To him, brazen women were only good for one task and at the moment, his stomach churned with the thought of bedding a whore.

He averted his eyes, especially when two of the women started to approach. He'd even briefly thought about fleeing, but he was no coward. The lasses reached Laird MacKay and Ruairi, rubbing their hands over the shoulders of the men.

"Would you like some company?" a brown-haired wench asked Ruairi.

"Nay, lass. I am happily wed."

Not hearing the answer she wanted, the woman moved behind Laird MacKay. "And what about you?"

"I'm wed as well."

When the woman glanced at Fagan, he held up his hands. "Nay, I'd like to keep my head and the other parts of me where they are. I'm wed too." He grasped Ian by the shoulders. "But my friend here is nae yet wed."

Ian cringed.

One of the women stood by his side and ran her fingers all over his chest. He stilled her hand in order to deter her affections, and that's when he caught sight of something from the corner of his eye.

Elizabeth.

Her eyes welled with tears.

Ten

ELIZABETH TRIED TO HIDE HER INNER MISERY BUT wasn't sure she was successful. She didn't think it possible, but Laird Munro had a way of slicing open her wound again. It was bad enough when the man vehemently denied the kiss they'd shared, but now she was forced to watch as he held the hand of some harlot right in front of her bloody eyes. Elizabeth was perfectly aware that she'd always had her heart open wide, but the shock of defeat held her immobile.

"Thank you, Lady Elizabeth, for your company in the gardens, but I don't want to keep Mother waiting. Pray excuse me, and we'll hope to see you later again this evening. Be sure to save a dance for me."

She'd barely heard Lord Kinghorne's words. "Thank you, my lord." As he walked away, she hadn't even noticed Fagan's hand on her shoulder.

"Lady Elizabeth, ye do remember Laird Fraser and Laird MacKay, eh?"

"Yes. It's a pleasure to see you again."

Fagan's voice softened. "Is everything all right? Ye look distraught."

She made the mistake of glancing at Ian. He was speaking in hushed tones in the courtesan's ear as the woman nodded in return. The courtesan pulled the other harlot by the arm down the hall, more than likely waiting for the time when Laird Munro agreed to meet her again. When Elizabeth lifted her eyes, Ian's expression darkened.

"If Kinghorne did nae behave and did something, ye need to tell me," said Fagan. She hadn't realized he was still speaking.

"Lord Kinghorne was nothing but a gentleman. Why don't you stay and finish your conversation with the men? I'll wait for you on the first bench in the gardens."

"The conversation is nae that exciting, lass. I can accompany ye to the garden."

"I'd rather have a moment alone if that's all right with you."

"Hmm… Grace always tells me those words have two meanings. Ye either want me to come along and talk with ye about something, or ye truly desire to be left alone. I have nae mastered the subject yet, lass, so ye'll have to tell me. Which is it?"

Elizabeth patted him on the arm. "You're safe, Fagan. I can assure you that my words meant the latter, but thank you for your concern."

Trying not to think of anything, Elizabeth sat alone on a bench in the garden. Men and women passed her in their finery, but she didn't know a single soul. She probably would've had better luck if Uncle Walter had accompanied her and made introductions. Sadness washed over her when she remembered that he was no longer here.

She glanced down, fingering the material on her gown. Even choosing the daring dress to entice Ian hadn't worked. When she spotted black boots, she lifted her eyes and was greeted by the handsome stranger from last night. He had warm, brown eyes and appeared just as she'd remembered him. His wavy, black hair hung down to his shoulders. He wore tan breeches, a loose-fitting tunic, and wisps of hair curled against the V of his open shirt. His exotic look was captivating.

"Pardon the intrusion. I know that we haven't been formally introduced, but I am King Henry VIII." When he gave her a low bow, she laughed.

"I must say, Your Majesty, you look very well and have certainly traveled far from Windsor where you've been interred for the last sixty-six years."

His smile widened. "I am Will Condell, an actor commissioned to play King Henry at the Globe Theatre in Southwark." He gestured to the bench. "May I?" His accent changed, but he was easier to understand than most of the Highland lairds she knew.

"Please, sit. It's a pleasure to make your acquaintance, Mister Condell. I am Lady Elizabeth Walsingham."

He lifted her hand and brushed a kiss across her knuckles. "The pleasure is mine, my lady." His eyes never left hers, and she was flattered by his interest.

"The palace must provide you with a lot of inspiration to play a role such as King Henry."

He casually leaned back on the bench. "That it does. The king was without a doubt a lover of sport. He loved to play tennis." Mister Condell grinned mischievously. "He also had a way with the ladies and his many wives."

An amused expression crossed her face. "Oh, yes, but I certainly wouldn't have wanted to be one of the many women among his court."

"I agree, Lady Elizabeth. Your head is lovely where it is."

"Your accent was very believable. I never would've known you weren't an English gentleman."

He reverted back to the English accent. "I've been an actor for many years. In order to play different roles, I have to speak many accents fluently."

"How many accents can you do, Mister Condell?"

"Let me see. I can speak in French, a bit of German, some Italian, you've heard the English, and of course, I can speak my native Spanish tongue." Elizabeth was amazed as the man kept changing his accent after speaking only a few words.

"And what about my language? Are ye able to speak Scots?" Laird Munro's expression held a note of mockery, and Mister Condell flew to his feet.

"I have not had ample opportunity to study the Scot's language, but I'm always willing to learn." The man extended his hand to Ian. "I am Will Condell, an actor at the Globe Theatre."

"Laird Munro…" Ian glanced around the garden and then at Mister Condell. "And as of this moment, I am the chaperone for the lass."

❧

Ian knew what Elizabeth was doing. He'd hurt her by denying the kiss between them. And the English harlot had only made matters worse by adding salt to an already open wound. Last eve he realized Elizabeth was no longer a child. But if she thought to use her feminine wiles to make him jealous by consorting with a man who was fair of face, her actions wouldn't work. Nor would he permit her to throw herself into the arms of the first man—well, the second man she'd met at court.

He wasn't worried over Kinghorne because the earl couldn't separate himself long enough from his mother. But for some reason, this *actor* unsettled him. Condell stood tall, confident, and could almost look him in the eye. This was the first time Ian could remember a man standing before him who was not cowering in his boots.

Ian didn't like him at all.

When the man smiled, Ian wanted nothing more than to ram Condell's straight, white teeth down his throat.

"I'm certain Lady Elizabeth is in good hands with you as her guardian, Laird Munro." Condell's gaze narrowed, and he lowered his voice. "But I'm no coward." He turned around and brought Elizabeth's fingers to his lips. "Lady Elizabeth, until we meet again."

"Of course, Mister Condell. It was a pleasure." As soon as the man walked away, Elizabeth cast a look of death upon Ian. Her expression was thunderous, and she closed the distance between them. "How dare you! You have no right to interfere in my life. Lest you forget, Laird Munro, you wanted no part of mine."

Her angry gaze swung over him, and then she poked him in the chest with her finger. She continued to speak through clenched teeth. "You have no trouble consorting with a harlot before my very eyes, but you cause me grief for talking to a man on a bench in the garden in the light of day. I'll never understand you."

Ian stopped her escape with a firm grip on her arm, and his eyes softened. "There are many harlots at court." When her eyes blazed, he added, "I have nay desire to take any to my bed." He brushed his thumb over her cheek. "I would ne'er deliberately hurt ye, Elizabeth."

There was a heavy silence as tears fell down her cheeks.

"You already have."

She walked away from him, and he called after her. He did not blame the lass when she did not look back. For being a Highland laird, he was certainly making all the wrong decisions. He sat on the bench and wondered at what point in his life everything went awry.

"Did ye find Elizabeth?" asked Fagan. As soon as Ian glanced up, his friend's expression changed to one of concern. "What the hell happened?"

"Where is Ruairi?"

"He's still with the Fraser and the MacKay." Fagan sat on the bench beside him. "Munro, is there something ye want to tell me?" When Ian didn't respond and rolled his neck from side to side, Fagan added, "We've been friends for years. I know something has been troubling ye. What the hell is going on?"

Ian thought hard about opening his mouth to his friend. Granted, they'd talked about everything— mercenaries, spies, crops, drinking, and wenching—but he gave pause. Although Ruairi and Fagan were his best friends, Elizabeth was their sister-in-law.

"For God's sake, *tha thu gus mo liathadh. Sput a-mach e.*" *You're driving me gray. Spit it out.*

"Lady Elizabeth told me that she loved me." Ian spoke in a rush of words, and Fagan chuckled.

"'Tis nay great secret. Everyone knows that."

"She's almost sixteen years younger than me. How could she know the meaning of the word, and what in the hell could she possibly want with the likes of me?"

Fagan rubbed his chin. "Mmm… I've been pondering that thought for many years. In fact, we've all wondered at what point the lass had lost all sense of reason, but she's always loved ye. She cares for ye, and ye know damn well that she's nay longer a child. What did ye say to her? I hope ye denied her in kind."

"I think I've managed to make matters worse."

There was a gleam in Fagan's eyes. "We always do."

"What do ye mean?"

"We're men. It's in our verra nature to speak the wrong words to women." Fagan pulled out his flask and handed it to Ian. "I've noticed ye've been troubled over Elizabeth a lot lately. I have to ask ye. Have your feelings toward her changed? What *do* ye think of the lass?"

Ian took a swig, which was not nearly enough. "I donna think of her. She is your sister-by-marriage."

"Och, aye. That almost sounded believable. I remember telling Ruairi the same about Grace, and now she is my wife. Tell me the truth. There have ne'er been secrets between us."

"The lass pities me."

"Is that what ye think? Hell, Munro. She looks upon ye the same way Grace gazes upon me and the way Ravenna looks at Ruairi. That's nae pity ye see in her eyes, ye daft fool."

"Nay lass has ever paid me so much attention. In truth, I donna know what she sees."

"Elizabeth is a kind soul. Whatever she sees, she knows there's kindness within ye too. Now tell me what ye did to make matters worse. I've had to dig myself out of a few troubles with Grace. Mayhap I can help and offer ye words of wisdom."

"I donna even think ye can help me with this." Ian rubbed his hand over his brow. "I was a fool and kissed the lass when I was in my cups. The next morn, I denied it ever happened."

❧

Elizabeth made her way around the entire garden before she decided to turn around and return to where her brothers-in-law waited for her. Fagan was sitting with Laird Munro on the bench when she approached them, and both men stood.

"Is Ruairi still talking with Laird—"

"My apologies for the delay. I hope Fagan and Munro kept ye entertained in my absence," said Ruairi as he walked up behind her.

"Yes. I cannot say that I've lacked for entertainment," she said dryly.

"'Tis about time for the noon meal. Let's make our way to the great hall."

Elizabeth sat between Fagan and Ruairi at the table and said a silent prayer of thanks no sharp weapons were within her grasp. And God decided to grant her a boon because Laird Munro was sitting on the other side of Fagan so she didn't have to look at him. Although, removing the dagger that was strapped to her thigh was an option. She tapped the hidden blade through her skirts, the thought of impaling the man through his heart making her smile.

Searching the faces of the men in the hall, none were Mister Condell or Lord Kinghorne. Just as well. She needed a break from men, Scottish men in particular. Granted, she had found great pleasure talking with Mister Condell, especially since he was as interested in the history of Henry VIII's reign as she was. How exciting it must be for the actor to play an English king at the Globe Theatre. Perhaps if she'd ask Ruairi nicely, he would accompany her to see Mister Condell playing the part of King Henry.

There was only so much swordplay Elizabeth could stand to watch in the Scottish Highlands. She yearned to attend the theater, and most of the music she'd heard in the Highlands was only that of Scottish bagpipes. A little culture wouldn't hurt her brother-in-law either. Ravenna would probably thank her for exposing Ruairi to the arts of the stage. Maybe then his tastes in tapestries would change from death and battles to life and celebrations. One could only hope.

When they finished their meal, Fagan stood. "We have to see the Fraser. Munro will escort ye wherever ye'd like to go."

"No!" Elizabeth cleared her throat. "What I meant to say was Laird Munro doesn't have to escort me. Why don't I come along with you?"

"Nay, lass. We have important matters to discuss. Ye stay with Munro," said Ruairi.

She didn't miss the odd look Ruairi gave Fagan before her brothers-in-law walked out of the hall, and she wasn't ready to have another conversation with Ian so soon. Her goblet suddenly held much interest, especially when the man slid closer to her on the bench.

"Lady Elizabeth, have you finished your meal? Mother and I were just going to dine. Perhaps you could join us."

Elizabeth glanced over her shoulder as Lord Kinghorne greeted her with a smile. His elderly mother stood by his side wearing a blue dress that blanketed her from neck to toe. Her gray hair was tucked up under a large hat that partially covered her face. The woman poked the earl with her elbow.

"Patrick, was this the young lady you were telling me about? I'm asking because you haven't introduced us. Where are your manners, my dear boy?"

"My apologies, Mother. Lady Elizabeth, pray allow me to introduce you to Lady Glamis."

Elizabeth stood, and the woman patted the top of Elizabeth's hand.

"A pleasure to meet you, my lady."

Lady Glamis glanced to Elizabeth's right and stared with astonishment. "And who do we have here?"

Elizabeth grasped Ian's arm, and he stood. "Lady Glamis, please allow me to introduce to you Laird Munro."

"'Tis a pleasure to meet ye, my lady." Ian gave Lady Glamis a slight bow. Elizabeth almost chuckled when he once again stood to his full height, and the woman tilted her head back—as if she was breaking her neck—to look up at him.

"If you don't mind me saying so, you are quite a large man."

"Mother…"

"'Tis nae the first time those words have fallen upon my ears, my lady. I'm Lady Elizabeth's chaperone."

"Then I dare say Lady Elizabeth is very well protected, Laird Munro." Lady Glamis gestured to the table. "Would you care to join us?"

When an uneasy expression crossed Ian's face, Elizabeth was tempted to make him suffer. But truth be told, she wasn't in the mood to converse with anyone either. "My apologies, my lady, but Laird Munro was escorting me to the gardens." When she gazed at him and gave him a knowing look, he placed his hand at the small of her back.

"Aye, mayhap we'll see ye again soon. 'Twas a pleasure to meet ye." He tipped his head to the earl. "Kinghorne."

As they walked away from the table, Lady Glamis spoke. "Patrick, I don't know what you're talking about. The laird was very kind."

"I know ye're verra cross with me, but I thank ye for that," said Ian.

"Cross does not even begin to describe what I feel." When Elizabeth was about to step out into the gardens, Ian escorted her the other way. "Where are we going?"

"There is something I want to show ye."

They passed the chapel some time ago, and she wondered where he was taking her. As they entered one of the halls she hadn't come across before, it wasn't as crowded as the others. They'd only

passed one man before they came to a set of marble
stairs.

"Are we allowed to be here?" she whispered.

"Ye donna see any guards, do ye?"

Elizabeth followed Ian up the stairs, and they
stood before a large, wooden door. He moved to the
side and gestured to the latch. "Open it." When she
hesitated, he folded his arms across his chest. "Are ye
going to open the door, or are ye going to stand here
and be stubborn?"

She shrugged with indifference. "I haven't decided."

Ian sighed and opened the door. As soon as she set
foot inside, she brought her hand to her chest.

"It's magnificent."

"Aye, I thought ye'd enjoy it."

The library was something she never could have
imagined. The walls were lined with more books
than she could count. Two men were reading
silently in the corner, but she'd barely given them a
second glance. Winding stairs led down to the first
floor, but she would explore that one later. A single
wall displayed artwork—and not scenes of death
and battle. As she studied the paintings of English
landscapes, flowers, and a man holding his dog,
she smiled.

"I see it in your eyes. Donna get any ideas, lass.
Ruairi will nae take down his tapestries."

She walked to the next painting. "You've read
my mind." When she glanced over Laird Munro's
shoulder, she studied the intricate wood carvings on
the ceiling. "Have you ever seen anything so grand?"

"I have." He closed the distance between them

and lifted his hand to her cheek. "Elizabeth, there is something I need to tell ye."

Intense astonishment touched her pale face. She bowed her head, and then she curtsied. "Your Majesty."

Eleven

Ian turned, giving his liege a low bow. King James's brown hair was combed back and his beard hung nearly the length of his chest. He wore a white doublet and hose, accented with black and silver breeches. A large chain hung around his shoulders, set with gold and other fine jewels. His black shoes were adorned with silver and pearls, and Ian only knew that because he studied them.

"Good day to you," said the king. "Please rise." He gazed at Ian and then at Elizabeth. "You must be Lady Elizabeth."

"Yes, Your Majesty."

"I apologize for not greeting you when you arrived at court, but I have pressing matters that require my immediate attention. Please accept my deepest condolences on the loss of your uncle. Mildmay was a good man, a man I was proud to call my friend. If you want for anything during your stay, please do not hesitate to ask."

"Thank you, Your Majesty."

The king gave a brief nod to Ian. "Laird Munro."

"Your Majesty."

The king's black, gold, and silver cloak flowed behind him as he descended the stairs with four of his guards. The man had an air of regal grace and authority. When Ian heard the king exit the library through the door on the first floor, he took a deep breath. He gazed at Elizabeth as she held her fingers over her lips and then slapped him on the arm.

"That was the bloody king." Satisfaction pursed her mouth, and he chuckled.

"Aye. That was the king."

"I simply can't wait to tell Ravenna and Grace that King James spoke to me. You *did* hear him."

"Och, aye. I heard him." From the excitement in Elizabeth's voice and the expression on her face, he was amazed she wasn't jumping up and down like a child given a toy.

"I should've told him there wasn't enough room for all of us, and I wasn't staying at the palace, but my words failed me. And to think my uncle was the king's friend."

Ian placed his hand on her shoulder in a comforting gesture. "I'm sure Mildmay is sorely missed by the king." When he removed his hand, she cast a puzzled gaze.

"My apologies. I was distracted by His Majesty. What did you want to tell me?"

"Pardon?" An inner torment gnawed at him because Elizabeth's eyes were lit with happiness. He didn't have the heart, nor could he find the strength, to tell her that he'd lied. God knew he was a daft fool, but at this moment, she didn't despise him. He didn't want to take the chance that she would again.

"I only meant to say that I brought ye to the library because I thought ye'd enjoy it. I know how much ye like your books."

"Thank you. I do like it very much. Do you mind if we stay awhile?"

"Of course nae. Take as much time as ye'd like. I'll wait for ye over there."

Ian sat in a soft chair as Elizabeth wandered around the second floor of the library. Her behavior reminded him of a bee that flew from flower to flower, except that the lass traveled from book to book. She ambled past a shelf, running her fingers over the spine of the leather bindings. Every now and then, she'd even stop and sift through the pages of a tome. And when a smile crossed her face, the sight warmed his heart.

Even though he was hesitant to admit it, the lass looked lovely in the black dress. He just didn't like other men staring at her wearing that gown. Settling back into the cushion of the chair, Ian closed his eyes. Fagan was right. Elizabeth had become a beautiful woman.

❧

A loud snort escaped Laird Munro and reverberated through the library. The man flew to his feet, withdrew his sword, and his eyes darted from left to right.

"Elizabeth!"

Elizabeth's sense of humor took over, and she laughed in answer. As she approached him, her lips were trembling with the need to smile. "Slaying the beastly dragons, Laird Munro?" His state of foolishness quickly turned to annoyance as he sheathed his weapon in the middle of the library. When he glanced around the room in a nervous gesture, she added, "No one is here. The men took their leave about two hours ago."

"Two hours?" His eyes widened.

"Yes. I suppose that's what happens when you spend the night drinking and not getting any sleep. Perhaps you'll seek your bed this eve and get some rest." When the memory of his lips on hers came to mind, she decided a change of subject was in order. "Should we seek Ruairi and Fagan now? Do you think they're done talking with Laird Fraser?"

"Aye."

As they reached the door, she paused in front of it, lifting her hand to stay him. "Thank you. You were kind."

His eyes brightened with pleasure, and then he gifted her with a smile, the kind of look that would melt the winter snow. Good heavens. She forced herself to settle down, clinging to the reality that he'd hurt her. Furthermore, she had no intention of falling under that spell—again. They walked out into the hall, and he closed the door behind them.

"I'm glad ye enjoyed yourself, lass. Ye even spoke to the king. Many of his subjects donna get the chance."

"I can't wait to tell Ruairi, but somehow, I don't think he'll be as excited to hear the news. Do you think we can stay after we sup this eve? Lord Kinghorne said musicians will play, and I'd love to listen. Who knows? Perhaps you can find another chair in the corner in which to relax and rest your eyes."

"And if ye say any such words to Fagan or Ruairi,

they'll have my head for falling asleep and neglecting my duties of watching over ye."

"I'm certain that I could be persuaded to keep my mouth closed if you'd quit interfering when a man tries to talk with me. Maybe then I'd consider making a deal."

He gave her a measured gaze. "Are ye blackmailing me?"

"Perhaps. Is it working?"

Laird Munro didn't respond, not that she thought he would. They made their way back through the halls of court, and when they passed the same harlot who'd had her hands all over Ian, Elizabeth stiffened. But something stirred within her when she felt his hand resting at the small of her back. His behavior toward her wasn't as aloof as it had been before. She wasn't sure what had changed, but maybe it was a blessing he couldn't recall the kiss between them. He was returning to the same kind laird that she'd always known. When "loved" came to mind, she mentally chided herself.

Her brothers-in-law stood in the hall with Laird Fraser. When Ruairi's eyes met Elizabeth's, he smiled. "And how did ye enjoy the library, lass?"

She glanced at Ian, and he shook his head in an appeasing gesture. "Go on and tell him. 'Tis written all over your face."

Elizabeth wrapped her fingers around Ruairi's arm, trying to stay her excitement. "You're never going to believe this. We saw King James in the library, and he talked to me," she blurted out in a rush of words.

"He did?" asked Ruairi.

Fagan folded his arms over his chest. "And what did he say?"

"Good day to you." Ruairi laughed, and Fagan rubbed his hand over his brow. "That wasn't all he said. He gave his condolences for Uncle Walter and said if I needed anything at court not to hesitate to ask. I was so excited that I forgot to ask him for more rooms for you."

"I'm glad ye did nae. I donna want to stay here. I'd have to sleep with one eye open," said Fagan.

"Please tell me ye seized the opportunity to ask the king when the Highland lairds were going to be granted their audience, Munro," said Laird Fraser.

"There was nay time."

"Damn." When Elizabeth's eyes widened, Laird Fraser added, "My apologies, Lady Elizabeth."

She waved him off. "Think nothing of it. I'm quite used to foul language."

"I imagine so, having to live with Sutherland and Murray under the same roof."

"Actually, I was referring to my sisters, Ravenna and Grace."

"Elizabeth, there is a tennis tournament commencing at the court. Would ye like to attend?" asked Ruairi.

"Yes. I've never seen anyone play the sport before."

"Then ye're in for a treat, Lady Elizabeth," said Laird Fraser in a dry tone.

❧

Ian wondered if this brutal torture would ever come to an end. Why would grown men want to hit a ball back and forth between them? At least practicing swordplay kept men alert and made them fit for battle. But this futile display was yet another example of the pampered English having too much time on their hands. He gazed at the men and women who were watching the men hit the ball, realizing he was among the many spectators encouraging this madness.

An elbow poked him in the side. "Did ye tell her?" asked Fagan.

Ian kept his eyes on the game and spoke in a low voice. "The king came into the library as I was about to say the words."

"Leave it to the royals…always interfering. Ye have nae changed your mind about telling her the truth, have ye?"

"Nay. I'll take your counsel on this, but I'll have to find another time to speak with her." He paused. "Why is it ye're helping me?"

Fagan let out a heavy sigh. "I've often told Ruairi that sometimes I'm the only one who knows what's best for him. And I'm giving ye the courtesy of telling ye the same."

"Aye, but the lass is your sister-by-marriage, and Grace is your wife."

"And I love them both verra dearly, but ye are my friend, my brother. Tell me. Is it wrong to want to see ye with happiness in your life? Ye've always had this stubborn way about ye, Munro, and God knows how ye've managed to plant this ridiculous notion in your head that ye're nae worthy of a woman's love. Granted, ye're verra large, and most lasses run at the sight of ye, but ye're a good man nevertheless. Elizabeth saw that in ye many years ago."

"And ye still think 'tis nae wise to tell Ruairi? The man is nae daft. He'll have my head when he finds out what happened between me and Elizabeth."

"'Twas only a single kiss." As if Ian needed his friend to remind him. "I would nae mention anything until ye know how ye truly feel for the lass. Take this time to woo her and make amends for your foolishness. I can nae say that Ruairi was nae cross with me when I told him about Grace, but we're all as brothers, kin, and ye donna turn your back on family. Besides, if ye wed Elizabeth, that's one less Walsingham under Ruairi's roof. More than likely, the man would thank ye for taking the lass out of his hands."

Ian cringed. "Did ye have to mention marriage? Do ye want me to run back to Scotland and nae look back?" He wiped the irritated expression from his face. "Although it pains me to admit, ye're probably right."

"I usually am. Mayhap ye can tell that to Grace, eh? She seems to think I'm always in the wrong."

When the tournament was over, which was not soon enough, they walked back to the great hall to sup. The tables were filling quickly, and Elizabeth sat on a bench at the table with Ruairi flanking her on one side and Laird Fraser on the other.

"Fraser, why donna ye come over here with me? I'd like to chat with ye," said Fagan.

Thankfully, the Fraser didn't think twice and moved next to Fagan. As Ian swung his leg over the bench to sit next to Elizabeth, he cast a quick glance at Ruairi. When his friend didn't look suspicious of Fagan's request, Ian let out the breath that he didn't know he held.

"Ye've had quite the day, lass." Ian patted Elizabeth's arm. When she looked away hastily and then moved restlessly, he added, "'Tis nae often someone speaks to the king."

Warily, she glanced down at his hand that still rested on her arm. She was trembling beneath his touch. "Yes." Clearing her throat, she lifted her goblet and took a sip of wine.

He leaned in closer, whispering in her ear. "Do ye need—"

"No. I do not."

An amused expression crossed his face. "How do ye know what I was going to ask—"

"*Uisge beatha.* The last time you sat beside me and offered me your drink, I was found in my father's study asleep in his chair."

He chuckled. "Aye, but ye held your drink, lass. I told ye before that I've been found in worse places than that." He pulled out his flask and held it up. "Are ye sure ye donna wish to partake?"

"Oh, I'm certain."

"Suit yourself." Ian shrugged and took a swig.

"I need to be able to walk if I wish to dance."

He placed the flask on the table. "Now that's where ye and I have a difference of opinion. Ye see? I would need a lot more *uisge beatha* if I wished to dance."

Elizabeth flashed him a look of disdain. "I don't think you have to worry about dancing with anyone, Laird Munro."

He nudged her in a jesting manner. "And what if I wished to dance with ye?"

"Now why would you want to do that?" she asked

in a dry tone. When his mouth curved with tenderness, she briefly closed her eyes. "Ian…" She leaned closer, lowering her voice. "Your intentions were clear. I can't do this to you or myself. And your actions—your words—are not making this easier for me."

"Elizabeth, I know that I said—"

A loud scrape came from beside them, and her eyes lit up. "The musicians are here, and the men are clearing the tables to make room to dance. I'd find your sleeping chair now if I were you, Laird Munro."

❧

The great hall was a fine display of color, and for a moment, Elizabeth was in a mystical trance as she stared at the beautiful gowns. She found herself glancing at the feet of the women to make certain they touched the ground. The ladies danced the pavane with so much poise they looked like angels floating on wispy clouds in the heavens above. But the men were certainly not to be outshined by the women. The gentlemen looked debonair. With every step, they moved with an easy grace.

And then reality crept back in.

Elizabeth was hesitant to admit the truth, but she couldn't deny it any longer. She was a wallflower. And frankly, she was in a state of foolishness. No one had asked her to dance, and not a single man dared look in her direction. Granted, Laird Munro was hovering over her like a wolf stalking its prey, and Fagan and Ruairi were huddled in the corner with the other Highland lairds not that far away.

Her eyes darted around the hall for the hundredth

time. Lord Kinghorne and Mister Condell were her only chance, and neither was to be found. This wasn't how she imagined her first dance at court. Just as she was about to give up hope, a male voice spoke from beside her.

"Lady Elizabeth." Her tight expression relaxed into a smile, and Lord Kinghorne gave her a bow.

She curtsied in response. "Lord Kinghorne, a pleasure to see you." The man had no idea how much that was true.

"I promised Mother the first dance, but please save one for me."

Elizabeth tried to wipe the displeasure from her face. "Of course."

She'd spent the last hour standing against the wall, only to be told by an earl that he'd rather dance with his mother. She was losing her mind. When that nagging voice in her head refused to cease, she thought she had.

As Lord Kinghorne danced with his mother, Elizabeth felt like a child waiting for her turn in line. To her astonishment, a young gentleman was approaching her, and she tried to mask the eagerness in her eyes. He stood no more than three feet away then without warning, he spun on his heel and did not look back.

All pleasure left her, and she stiffened as though he had struck her. When she looked away in frustration, Laird Munro was lifting his hand from the hilt of his sword. Her accusing gaze was riveted on him.

"Did you make him flee like a dog with his tail between his legs?"

A soft gasp escaped Ian, and he placed his hand over his heart as if her words had slayed him. "*Me?* I did nay such thing. I did nae even talk to him."

"You know very well that you don't even have to. Have you been doing this all night?" When he didn't respond, she threw back her head and placed her hands on her hips. "I thought we had an agreement. Do you want me to tell Ruairi you fell asleep in the library while you were supposed to watch over me and care for my safety? I thought not. I strongly suggest you take your leave. You can keep an eye on me from over there with the other Highland lairds." When he opened his mouth to speak, she lifted her hand to stay him. "Now, Laird Munro. I insist."

"Eliz—"

"Go away, Laird Munro."

The man was driving her mad. As he bristled off to lick his wounds, Lord Kinghorne walked toward her with a smile on his face and an extended hand.

"Lady Elizabeth, may I have this dance?"

She practically pulled the man onto the floor. "It would be a pleasure, my lord."

"Thank you for saving me a dance, Lady Elizabeth." When he bowed, Elizabeth curtsied in return. His hand touched hers in the air, and they turned in a circle.

"To tell you the truth, I do not think many men were up for the task, my lord. I tend to believe my chaperones take their responsibility too seriously."

An amused expression crossed the earl's face. "I wouldn't be too hard on them. They're only doing what comes naturally, and that is to protect those they love."

"I suppose."

"They're watching over you. In truth, I'd never let Mother wander through the halls of court without an escort."

"Of course not." When they switched hands, Elizabeth wondered if she'd ever have a conversation with Lord Kinghorne that did not involve his mother.

"Mother and I are having tea tomorrow in the garden. Would you care to join us?" The earl glanced over his shoulder.

"May I cut in?"

❦

"I thought ye were going to take my counsel. What the hell are ye doing?" asked Fagan.

Ian placed his back against the wall as he watched Elizabeth with Kinghorne. "I was trying to build up the nerve to ask her to dance."

"And ye thought to frighten off the lads by looking as though ye'd behead them in the middle of the great hall if they approached the lass? That was your idea?"

He shrugged. "It worked."

Fagan gestured to the dance floor. "Aye, it worked verra well. Elizabeth is dancing with Kinghorne."

"The man is nay threat. He loves his mother too much to ever love another woman. More than likely *ye'd* have a better chance than Elizabeth of getting into his bed."

"Nevertheless, ye daft fool, ye are supposed to be out there with her now. What did ye speak to her about at supper?"

"I was about to tell her that—"

"God's teeth, Munro. Ye were going to tell her that

ye remembered the kiss between ye in the middle of
the great hall with hundreds of people around? Think,
man. Choose a private moment and tell her, and listen
to what I'm telling ye to do. I doubt the lass even
knows ye're trying to woo her."

Ian wasn't about to admit the truth to that matter.
"Ye do realize that I'm taking the advice from the
same man whose wife blackened his eye?"

"And ye do realize that Grace is now my wife, eh?"
asked Fagan in a mocking tone. He gestured to Ian's
belt. "Get out your flask." When Ian handed his friend
the whisky, Fagan smiled. "Nae for me. Take a swig."
Ian wasn't about to refuse Fagan's orders because he
needed all the help he could get. "Now get your arse
out there, and ask the lass to dance."

He imposed an iron control on himself. "I can do it."

"Ye're the Munro. Of course ye can." Fagan took
the flask out of Ian's hand. "And ye can nae dance
with that sword. Give it to me." Ian handed his scabbard to Fagan as his friend slapped him heartily on the
back. "Hold nay prisoners in your wake."

Ian walked around a large circle of women, stepped
between two men, and finally made it to the dance
floor. When he reached for the hilt of his sword, the
security he'd always depended on was gone. He felt
vulnerable. He'd faced men on the battlefield and
looked into the eyes of the devil himself, but at this
moment, he was petrified.

With all the courage Ian could muster, he straightened his spine and willed himself to approach Elizabeth.
He'd almost reached her when he froze mid-step.

Condell.

❧

"Your mother is asking for you, my lord," said Mister Condell.

"Yes, of course." The earl gave Elizabeth a bow. "Excuse me, Lady Elizabeth."

Mister Condell assumed the earl's place and gave her a roguish grin. "My apologies, but I can't stand to see any lady suffer. Did you have to hear all about Lady Glamis's ailments, or did he spare you the details?"

Elizabeth laughed. "Lord Kinghorne does care for his mother."

"That he does, my lady. That he does." His gaze dropped from her eyes to her shoulders to her breasts. "You look beautiful, Lady Elizabeth."

Her heart danced with excitement. "Thank you, Mister Condell. When is your next performance, Your Majesty?"

"I'll be playing King Henry again on the morrow, my lady. Perhaps you'd like to attend the theatre one afternoon you're here at court."

"I would like that very much."

His eyes lit up, and he spoke in a conspiratorial voice. "I have to confess that the only reason I'm attending court is because the king favors my acting ability. And do you know why that pleases me the most?" As if on cue, the music ended. He grasped her hand and bowed, his eyes never leaving hers. "I would've never had the pleasure of meeting you, Lady Elizabeth."

Without warning, the king's guard clamored into the great hall with swords drawn. "No one is to move!"

Twelve

Ian dashed to Elizabeth's side even though one of the king's guards had given him a scolding look for disobeying his command. He never cowered before the English and wouldn't start now. He lowered his hand, patting around his waist for his weapon.

"Damn." Fagan still held Ian's sword.

Elizabeth gazed at him, her face clouding with uneasiness. "What is happening?"

"I donna know, but there is nay need to fear."

"Don't worry, Lady Elizabeth. I'm sure all will be well," said Condell. "Remember that I *am* King Henry."

When the man changed his voice to an English accent and gave her a roguish grin, Ian scowled at the actor over Elizabeth's head. A loud commotion at the door brought his attention back to the guards. Eight men stood at the entrance to the great hall as more were shouting out in the hall. Ian could only imagine what madness was upon them now.

Lord Kinghorne stepped from the crowd and spoke in a haughty tone. "I demand to know what this is all about."

One of the guards approached the earl, speaking in low tones. Frankly, Ian couldn't make out a single word with all the voices in the great hall talking at once. When Kinghorne finished his conversation with the guard, he made his way to Elizabeth.

"My lord, what has happened?"

A worried expression crossed Kinghorne's brow. "The king's guard wants everyone to remain here in the great hall until they search the castle."

"For what purpose?" asked Elizabeth.

"A man has been found in the gardens."

"They found the man responsible for—"

The earl's mouth was tight and grim. "No, Lady Elizabeth. They discovered another man of the Privy Council was attacked on the grounds."

She gasped. "Is he all right?"

Kinghorne's eyes darted to Condell's and then back to Elizabeth's. "He lives but is not conscious. Pray excuse me while I see to my mother."

A shadow of alarm touched Elizabeth's face. "Another one? This is the second man who's been assaulted since we've been here. Why would someone want to kill the members of the council?"

Ian hesitated, measuring Elizabeth for a moment. She was an intelligent woman. He knew it was only a matter of time before she recognized the connection. She looked up at him with an effort.

"Was my uncle—"

He grasped her arm and narrowed his gaze. "Now is nae the time or the place, lass. Come with me."

Her voice broke. "Yes. Of course." Elizabeth made

her excuses to Condell, and the man wisely did not stand in her way.

They approached Fagan, and he handed Ian back his sword. He breathed easily when he was finally able to put his weapon back in its rightful place. But his relief altered instantly into worry because Elizabeth left his side and walked to Ruairi with hurried purpose.

"What did Kinghorne say?" asked Fagan.

"Someone tried to kill another member of the king's council. I'm nae sure if the man lives or dies." He lowered his voice. "We may have another problem, and ye know from past experience those donna always turn out in our best favor. Lady Elizabeth asked me if Mildmay was murdered."

"What did ye say?"

"I did nae answer her. What the hell was I supposed to say?" He turned when a female voice caught him unawares.

"The truth, Laird Munro."

❧

Ruairi placed his hand on Elizabeth's shoulder. "Lass, I'm nae sure what is afoot with the king's men, but there is nay reason to believe Mildmay's death was nae an accident."

Her brother-in-law's appeasing words only irritated her more. "Surely you can't help but wonder if my uncle's death truly happened the way it did. Don't you think these events are too similar not to question? Isn't it *possible* that someone made it look like Uncle Walter died in a carriage accident so that no one would question his death? Mark my words. If there is someone out there murdering men of the Privy Council, we must find the man responsible…for Uncle Walter."

Ruairi gave an imploring gaze to Fagan and Ian. "*Cuidich mi*." *Help me*.

The men exchanged carefully guarded looks, and then Fagan spoke in an odd tone. "Elizabeth, your imagination is—"

"You are free to go about your business!" shouted one of the king's guards.

"Fagan, if you're going to say that all of this is my imagination, I strongly caution you not to open your mouth again."

"Lass, ye're becoming more like your sisters every day. I swear that ye sounded exactly like Grace."

"It's been a long day. I'm weary. Are you ready to take your leave?"

"Aye." The men all answered.

Lord Kinghorne was escorting Lady Glamis out of the great hall when they met at the door. Although the earl drove her mad with every sentence about his mother, he was a good man in Elizabeth's eyes. As she gazed down at the frail, hunched over woman, there was a spot of blood on Lady Glamis's silk slipper.

"My lady, why don't you come with me for a moment?" Elizabeth led the woman over to a solitary wall outside the hall and lowered her voice as Lord Kinghorne cast a puzzled gaze. "Lady Glamis, there is blood on your slipper."

The woman fumbled to adjust her hat and was stammering with confusion. Seeing the discomfort on his mother's face, the earl spoke. "I was afraid this was too much for Mother. I'm taking her back to her chamber now. She needs to rest. Thank you for your concern, Lady Elizabeth. I don't think many women would be as kind."

"We only have one mother in this world, my lord, and I would hope everyone would be so kind."

Lady Glamis patted Elizabeth's arm. "Thank you, my dear. Come along, Patrick. I need to lie down."

"I'll see you on the morrow, Lady Elizabeth," said Lord Kinghorne.

After a long day at court, Elizabeth sat back on the seat of the carriage and closed her tired eyes. As she rested to the rhythmic movement of the carriage, she wondered if her brothers-in-law thought her an idiot. Just because she wasn't a man didn't mean that she didn't have a brain and couldn't have opinions of her own. And if the men wouldn't listen to her, perhaps her sisters would. She had thought about sending a missive to Apethorpe Hall, but her questionable words would be the last thing anyone there needed to hear.

Poor Aunt Mary was recovering from losing Uncle Walter, and Ravenna needed to spend more time worrying about the child she carried rather than seeing to the needs of everyone else around her. Sending a letter would only alarm those Elizabeth cared the most about. But she'd be sure to keep her eyes and ears open at court because if she saw anything that cast a single shadow of doubt about Uncle Walter's sudden demise, she and her family would want to know. And she owed it to her uncle to find out the truth.

❧

Other than Ian, Fagan, and Ruairi, only one man sat

in the dining hall at the inn. Ian embraced the silence as his friends did the same. But that didn't stop that nagging feeling in the back of his mind that refused to be stilled.

Ian took another drink from his tankard and then lowered his voice. "The king is verra well guarded."

"If ye donna have access to the king, what better way to fracture the realm than by killing off his advisors," said Ruairi.

"Och, well, I'm just glad this does nae have anything to do with fathers-in-law, the Stewart, mercenaries, or the Walsingham sisters," added Fagan.

Ruairi sat forward. "I donna want Elizabeth questioning Mildmay's death, especially at court. She would nae understand how perilous these questions could be if they fall upon the wrong ears. And the last I need is for the lass to be planting ideas in Ravenna's head. My wife is supposed to be retired from service, and she carries my second child."

"And let's nae even think about the repercussions if Elizabeth opens her mouth to Grace. *My* wife has had more than enough adventures with Casterbrook," said Fagan dryly.

Ruairi finished what was left of his drink and stood. "I seek my bed. I'll see ye both on the morrow."

As soon as Ruairi walked away from the table, Fagan spoke. "Ye're a coward. I saw ye stop when that man asked Elizabeth to dance. Munro, I've seen ye slay men on the battlefield and nae think twice. Yet, ye let an Englishman frighten ye off. I'm verra disappointed in ye."

"Aye, well, I'm sure the lass would've rather been

seen on the arm of King Henry than with the likes of me."

Fagan snatched Ian's cup away. "Ye better seek your bed. Ye're delusional."

He reached over and grabbed his tankard back. "*Condell*," he spat, "is an actor playing King Henry at the theatre. Ye know how much Elizabeth is fascinated with the topic. They share a common ground… something the lass does nae have with me." As he took another drink, he scowled into his tankard.

Fagan sat back casually in the chair. "Oh, that's what's concerning ye. For a moment, I thought ye were foolish enough to believe ye were nae as…bonny in the lass's eyes as the actor. Please tell me that I'm wrong because the Munro I know does nae give up without a fight, especially to the English."

"I donna know what the hell I'm doing." He threw up his hands in frustration. "I'm certain that I feel something for the lass, but I'm nae sure what. And when I see her with any other man, I want to behead him."

"If that's nae love, I donna know what is."

"Love? I ne'er said that I loved Elizabeth. Sometimes 'tis difficult to recognize the difference between the young girl who hung on my every word, and now the woman she has become."

"Open your eyes, ye damn fool, before 'tis too late, and she finds another to her liking—King Henry mayhap."

"Did anyone ever tell ye that ye're a pain in the arse?"

"Ruairi, now and then Ravenna, but mostly Grace."

Ian sighed. "Since I did nae get the chance to tell Elizabeth the truth, when do ye think I should tell her?"

"Now. Ye need to be alone. She's probably nae sleeping because of the events this eve. Take your leave, Munro. Tell her the truth, and shame the devil."

Ian slapped the table and stood.

"Munro, *dean do dhìcheall.*" *Do your best.*

"*Chi mi rithist thu.*" *I'll see you later.* "Wish me luck."

Fagan held up his tankard in mock salute.

⁂

When there was a knock at the door, Elizabeth rose from the chair that she'd been sitting on for the last hour. She couldn't sleep because never had death been so close to her door. She always felt safe within the castle walls, at Ruairi's, in Scotland. And in the past two days, one man was killed and another—well, she wasn't sure if he lived or had died.

She wrapped her robe tighter around her body and then opened the door a crack. A young boy with unruly brown hair shifted from foot to foot.

"M'lady, I bring a message."

"At this time of night?" She opened the door and glanced down the empty hall.

The boy shoved a note into her hand. "Oh, I almost forgot." He reached around his back and handed her a single red rose. "Here."

She was so shocked that when she looked at the boy, he was already descending the stairs. Elizabeth closed the door and sat on the bed. Placing the rose beside her, she opened the note.

My Dear Lady Walsingham,

We all are men, in our own natures frail; few are angels.

—King Henry

Please accept my deepest apologies that your first days at court have been overshadowed by this unfortunate chain of events. When the rose you hold is faded and the sweet smell is gone, the memory of your beauty and our dance will still dwell on.

With warmest regards,
Will Condell

Mister Condell's actions were kind, thoughtful, and Elizabeth couldn't stay the smile that crossed her lips. She lifted the rose to her nose, and the fragrant scent invaded her senses. When there was another knock, she thought perhaps King Henry had another gift in store. She couldn't wait to find out. As she opened the door with the flower in hand, her smile slowly faded.

"Might I have a word with ye?" Before she could answer, Laird Munro pushed his way into her chamber and closed the door. He glanced at the rose and cast a puzzled gaze. "Where did ye get the flower?"

In a nervous gesture, Elizabeth approached the bed and picked up the note. "It was a gift from Mister Condell."

"He was here? At this time of night?"

She laid the bloom and note on the table. "No. He sent a messenger. He apologized for this evening."

"What the hell…er, what was he apologizing for?"

"The man who was killed yesterday and the man who was injured—or worse—this evening."

"I've come to talk with ye. I need to tell ye something, and ye need to listen."

A warning voice whispered in her head as Ian hesitated, measuring her for a moment. Her misgivings increased even more with the silence that loomed between them. When he didn't speak and tapped his fingers on the hilt of his sword in a nervous gesture, she decided to put him out of his misery.

"I'll make this easy. I know what you've come to say."

His eyes lit up. "Ye do?"

"Yes. Uncle Walter did not die in a carriage accident."

Ian stood motionless in the middle of the room. He closed his eyes, tilting his head back. "Why does naught ever happen in my favor?"

"Pardon?"

He reached out and caught her hand in his. "As Ruairi told ye, we have nay reason to think Mildmay's death was nae an accident."

"Laird Munro, two men in two days, both from the king's council, and you see no reason to question my uncle's death? Need I remind you that Uncle Walter was part of the Privy Council?"

A muscle ticked at Ian's jaw. "Now ye listen to me verra carefully, lass. I donna want to hear more questions from ye about the cause of Mildmay's death, especially at court. Do ye understand? These are dangerous times. I donna want to see ye hurt."

"Why, Laird Munro? Are you telling me there was something more to my uncle's *accident*?"

His eyes darkened. "I am telling ye to stop this madness before ye say something ye should nae."

She lifted her chin, meeting his gaze, and responded sharply. "I have *every* right to speak my mind." She abandoned all pretenses.

"Ruairi is your laird. He told ye to stop, and I suggest ye heed his command."

"Heed his com—" She growled. "Ruairi is not my laird. Lest you forget, I am English. He is my brother-in-law."

"He is also your guardian and your chaperone," Ian snapped. "Lest ye forget," he replied in a mocking tone, "ye are still young enough for him to bend over his knee. Ye will show him respect."

"Get out!"

"What?"

Ian seemed puzzled by her fit of rage, especially when she pushed and shoved his massive frame step by step to the door. "Take your leave before I kick you out. I may be much smaller than you, Laird Munro, but Ravenna showed me how to hurt a man. For your own safety, get the hell out!"

If the man was astonished by the curses that fell from her mouth, he didn't say. And for once, Elizabeth really didn't care.

❧

Ian didn't even reach the last step before Fagan opened his mouth. "What the hell did ye do? Elizabeth did nae even break her fast this morn. She's waiting in the carriage."

"Where is Ruairi?"

"Seeing to the horses."

"Remind me the next time I decide to take your advice about anything to flee the other way."

As Ian was about to step out of the inn, Fagan grabbed his arm to stay him. "What do ye mean? I knew the lass would be cross with ye when ye told her the truth, but I did nae think ye'd fire her ire as much as ye had."

"I did nae tell her."

"Have ye learned naught? Will there ever be a time when ye listen to what I tell ye?"

"*King Henry* sent her a note last eve accompanied by a single rose, apologizing for the events that happened at court."

"Damn. I always forget about flowers. They say 'tis the way into a woman's heart."

"Now ye tell me." Ian shook his head. "In truth, I donna think if I'd given the lass flowers it would've mattered."

Ruairi stepped through the door. "What would've mattered?"

"I am the reason Elizabeth is cross this morn," said Ian. "If her willfulness is anything close to what ye experience with your own wives, then I pity the both of ye."

"Ye have nay idea," said Fagan.

"The lass insists that Mildmay's death was nay accident because of the two other men. I told her to cease her questions and stop this madness."

"Let her be cross with ye," said Ruairi. "She must mind her tongue at court."

"Aye, well, she would nae listen to reason and became even angrier when I told her that she must heed your command because ye're her laird." When his friends shuddered, Ian added, "But that was nae the worst part of what I said. I did nae realize the words came out of my mouth until 'twas too late."

Ruairi sighed.

"I may have told her that she's still young enough for ye to bend over your knee if she did nae listen. *Sin e. Sin agad e.*" *That's it. There you have it.*

"*Dé thubhairt sibh?*" asked Fagan. *What did you say?*

He didn't think Fagan wanted the answer repeated. In short, Ian knew his words were wrong the first time he'd said them. God help him. He certainly had a way of creating a fine mess.

Ruairi patted him on the back. "I'm sorry, Munro, but ye're on your own for this one."

Thirteen

ELIZABETH DIDN'T ATTEMPT TO STEAL A GLANCE AT Laird Munro when she walked into the hall of Hampton Court Palace. If she had, she would have throttled him where he stood. Her brother-in-law would've never turned her over his knee, as if Ravenna would have ever permitted such a thing. What made matters worse was the fact that Ian only said the words to goad her into ceasing her questions about Uncle Walter.

"Pardon us." Two women around the same age as Elizabeth wore matching blue gowns. Blond curls framed their identical oval faces, and they had perfect white, straight teeth. One girl nudged the other in the arm. "Tell her we're twins."

"I think she can see that for herself, Gillian." The woman smiled at Elizabeth. "I'm Lady Margery Tullibardine, and this is my sister Lady Gillian."

"It's a pleasure to make your acquaintance. I'm Lady Elizabeth Wal—"

"Yes, we know." One of the twins, perhaps Lady Margery, gestured to Ian, Fagan, and Ruairi. "We heard you were being escorted around court by Highlanders. We didn't believe the rumors to be true—until now."

"If you don't mind us asking, Lady Elizabeth, why are those men accompanying you?" asked the other sister.

"I'm afraid the tale is not that exciting. Two are my brothers-in-law."

"We were just going to take a walk in the garden. Would you care to join us? We'd love to hear all about it."

"Yes, I'd be delighted. Please give me but a moment."

Elizabeth approached Ruairi, smiled at Fagan, and paid no heed to Ian. "I'm going to take a walk in the garden with the Tullibardine sisters. I'll meet you here in an hour."

Ruairi gazed at the sisters in awe. "I have nae been in my cups, but I'm seeing double."

She laughed. "They're twins."

"Apparently. All right, lass. Donna wander anywhere else, especially alone."

"I won't."

Elizabeth ambled along the garden paths with the twins flanking her on each side. The sky had turned gray, and she hoped the weather was not going to turn for the worst. Then again, she was having a difficult time removing the dark cloud that hung over her head and followed her everywhere. Of course, the shadowy mass could've been Laird Munro. With that thought, she gazed around the garden in the hope she'd see Mister Condell.

"We've never seen you before. Is this your first time at court, Lady Elizabeth?"

"Yes, Lady Ma...er, I'm not sure with whom I'm speaking."

"I'm Lady Margery. I'll tell you a little secret." She stopped and smiled. "You can tell us apart because I have a small scar here on my chin. Can you see it?"

Elizabeth leaned closer. "Yes."

"One of my father's dogs bit me in the face when I was a child, and the wound left a mark."

They continued to walk along the edge of the garden. "I'm sorry that happened to you. My sister was attacked several years ago," said Elizabeth. "The animal left quite the nasty scar on her leg, and now she is deathly afraid of…dogs." When she realized "wolves" almost escaped her lips, she bit her tongue. She wasn't in the mood to explain Angus.

"Oh, I'm not afraid of them. What happened to me was a careless accident. I was young, and our dog had puppies. When I tripped over my own two feet, their mother thought I was a threat and bit me. It was entirely my fault."

"I wish you could talk some sense into my sister. She thinks all dogs are out to cause her harm," said Elizabeth.

"Your sister, Lady Ravenna?" asked Gillian.

Elizabeth's jaw dropped. "Yes. How did you know?"

"We'd heard Father mention your sister in passing when he was talking about your chaperones. Was she the one betrothed to Lord Casterbrook?"

Elizabeth became uneasy under the twins' scrutiny. "Umm…no. That was my sister, Lady Grace."

Margery placed her hand on Elizabeth's shoulder. "Is it true then? Did Lord Mildmay kill Lady Grace's betrothed?"

Elizabeth paled.

❦

Fagan sat on a bench in the garden. "Ye could always try flowers."

"We've been down this path before. Condell is one step ahead of me," said Ian.

"Then ye need to figure out what to do before Condell does it, and Elizabeth's heart is gone forever. Let's think about what the lass favors." Fagan's expression stilled. "We know she likes her books, and she shows an interest in the history of King Henry."

When Ian let out a defeated sigh, Fagan offered a look of apology a little too late. "Not your Condell playing King Henry, of course." When Fagan saw the look on Ian's face, he added, "Donna forget that Condell is an actor used to playing a part, but ye have him at a clear advantage. Ye've known Elizabeth for years, and he's only talked with her—or been trying to woo her—for a few days. If I recall correctly, the lass said she loved *ye*, not Condell."

"Elizabeth asked Ruairi if he'd escort her to the theatre to see *Henry VIII* this afternoon. What if I escorted her?"

Fagan stood. "Now ye're thinking, not to mention that Ruairi would thank ye for putting him out of his misery of attending the play." He slapped Ian in the chest and gestured over his shoulder. "I'm taking my leave. Now's your chance to make amends—again. Good luck, Munro."

Ian turned as Elizabeth approached. "Did ye enjoy your walk?"

"Oh, the experience was quite enlightening."

"There is an archery tournament taking place within the hour on the south side of the gardens. Would ye like me to escort ye? I donna mind."

"And if I say no, will Ruairi turn me over his knee and scold me like a willful child?" When she added a smile of defiance, he thought this might be an opportunity for a bit of the truth.

He closed the distance between them. Lightly, he fingered a loose tendril of hair on her cheek, and her breath quickened. When his gaze met hers, his heart turned over in response, and he couldn't find the strength to pull away. "Please accept my apologies for my careless words. The last I want in this world is to see ye hurt, Elizabeth. I know the events at court have unsettled ye, and in truth, I donna know if there was more to your uncle's death or nae. But I do know that ye can nae have your questions fall upon the wrong ears."

When she started to speak, he held up his hand and added, "I want to make things right between us. Let me start by being your escort later this afternoon to the theatre, if ye'll have me."

She stared, wordlessly.

"Please say something, lass. I can nae read your thoughts." Life would be so much simpler if he could.

"I'm still angry with you, but your apology is accepted. I'd love to attend the theatre. But I do have questions about my uncle that I want answers to. Do you understand?" Her question was more of a demand.

"Aye, but now is nae the time."

She nodded, giving him a brief moment of compliance.

Ruairi and Fagan approached them with Lairds Ross, Fraser, and MacKay. When all the lairds were smiling, Ian thought for a moment that one had finally been granted his audience with King James. When he gave the Fraser a questioning gaze, the man returned a knowing smile.

"Did ye honestly think it would be that simple, Munro?"

"Damn." There were only two occasions a Scot would ever smile at court, the first of course, being told he could take his leave from this dreaded nightmare. And that wasn't the reason for the Fraser's merriment.

"We're off to watch the English look like fools in the archery tournament."

And there was the second cause.

Fire lit Elizabeth's eyes as she boldly met the Fraser's gaze. "Laird Fraser, I—"

"My apologies, Sutherland. I keep forgetting your sister-in-law and your wife are English."

The lairds stepped around Elizabeth, and Fagan patted her on the shoulder in a comforting gesture as he passed. Her expression clouded with anger, and her eyes met Ian's. Instinctively, he raised his hands, giving up in battle before one had even begun.

"Ye can nae be cross with me. I did nae say anything."

"No. You didn't, and there lies one of the problems," she responded sharply. "Let's go on then. I'm looking forward to watching my countrymen play themselves as fools for your enjoyment."

Ian was tired of being the object of Elizabeth's wrath and thought it best to keep his mouth shut for his own good. They made their way to the open field at the south end of the gardens. The skies were gray, and the sun was nowhere to be seen.

"I hope the storm passes," said Elizabeth.

He prayed that was true because he couldn't imagine being cooped up within the castle walls with the

English…and a murderer. He'd have to watch his back at every turn. At least out in the open he could see any threat coming upon him.

The men waited while the targets were placed. A crowd started to gather, including the twins that Elizabeth had met earlier. A man stepped up to shoot his first round in the archery contest, already wiping the sweat from his brow. Lifting his bow, he visibly trembled, studying the target. In fact, he examined it so long that Ian could have easily released an arrow several times before the man even took the shot. Finally, Ian watched as the arrow whizzed through the air, missing the goal by several feet.

The next contender patted the man on the back and then stepped forward. He raised the bow, studying the target briefly, and then released the arrow. He had an admirable aim, hitting the center mark with astounding accuracy.

As the crowd cheered, Elizabeth left Ian's side and stood next to the twins. He was glad to see she found other women around her age to talk with at court. Even though he understood why Mildmay and Ravenna had sheltered the Walsingham sisters from the aristocracy, being from a family of spies and all, he recognized Elizabeth's need to feel she belonged among her peers. Perhaps her time at court with the English wouldn't be as mundane as his. And he had to admit that he'd grown rather fond of seeing a smile on her face.

The men and women around him fell silent, but he couldn't tear his eyes away from her. His gaze roved and lazily appraised her. Every time he saw her, spent time with her, she stoked a gently growing fire.

Although he had to fight his own personal battle of restraint, he hungered from the memory of his mouth on hers. The lass continued to stir something inside him that he'd never thought possible.

The tournament entranced her, and he was taken aback that she'd actually shown an interest in the sport. At least shooting arrows was more exciting than tennis. He'd give her that.

When the crowd cheered, Ian glanced at the target. The arrow was dead center. His eyes searched for the archer. Ian spotted him with bow in hand…standing before Elizabeth.

Condell.

⁓

"That was a fabulous shot, Mister Condell," said Elizabeth. "I didn't know you could shoot."

His eyes twinkled with amusement. "There are many things that I do very well, Lady Elizabeth."

She cleared her throat. "Yes, well, Mister Condell, pray allow me to introduce to you Lady Margery Tullibardine and her sister, Lady Gillian."

"Do my eyes dare deceive me?"

Lady Margery laughed. "I'm afraid not, Mister Condell. Have we met before? I must admit you do look vaguely familiar."

"Now I recognize you," said Lady Gillian. "You're the actor who is playing King Henry at the Globe Theatre, are you not?"

He placed his hand over his heart and gave Lady Gillian a slight bow. "That I am, my lady."

"We saw the play last week while Father stayed in

London, and your performance was exhilarating," said Lady Margery. "I don't know how you managed to remember all your lines, and you spoke in an English accent very well."

Mister Condell smiled from ear to ear. "I am humbled by your generous words, my lady. Perhaps you will be successful in talking Lady Elizabeth into coming to see me, and the troop, perform. There are many talented actors among us."

"Lady Margery and Lady Gillian do not need to talk me into anything. I'll be there for your performance later this afternoon."

He smiled with an air of pleasure. "I'm glad to hear it. You must be my honored guest. I will hold a chair for you in the front row."

"That would be lovely, Mister Condell, but could you please hold two?"

"Oh, yes. I had almost forgotten about your chaperones." He glanced at the twins. "If you ladies will please excuse me, it is almost time for my turn."

"Good luck, Mister Condell," said the sisters at the same time.

He gave a slight bow and then turned to Elizabeth. "Lady Elizabeth, until this afternoon."

When he spoke in an English accent, the twins laughed in response. The moment Mister Condell walked away, Lady Margery poked Elizabeth in the arm. "It's clear the man has taken a fancy to you."

"He's very handsome," added Lady Gillian.

"Mister Condell is only being kind." She wouldn't dare mention the message or the gift of the rose that he'd sent her last night.

"Do you favor him? I only ask because my heart flutters at the sight of him," said Lady Gillian.

"Gillian, how could you ask Lady Elizabeth about such a private matter?" asked Lady Margery in a scolding tone.

Elizabeth almost chuckled. The sisters had no trouble inquiring if Uncle Walter had killed Daniel, but Lady Margery thought it was improper to ask about Elizabeth's feelings toward Mister Condell. She wondered if she'd ever understand the logic of others.

Her attention was drawn back to Mister Condell as he was about to take another attempt at the target. The man was boldly confident, and she liked that. He moved into position and adjusted the arrow. Lifting the bow, he aimed, releasing his shot.

Dead center.

The crowd cheered, and so did Elizabeth. When Mister Condell's eyes met hers, her expression brightened, and they shared a smile. She was proud of him for doing well.

She glanced over her shoulder, and Ian stood tall, his hand resting on the hilt of his sword. His vexation was evident. They stared at each other, and it wasn't long before she detected bitterness, hurt—perhaps a little of both. Without warning, he stormed off, and his broad back thundered from the tournament. The man was confusing in every way.

❧

Ian was ready to turn the archery tournament into a bloody battle in the middle of the field. If not for

Fagan who rested his hand on Ian's shoulder with a restraining grip, there would've been bloodshed.

The way Condell gazed at Elizabeth made Ian's blood boil, especially when the lass seemed to return the actor's favor. Whatever this was between Elizabeth and Condell, Ian couldn't let it continue. He needed to tell the lass the truth and decided no matter what, it would be tonight. Enough was enough.

Fagan's grip tightened. "If I have to remove Condell's dead body from where he stands, I am nae going to be pleased."

Ian took a deep breath. "I have my wits about me, but mayhap 'tis best if I remove the bastard from sight."

"Aye. Take your leave before ye do something foolish."

He spun around, never wanting to run someone through more than he did King Henry with his bonny face and flirtations with Elizabeth. He wondered if men had ever felt the same way about the true King Henry during his reign at court, since the man also had a bold reputation with the lasses. A smile crossed Ian's face when he knew one of the kings couldn't stir more trouble because he'd been long since dead and buried. The thought pleased him, because if Condell continued to step in Ian's path, the arse would soon be joining King Henry in a cold, dark grave.

Ian increased his gait, needing to place as much distance between himself and Condell as he could. Elizabeth was being pulled out of Ian's grasp right before his eyes. Fury almost choked him. Curses flew from his mouth. Blood pounded in his ears. What he needed was a bit of swordplay to calm the raging storm.

When he realized he was alone in the garden because most of the crowd was gathered at the tournament, he withdrew his sword and swung at the first object in his path. God bless the dozen roses he had just beheaded. The flowery blooms met their end of days, and he felt a moment of brief satisfaction. He sheathed his weapon and sat on a bench.

All his life, he'd never mattered to anyone. Elizabeth was the only woman who had ever seen him for who he truly was. He couldn't deny the evidence. He recognized that Elizabeth was the only woman he'd ever *permitted* to get close to him.

He was a fool for denying his feelings for her. She believed in him, and time after time, all he did was push her away. His mind became filled with sour thoughts. Had he made too many mistakes? A dire thought plagued him at that moment.

Had he given up his only chance at happiness?

A female voice startled him.

"I do believe you've won the battle, Laird Munro." Elizabeth's eyes narrowed with suspicion. "That is your handiwork, is it not?" When she gestured to the fallen blooms, she sighed and sat on the bench beside him. "Is England that unbearable that you can't even enjoy an archery tournament?"

He leaned over, placing his elbows on his thighs. When he realized he was hunched over like a defeated dog, he sat up straight. "'Tis naught England or the tournament, lass. I have greater troubles." He rubbed his hand over his brow and then met her gaze. "I've made mistakes, and now, I'm afraid 'tis too late to make them right."

When his hand came down on hers in a possessive gesture, her eyes widened. "I'm nae verra good with words, but I will try. I was a blind fool nae to see what was before my verra eyes. I avoided Sutherland lands all those years because of ye."

Elizabeth merely stared at him.

"The truth is that for the first time in my life I was frightened. Aye, the battle-hardened Laird Munro was cowering like a wee bairn. Nay one—I should say nay *woman*—has ever cared about me the way that ye do. Your eager affection unsettled me because I could nae determine why ye held such feelings toward me. I am much older than ye. And I know damn well...er, I know there are better men out there who are younger, bonnier, and more suitable than the likes of me."

He looked at their entwined hands. As if the sight gave him strength, his gaze once again met hers. "I remember the kiss in my chamber. How could I nae? I think of holding ye in my arms every waking moment. I denied the time between us because I did nae understand what I was feeling. I can nay longer deny in my heart what I've known all along. I want ye—I'm begging ye—to give me another chance to win your favor."

"Why?"

Of all the words he'd expected Elizabeth to say, that was not one. "Why?" he repeated.

She pulled her hand away. "Yes. I've been nothing but kind to you, and you've hurt me at every turn. You disregarded me when I had never once given up on you. You looked me in the eye and denied what happened between us even after I'd given you a chance to tell the truth. You *lied* after I gave you my heart and soul."

Tears fell down her cheeks. "Now that Mister Condell makes attempts to woo me, you finally find your voice. Why? Tell me *why* I should give you another chance, Laird Munro. Are you too proud? Is jealousy for Mister Condell the only reason you beg me for another chance? You owe me a reason. You owe me that much."

"*Gràdh geal mo chridhe.*"

She gave him a look of amusement. "Gaelic, Laird Munro?"

He briefly closed his eyes and prayed for strength. "I needed to say the words in my own tongue first because I needed to find the courage to say…" He lifted his hand and gently brushed his fingers against her cheek. "Ye're the bright love of my heart, Elizabeth." As if fate was once again laughing in Ian's face, pellets of rain fell, stinging their faces.

But neither moved.

Fourteen

ELIZABETH WAS SPEECHLESS. SHE WAS EXPERIENCING A wide gamut of emotions from Ian telling her that she was the "bright love of his heart" to his admission of guilt, lies, and deceit. She'd waited so long to hear his words of love, but for some reason, she wasn't feeling as exhilarated as she thought she should've been.

He decided that he'd rather hurt her than admit the truth, even after she'd given him ample opportunity to acknowledge their kiss. She was disappointed that he wasn't the man she thought him to be. Furthermore, what if she gave him another chance only to have him turn around and cause her additional pain? There were only so many times her poor heart could be mended.

As the rain fell harder, men and women darted along the garden path trying to seek shelter from the storm. Elizabeth didn't have enough strength to think, let alone move her body from the bench. Firm hands pulled her from behind, and she immediately recognized the Scottish accent.

"Lass, come out of the rain." Ruairi placed his arm

around her and glared at Ian. "Munro, what the hell are ye doing?"

Ruairi hastily escorted Elizabeth inside the castle walls. She was numb, cold, wet, and confused. The servants were handing out towels for those who were foolish enough to get caught in the rain. Ruairi wrapped one around her and handed her a cloth.

"Thank you."

"Why did ye nae have enough sense to come into the castle?" Ruairi glanced over her shoulder. "Munro, why were ye sitting with Elizabeth in the heavy rain? Ye did nae think to take her inside?"

When Ian didn't respond, she hesitated, torn by conflicting emotions. She didn't feel the sudden need to come to his rescue like she always had in the past. Trying to weigh all the events, she was swimming through a haze of mixed feelings. She remained frozen in limbo, where all actions and decisions were impossible.

Ruairi wrapped his arm around her, moving his hand up and down her frame. "Ye're trembling. Let me get ye something warm to drink."

"I'll do it," said Ian.

"Ye're going to catch the ague if ye donna change your wet clothes. Ye did nae bring anything else to wear, did ye?" asked Ruairi.

"No. Do you think it would be all right if we returned to the inn? I'd like to put on some dry clothes and rest for a while. Laird Munro offered to escort me to the theatre later this afternoon."

For a moment, Ruairi stared, wordlessly. "He did?"

She patted her hair dry. "Yes. Does that surprise you?"

"Aye, especially because Munro does nae favor

plays or art of any kind. Well, I must say that is nae exactly true. He favors my wall hangings. But the only culture he shows an interest in is his own."

"*Tha e fliuch an diugh*," said Fagan, shaking off the rain. *It is wet today.* "*Tha tàirneanaich agus dealanaich ann.*" *There's thunder and lightning.* He looked at Elizabeth, and his eyes widened. "Why are ye all wet? Where is Munro?"

"He took his leave to get her something warm to drink. We'll take Elizabeth back to the inn so that she can change her wet clothes. Munro will be escorting the lass to the theatre this afternoon." Ruairi spoke in an odd tone, and Fagan averted his eyes.

"To tell ye the truth, I much prefer Mistress Betts's cooking over the food at court anyway, and I find myself needing a respite from all the English...er, people attending court."

Elizabeth laughed to cover her annoyance. "You do realize that if Grace heard those words upon your lips, your other eye would be blackened. Need I remind you the Walsinghams, including your wife, are English?"

"*Cuidich mi*," said Fagan. *Help me.* He cast Ruairi an imploring look, but her brother-in-law only chuckled, giving his captain a friendly punch in the arm.

"Ye and Munro have much to learn. I keep telling ye both, and yet, ye donna listen."

"Here ye are, Lady Elizabeth." Ian handed her a cup of warm broth.

"Thank you." She took a sip, the warm liquid feeling delightful the entire way down.

"Would ye like me to ride back to the inn and have

Mistress Betts pack ye some warm clothes for court? I donna mind," said Ian with an eager affection.

"No, thank you. I told Ruairi and Fagan that I wouldn't mind returning to rest for a while before we attend the theatre this afternoon. Would that be all right with you?"

He bobbed his head without missing a beat. "Aye, I could use a respite from court."

Elizabeth smiled at Fagan. "I hope you took notice. Laird Munro doesn't favor the English either, but he was able to hold his tongue this time. The task is not difficult. You should try it more often. Doesn't my sister—or I should say my *sisters*—tell you it's best not to say anything when you don't have anything nice to say?"

"I donna why I miss Grace. She's right here."

❧

A storm was brewing, and it wasn't the one that happened an hour ago at the palace. Ruairi was silent the entire way from court. That meant there was something on his mind. Ian only hoped that his attempts to woo Elizabeth were not the reason his friend was troubled.

As soon as they arrived at the inn, the lass retired to her room. He couldn't say that he blamed her. His confession had probably taken her by surprise. From the expression on her face when he'd told her his true feelings, there wasn't any doubt about that.

Ruairi slapped Ian on the shoulder. "Let's have a wee dram, shall we?"

He wouldn't have thought Ruairi's request was

odd, but Fagan had conveniently disappeared. And the man never declined a drink in his life. They made their way into the dining hall and sat at the same table in the corner. There were ten men and a handful of women in the room. For several moments, his friend didn't say a word, even when the young lad from the kitchen approached them and set two tankards of ale on the table. The boy walked away, and Ruairi met Ian's gaze.

"We've been friends for years and always held the other's back. Ye're my brother. More often than nae, we even think the same." Leaning forward in his chair, in a controlled voice, Ruairi said, "So tell me what is happening between ye and Elizabeth."

Of course, Ian's first reaction was one of complete denial to save his own arse, but his friend saw right through him.

"I'm nae blind nor am I stupid."

Ian had never lied to Ruairi, even in the worst of times, and wouldn't ruin their friendship by starting now. Besides, he could no longer stand the anticipation. Since there was no way to explain his foolish behavior, he blurted out the words in a single breath, ready to face the consequences of his actions. "I love her."

His confession wasn't as difficult as he thought it would've been, but Ruairi's expression was a mask of stone. If his friend pulled out his *sgian dubh* and stabbed him through the heart, he wouldn't have been surprised. Ian's misgivings increased by the minute, especially when Ruairi hadn't moved or had yet to say a single word. When a muscle started to tick at his jaw, Ian unknowingly shifted in the seat.

"Did ye ruin her? I will have the truth." Ian knew he was in trouble when Ruairi spoke through clenched teeth.

"Nay. I give ye my word."

He sat back in the chair and grinned with no trace of his former animosity. "'Tis about damn time, Munro. The lass has been pining after ye for years. I'm glad to see ye finally took notice."

Ian lifted his fallen jaw. "Ye're nae cross with me?"

"The only reason I'm cross with ye is for taking so long to see what was before your verra eyes. I'm nae sure what my wife or Grace will think on the matter, but I thank ye for one less Walsingham under my roof." Ruairi lifted his tankard in mock salute.

"Donna be too pleased. I'm nae sure if there will ever be a wedding in my future." Ian glanced at his cup, trying to keep the sound of defeat from his voice, but wasn't certain he was successful.

"Och, aye. Ye and Elizabeth will be wed. There is nay taking back your words now. I heard ye say that ye love her, and I know she loves ye."

Ian chuckled. "If only it were that simple..." His voice became serious. "I'm afraid there is another contender fighting for the lass's affections."

"Who? Kinghorne? He loves his mother too much to love another woman."

"I'm not talking about the earl. I'm speaking of the actor, Condell."

"The man at the archery tournament?"

"Aye."

Ruairi raked his fingers through his hair. "Munro, just because the man is fair of face does nae mean he has even a chance of capturing Elizabeth's heart. The lass is smart. She would nae throw away three years of love that she held for ye for a mere actor. God's teeth! Ye're a Scottish laird. Furthermore, Elizabeth is a lady. Do ye think Ravenna or Grace would permit her to wed an *actor* who is below her station?"

Ian gave him a knowing look. "Grace wed Fagan, and he's your captain."

"The two love each other greatly. I donna think anyone or anything can keep them apart, and I would ne'er want to be the one to try." Ruairi cast a puzzled gaze. "Is that why ye're taking the lass to the theatre…because of Condell? If I discover there is a man killed in Southwark this eve, do I need to worry ye're the cause?"

"Why would I take her to see the enemy if I wanted to cause him harm? Although, I have been tempted to run the bastard through," he mumbled under his breath. "Nay. I try to win Elizabeth's favor, woo her, but I'm nae certain my efforts are working."

Mistress Betts walked into the dining hall, and Ruairi smiled. "I have an idea. Will ye trust me with something?"

"I donna think I like where this is going. Do I have a choice?"

"Nay."

Ruairi cleared his throat. "Mistress Betts, may I see ye for a moment?"

That was the instant Ian pondered if his friend had gone mad or if the man was a genius. The next he knew, he was sitting in his room with Mistress Betts standing behind him with scissors in hand. Ruairi sat on the edge of the bed as he gave the lass pointed instructions. Ian had no choice but to pray for the best and trust his friend.

"Are you certain, Laird Munro? Once I cut, there is no turning back."

"Dinna fash yourself over it, Mistress Betts, because if it does nae turn out right, ye will nae be to blame." Ian turned his head and gave Ruairi a hostile glare.

"It would nae be the first time ye've been cross with me. Go ahead, Mistress Betts."

As soon as the lass placed the scissors against Ian's shoulder, he held up his hand. "Wait." He glanced down at his long, red locks. Grabbing a section of hair into his hand, he lifted it level to his eyes. "*Mar sin leibh an dràsda.*" *Good-bye for now.*

There was a knock at the door, and Fagan called out. Ian cringed because the last he needed was an audience, especially this audience.

"*Thig a-steach,*" said Ruairi. *Come in.*

"*Dèan às!*" called Ian. *Be gone!*

The door opened, and he didn't even attempt to turn around because Ruairi and Mistress Betts were all he could handle. Unless he wanted to throw Fagan out the door, Ian didn't have a choice but to provide their entertainment. When Fagan sat beside Ruairi on the bed with an amused look on his face, Ian's mood darkened.

"Ye did nae think I was going to miss this, did ye?" When Ian scowled, Fagan added, "Ye're making the right decision." He held his hand over his heart. "The things we men must do for love."

"If ye donna shut your mouth, I will shut it for ye,"

Ian warned. He glanced at Mistress Betts. "Go ahead, lass. I want this to be done."

He sat perfectly still until the sound of the scissors stopped. When he glanced down, his eyes widened. "What the hell?" He picked up his fallen hair that lay in clumps on his lap as Ruairi and Fagan stood. "I must look the fool."

"Munro, it looks much worse than it is," said Ruairi. He placed his elbow into Fagan's gut.

"Aye, Munro. Ye do look a few stones lighter," said Fagan.

Mistress Betts brushed the fallen hair from Ian's clothes and picked up his mane on the floor with a wet cloth. She turned and smiled. "If there isn't anything else, I'll be taking my leave." She paused. "Lady Elizabeth will love the look of you."

His felt the heat rise into his cheeks, knowing his face must've turned ten shades of red. When Mistress Betts closed the door, Ian let out a heavy sigh. "Do ye think this is going to work?"

"Aye," said Ruairi. He gestured to the looking glass. "Why donna ye take a look and see for yourself?"

Ian stood and took a couple steps forward. He barely recognized himself. "What the hell have I done?"

❧

Elizabeth hadn't realized she'd fallen asleep until a little snort escaped her. After being in a damp dress, the warm bed felt heavenly. She didn't want to remove herself from under the blankets, but she was excited to see *Henry VIII*.

This was the day she'd been longing for, a chance

to attend the theatre. Even though Ian was escorting her, she'd made up her mind this afternoon was hers to claim. She wasn't going to think about Mister Condell's wooing gesture, and she refused to be plagued by Ian's words of love. Otherwise, she'd go mad. There would be no shadows across her heart. Her intention was to sit back and enjoy a play at the Globe Theatre in Southwark.

She rose from the bed and approached her trunk. She decided to wear the golden gown adorned with the laced bodice, ribbon waistband, and a wheel farthingale. Wanting to look her best for the theatre, Elizabeth pulled out her matching gold silk slippers and set them on the bed.

As she stole a glance in the looking glass, she said a silent prayer of thanks for Mistress Betts. Even though Elizabeth could pin her own hair on the top of her head, the woman always made the task look easier than it was. And she was grateful that Mistress Betts was willing to lend a hand.

Lifting her nightrail, Elizabeth secured her dagger to her thigh. The burly Laird Munro might be her escort, but she'd heed her sisters' advice. She needed to be able to defend herself, especially traveling the streets of London. She had just started to wonder if there was ever a time when her sisters had used their daggers in defense when there was a knock at the door.

Once her blade was in place, Elizabeth dropped her nightrail. "Yes?"

"It's Mistress Betts, my lady. Are you ready to dress?"

Elizabeth opened the door. "Yes, please come in."

Mistress Betts closed the door behind her and

approached the bed. "This is a lovely gown to choose for the theatre. I'm certain you'll be catching the eye of many men…or perhaps one man in particular."

"That was not my intention."

"I know he'll love the dress just the same."

Elizabeth's eyes widened. "Who will love the dress?"

"Laird Munro, of course." As Mistress Betts gave her a knowing look, Elizabeth had trouble finding her words.

"I must ask you. How did you know?"

"I see love in your eyes every time you gaze upon the man, my lady. And I've seen the way he yearns for you when you're not looking." Mistress Betts picked up the dress. "Love does not lie."

Perhaps, but Elizabeth didn't want to tell Mistress Betts that Laird Munro had lied to the woman he supposedly loved. "Yes, well, I don't want to be late for the theatre."

Mistress Bates secured the last curl on the top of Elizabeth's head, and Elizabeth stood. Smoothing her skirts, she gazed into the looking glass. "I do wonder why I've never had a lady's maid before. I realize now how dreadful of a job I've been doing all these years. My hair looks beautiful."

"As do you, my lady. Have a fabulous time at the theatre. I'm certain you'll be sure to see some welcome surprises." When Mistress Betts's eyes lit up, Elizabeth gave her a warm smile.

"Thank you."

After Mistress Betts departed, Elizabeth waited in her room another moment, wanting to clear her mind of any unwelcome thoughts. Lifting her skirts, she descended the stairs, amazed that she had arrived before Laird Munro. This was a first because Fagan, Ruairi, and Ian had been always waiting for her. A few men and women passed her as she waited by the front door of the inn. Just when she thought Ian had decided not to escort her this evening, Fagan came down the stairs.

"Are ye waiting for Munro?"

"Yes, he's coming, isn't he? I don't want to be late for the first act of the play."

Fagan gestured behind him, and she spotted the red, green, and blue kilt that Ian wore as he descended the stairs. This was the first time she'd ever seen him without his massive broadsword strapped to his waist. A plaid hung over his shoulder and was affixed with his clan badge. His unruly hair wasn't hanging down to his elbows in complete disarray and was pulled away from his boldly handsome face.

When he reached the last step, he moved his arm back as if he was searching for his sword and had forgotten it wasn't there. He gave her an uneasy smile.

"Lady Elizabeth, ye look verra bonny." He gave her a slight bow and then extended his arm.

She froze.

Ian's unruly locks were gone. His hair was shoulder length and neatly tied back at the nape of his neck. When she took too long to respond, his eyes met hers, and she placed her hand on his arm.

"I know ye've been waiting to attend the theatre, lass," said Ian. "I hope that ye find me suitable enough to be your escort this afternoon."

The man could've been dressed in rags, and Elizabeth

wouldn't have cared. She suddenly had a feeling many eyes were watching them and glanced around the room.

Fagan had his finger pointed at Ian and then hastily lowered his arm. Very casually, he leaned against the wall. Ruairi was standing with his arms folded over his chest, and both men held ridiculous expressions as though they were caught doing something they shouldn't have been doing.

Ian cleared his throat. "Lady Elizabeth." He reached behind him and handed her a single red rose. "A rose… for the bonniest lass who ever graced the Highlands."

She heard Fagan whisper. "I taught him that."

Fifteen

IAN SAT IN THE CARRIAGE ACROSS FROM ELIZABETH. She'd been in the same position since they'd left the inn with her hands folded on her lap, gazing out the window. She had yet to even glance in his direction. It wasn't his imagination. She couldn't even look him in the eye. He never should've listened to Ruairi and Fagan.

With his cut hair tied back and no sword at his side, Elizabeth probably thought he looked like a Scottish lout. And he more than likely didn't win her favor by gifting her with a single rose either, especially since Condell had done the same. Fagan's idea of a flower wasn't original, and Ian made a mental note that perhaps from now on he should follow his own instincts for courting the lass. He couldn't do any worse.

"I wish ye'd speak to me." Something out the window held Elizabeth's attention because she couldn't tear her eyes away.

"And what would you like me to say?" she asked in a dry tone.

"I told ye in the garden that ye're the love of my heart, and ye have nae said a word about it."

"Unlike you, I'd rather not say anything than look you in the eye and speak a lie."

He sat forward and grabbed her hand. At least now her gaze rested upon him. "Elizabeth, I was wrong to deny what happened between us."

"Could you please do me a favor?"

He brushed his thumb over her knuckles. "Anything."

"I only want to enjoy the play. I don't want to think or speak about you or Mister Condell. Is that too much to ask for one afternoon?"

Ian gave her a knowing smile. "Ye're right. What else is there to talk about? I love ye, and ye love me. 'Tis all that matters."

Anger lit her eyes like wildfire. "After all this time, you come forth now. How very presumptuous of you to believe that your abrupt declaration in the garden would solve everything between us. Let's not forget the fact that you've hurt me." Her eyes clawed him like talons. "Only when Mister Condell made an attempt to woo me, did you dare speak words of love. How convenient. You must think me a fool, some play toy that you can keep on a string to pull or release anytime you wish."

He was about to explain that he didn't feel that way when she spoke in a controlled voice. "I am the daughter of Lord Francis Walsingham, the niece of Lord Walter Mildmay, and the sister of Ravenna, Grace, and Kat. Walsingham blood flows through these veins, Laird Munro, and I am done being your game pawn."

The carriage stopped, and Elizabeth glanced out the window. She withdrew her hand from Ian's grasp as if

he were on fire. "Good. We're here. Let's try to have
a pleasant time, shall we?"

The door opened, and Elizabeth took the coachman's hand. She stepped down, leaving Ian sitting in
the coach with his mouth agape. Before he followed
her out of the carriage, he paused, wondering what the
hell he'd done now.

❧

Elizabeth was aware her rebellious emotions had
gotten out of hand, but once she stood in front of the
Globe Theatre, all her anger quickly fled. The grounds
surrounding the building were bustling with men
and women. As merchants sold their wares, she felt
as though she was at market day. There were breads,
cheeses, pastries, and pies, and men were cooking
meat on a spit. A pleasing smell wafted through the
air, making her mouth water.

Sitting on the south bank of the River Thames, the
circular three-story theatre was a magnificent sight. As
she approached the main entrance, the words "*Totus
mundus agit histrionem*" were inscribed. *The whole world
is a playhouse.* A crest displayed Hercules holding a
giant globe on his broad shoulders.

"What do ye think?" asked Ian. "Will ye stand
here, or do ye want to see the play?"

"I want to see the play." The man didn't need to
ask her twice. She took his arm and could barely wait
to set foot inside the theatre. As they walked through
the entrance, she briefly paused in awe.

A thatched roof covered a small part of the structure, and the majority of standing room in the theatre

was under the open sky. Thank heavens the rain had stopped. The main stage, which was about five feet high, was located in the center of the building and pushed up against one of the interior walls. Two other playhouse boxes flanked a balcony on each side of the stage, and columns supported a small house on the third level, where the theatre's flag hung.

Elizabeth was about to ask Ian if he was ready to take their seats when a trumpet sounded to signal the start of the play. As Mister Condell had promised, there were two empty chairs near the front of the stage.

"I'm pleased to see ye so happy, lass."

"I've been looking forward to this for a long time."

The play opened with the Duke of Norfolk, Buckingham, and Lord Abergavenny. The conversation between them expressed their mutual resentment over the ruthless power of Cardinal Wolsey.

King Henry VIII was introduced during the second scene, and that was the moment Elizabeth had been waiting for. She studied Mister Condell's every move. He accurately portrayed how much the king relied on the cardinal, Wolsey clearly having the king's favor. She wasn't astonished that Mister Condell played an alluring King Henry. When Queen Katherine entered to protest about the cardinal's abuse of the tax system for his own purpose, Elizabeth sat forward, hanging on their every word.

After the final act, Ian stood and stretched his back. "Did ye enjoy yourself?"

She couldn't stay the laugh that escaped her. "Yes. And don't think that I missed your bobbing head. I don't know how you can possibly sleep in a library or during *Henry VIII*. There are so many interesting things to see."

"I donna know. Ye would think all the excitement to be had in a library or at a play would keep a man awake," said Ian dryly.

"Do I detect sarcasm, Laird Munro?"

Ian shrugged. "Mayhap. Are ye ready to take your leave?"

"I was hoping to speak to Mister Condell and congratulate him on a fine performance." When Ian scowled, she added, "The man was kind enough to reserve seats for us. The least we can do is thank him properly." When she spotted Mister Condell making his way toward them, she poked Ian in the chest with her finger. "Here he comes. Do not be rude."

"I make nay promises, lass."

❧

When Elizabeth's eyes lit up, Ian tried to be the bigger man. He truly did. But as Condell approached them still wearing King Henry's courtly attire, Ian didn't even attempt to wipe away the disgusted look from his face—especially when the crowd bowed before the seedy bastard.

Elizabeth curtsied. "Your Majesty, your performance was grand. You should be proud."

Condell lifted her hand and brushed a kiss on the top of it. "You're far too kind, my lady." When he spoke in an English accent, Ian shook his head. "Munro, thank you for escorting Lady Elizabeth to see the play."

"Ye can let go of the lass now."

Elizabeth cleared her throat. "Will you be at court on the morrow, Mister Condell?"

"Yes. With you being in attendance, how could I not, my lady?"

Ian rolled his eyes at the same time Elizabeth gave him a scolding look. Condell turned, and his eyes narrowed. "Would you mind if I had a private word with Lady Elizabeth?"

"Aye, I would." When Ian casually reached for the hilt of his sword and realized it wasn't there, he silently cursed, especially when Condell realized what he was doing.

"How does it feel not having your weapon, your giant broadsword, strapped to your waist, Laird Munro?"

"'Tis nae the only weapon I carry," Ian warned. "Besides, I have been known to kill a man with my bare hands."

"Laird Munro, is that really necessary?" asked Elizabeth.

The actor turned his back on Ian. "I was hoping to ask you when we were alone, but I see your *chaperone* is not going to allow us a private moment together. As I told you before, the king favors my acting ability. He's granted me special access to unique places at court…for inspiration, you might say. Would you like to see Anne Boleyn's apartments above the gate?"

She gasped. "Truly?"

"Yes. I know you're fascinated with King Henry's realm. I thought you'd enjoy it."

Before Elizabeth could answer, a beautiful woman approached them with long, blond hair and more curves than Ian could count. "Condell, you're needed in the back."

"Of course. Lady Elizabeth, Laird Munro, allow me to introduce to you Mistress Alexander. She has done wonders in the ways of theatrical applications. She's in charge of costume design, hair, and transformations you saw in the production. Her work with clay and plaster masks is remarkable—lifelike. She can make anyone appear as someone else."

"It's a pleasure to meet you, Mistress Alexander. I never would've guessed Queen Katherine a man if I hadn't already known. Perhaps there'll be a time when a woman will be permitted to play the role."

"I should hope not, my lady. I wouldn't want to be out of work." Her expression grew serious. "Condell…"

"I'll be right there." The actor smiled at Elizabeth. "How about I meet you at noon at the gatehouse? I can have one of the king's guards let us in."

Elizabeth gave Condell a warm smile. "I'd be delighted. It was a pleasure to have met you, Mistress Alexander. And Mister Condell, thank you for holding seats for us. We enjoyed the play immensely."

"Munro…" Condell turned away without waiting for a reply.

"The man is verra bold."

"I do appreciate you not taking him to task in front of the entire theatre." When Elizabeth gazed at him, Ian's heart lurched madly. "I've tortured you enough for one afternoon. It's getting late. Are you ready to take your leave?" When he gave her a grin as though the answer to her question was obvious, she took his arm. "A little bit of culture never hurt anybody, Laird Munro. Remember that."

As they waited for the carriage, Elizabeth kept her

hand on his arm, and nothing had ever felt so right. At that moment, it wasn't hard to imagine the lass beside him as his wife. He made a vow that he would never again push her away. Even though he didn't understand her attraction to him, she was a grown lass and capable of making her own decisions. Who was Ian to question her judgment, especially when it was in his favor?

"Lord Kinghorne, I didn't know you were attending the theatre this afternoon," said Elizabeth.

When Ian turned and gave the earl a brief tip of his head, the man couldn't stop fingering the buttons on his doublet in a nervous or restless gesture—perhaps both. Even without his sword strapped to his waist, Ian frightened men. The thought pleased him.

"Lady Elizabeth and Laird Munro, what a pleasant surprise to see you here. I should have suspected you'd favor the theatre."

"Yes. Laird Munro was kind enough to escort me." Elizabeth glanced around the crowd. "Where is Lady Glamis?"

"She remains at court." He gazed around uneasily. "She wasn't feeling well so I thought it best she stay in her chamber and rest."

"I do hope she's well soon. I'm certain she'd love to accompany you to see the play. Mister Condell was simply wonderful as King Henry, don't you agree?"

The earl gave her an appeasing look. "Yes, indeed. If you'll pray excuse me, that's my carriage waiting. I'm sure that I'll see you both on the morrow."

Elizabeth studied the earl as he approached the waiting coach. "Was his behavior rather...odd?"

"He's English. Ye're asking me if he's odd?" When she placed her elbow into Ian's gut, he added, "He was more than likely worried about his mother. Mayhap he was trying to make haste to return to court."

"Perhaps."

Elizabeth stepped into the carriage. As soon as the door closed, she nestled back into the seat. "I had a lovely time. Thank you."

"'Twas my pleasure."

The lass was silent almost the entire way back to the inn, and he felt a certain sadness their time together was coming to an end. He decided to honor her request and keep his mouth shut about what was happening between them. She deserved to enjoy herself, and that certainly wasn't too much to ask. That's why he was taken aback when she spoke.

"I simply cannot go through this another time." She blurted out the words in a single breath. "Give me your word that you will never lie to me again."

Ian sat forward, and covering her hands with his own, he gave her a tender smile. "I told ye I was a fool. I ne'er wanted to hurt ye, but I am a man. Ruairi and Fagan told me 'tis in our nature to fire the ire of the lasses we love." He rubbed his thumb over her fingers. "I donna want there to be any more shadows between us. I meant what I said to ye in the garden. I do love ye, Elizabeth. I think I've always known it to be true, but I was too afraid to admit as much to ye and myself."

Her breath hitched. "Come closer, Laird Munro." He leaned forward, and she gently caressed his cheek. She pulled him so close that he could feel her breath.

Her lips brushed against his as she spoke. "I've waited so long to hear those words."

His mouth covered hers hungrily, and his lips explored her soft, ivory flesh. She drew his face to hers in a renewed embrace, and it was a kiss for his tired soul to melt into. When the carriage slowed its pace, Ian pulled back, and Elizabeth straightened her skirts. She looked him in the eye and did not falter.

"I will not have you deny again what happened between us."

He chuckled. "Ye donna have to worry about that, lass."

"Give me your word that you will not lie to me again."

"Aye. I give ye my word."

Her eyes studied him intensely. "Did my uncle murder Daniel?"

As the carriage came to a halt, Ian climbed out and extended his hand to assist Elizabeth from the coach. When she stepped down, she implored, "Please, Ian. If you truly want to move forward—"

"Ye need to talk with Ruairi."

"I want to talk with you."

He said the first thought that came to mind to deter her. "We can nae talk in the dining hall. Someone will hear us."

"Then come to my room later this evening when the servants are asleep."

He stared at her with rounded eyes, astonished by her suggestion. "I donna think that's a good idea, lass. Remember what happened the last time we were alone in my chamber."

"As I recall, that was the problem that started this

whole bloody mess between us, was it not? I remember perfectly well what occurred in your chamber. On the other hand, you—"

"I donna understand why ye will nae talk to Ruairi. He is your laird."

"How many times must I tell you that Ruairi is *not* my laird? Furthermore, you know my brother-in-law will not speak to me without Ravenna by his side."

"And I'm sure for good reason." He paused and took a deep breath. "I donna think 'tis my place to talk with ye about this. I am nae your family. Mayhap if I talk to Ruairi first, he—"

"For heaven's sake, Laird Munro. Meet me in my chamber later this eve."

❧

Ian waited until the darkened hours of the night and still had no clue if he should tell Elizabeth the truth about her family. As another alternative, he could've sought Ruairi and Fagan and asked for their advice, but he didn't, and it was too late now. No matter how much he pondered the matter, even if he had talked to Ruairi, the end result was the same.

Elizabeth wouldn't trust him.

There was no sense delaying the inevitable. Ian stood in the hall and lightly tapped on her door. When she lifted the latch, he turned his head. Not seeing anyone in the hall, he walked into her room and gently closed the door behind him. Even in a simple day dress, the lass looked beautiful by candlelight.

"Did anyone see you?"

"Nay."

Elizabeth gestured to the chair and sat beside him at the table in the small sitting area. "First, please let me start by offering you an apology."

Ian lifted a brow. "An apology? For what, may I ask?"

"I know my brothers-in-law are your best friends, and I understand why you wouldn't want to discuss my uncle or Daniel with me. I recognize that I've placed you in a difficult situation, but the truth is... I've always loved you, Ian. I can't deny it. And you say you love me too. I want us to talk with each other like we have in the past—honestly—with no secrets."

Her words pleased him beyond measure, and he pulled her to her feet. When her eyes froze on his mouth, he slowly lowered his head. Standing on tiptoe, Elizabeth pressed her lips to his, his hands locking against her back. She was soft and warm, and he was very conscious of where the lass's flesh pressed against his.

He made sure his touch was gentle because the last thing he wanted to do was frighten her. When he planted a kiss in the hollow of her neck, he felt her knees weaken, and he tightened his grip.

His lips recaptured hers, more demanding this time. When her body arched toward him instinctively, it was almost his undoing. Her innocent response to him was so powerful.

Before his actions got out of hand, he slowly pulled back, and something inexplicable passed between them. Clearing his throat, he whispered, "Elizabeth, we must stop, or soon I will be unable."

An unwelcome blush crept onto the lass's cheeks. He was perfectly aware that he needed to gain

Elizabeth's trust once again, but stealing kisses from her in the carriage or in her room in the middle of the night was not the way he wanted to go about it. He still wanted to woo her and win her love.

Ian gazed into her eyes. There was no other view he'd rather see. "*Tha gaol agam ort*. You need to understand those Gaelic words, lass, because ye'll be hearing them often. I love ye, Elizabeth." He lifted his hand and brushed her fallen tresses behind her ear.

"Are you trying to distract me, Laird Munro?"

He gave her a roguish grin. "Is it working?"

"Not as much as you'd hoped it would. Why don't we sit for a while?"

Once again he sat at the table and readied himself to face the inquisition. Trying to collect his thoughts, he paused, not even sure where to start.

Elizabeth cast a patient smile and then said, "The Tullibardine sisters overheard their father talking about me having Highlanders as my chaperones. Not only did Lord Tullibardine speak of Ravenna's marriage to Ruairi, but he went on to say that Uncle Walter murdered Daniel."

He chose his words carefully. "Lass, I still believe this conversation is best held with Ruairi."

Elizabeth sighed. "You speak words of love, yet, you still don't tell me the truth."

"I am nae lying to ye now."

"Perhaps not, but you're not very forthcoming with information that I know you possess. How do you expect me to trust you when you won't talk to me? Tell me, Ian. Did my uncle end Daniel's life?"

There was a heavy silence as Elizabeth cast an

unrelenting gaze upon him. Her question was like a double-edged sword. No matter what his answer, he had a pretty good idea what the consequences of his actions would be. His mind wandered, and he asked himself if he was willing to lose the lass by not speaking the truth. And then he realized that he'd answered his own question.

"Aye, Mildmay killed Casterbrook."

❧

Perhaps Elizabeth shouldn't have asked a question that she didn't want to know the answer to because Ian's response was a stab in her heart. She tried to keep her fragile control. Uncle Walter, a man who was like a second father to them all, had murdered Grace's former betrothed. Why? How could a man as gentle and caring as Uncle Walter kill another man? In her heart she had always known something had befallen Daniel because Ravenna and Grace had become masters at avoiding Elizabeth's prodding every time she inquired.

She felt as if her breath was cut off. "I want answers, and I seem to be the only member of the family who doesn't have them." When Ian rubbed his hand over his brow, she added, "Even the Tullibardine sisters knew the truth about Daniel. I suspect now *I'm* the fool for not even knowing what was occurring with my own family. Why is that?"

Ian's face remained closed, as if he was guarding another secret. But she wouldn't have it and refused to give up. "I want the truth."

"Ye know Mildmay and Casterbrook worked for the king."

"Yes. My uncle had been in the king's employ for as long as I can remember. He was His Majesty's most trusted advisor, his friend."

"Aye. Mildmay was the king's friend and advisor, but he was more than that."

A puzzled expression crossed her face. "What do you mean?"

He reached out and gently touched her arm. "Lass, this may be difficult for ye to hear, but I donna know any other way to say—"

"For heaven's sake, Ian, just tell me."

"Your uncle was a spy for the Crown."

Sixteen

ELIZABETH WAS RENDERED SPEECHLESS. SHE HAD TO study Ian to make certain he wasn't jesting. Even though he hadn't spoken another word, his face spoke for him. He was telling her the truth. Uncle Walter had been a spy. Her thoughts raced, wanting to put all the pieces together.

"Ye frighten me when ye donna say anything. I can nae read your thoughts, lass."

"Apparently, my uncle was not a very good spy if you knew he had worked for the Crown."

Ian sat forward. "Nay, that's where ye're wrong. Your uncle had been in service to the realm for a verra long time. Ye know he served Queen Elizabeth and then worked for King James as the king's advisor. Mildmay was a skilled man. He also loved ye and your sisters like ye were his own daughters."

She rubbed her fingers over her eyes. "So if my uncle was a spy for the king, why did he kill Daniel?"

"Casterbrook had ambitions of his own. Grace was only one of his pawns in a grander scheme."

"If he did use Grace for a purpose, I can understand

my uncle being cross, but to *kill* Daniel over his ambitions? That's not like Uncle Walter at all. The man that I'd known all my life was a gentle soul. I can't fathom he'd end anyone's life, let alone one betrothed to my sister." Her head was puzzled by new thoughts, and she wanted answers faster than she could comprehend them. "Do my sisters know of Daniel's treachery? Do they know our uncle murdered him?"

"This is why I wanted ye to talk with Ruairi, lass."

"It doesn't matter who tells me. I need to know the truth."

Ian's face clouded with uneasiness. "Grace was going to break off her betrothal before all this happened. Casterbrook harmed your sister, and for that, he was killed. If ye must know, it was Fagan and Mildmay's swords that sent the bastard to his maker. 'Tis naught I would nae have done myself if someone had harmed ye, Elizabeth."

"Grace never said a word about any of this."

"Ravenna and Grace decided nae to tell ye and Kat. Ye are…er, were young and innocent. Your sisters wanted to protect ye."

Elizabeth didn't even attempt to wipe away the look of disgust that crossed her face. "Of course Ravenna would've known too. I can't believe the gall of the two of them. They didn't think it was necessary to tell me anything, just let me hear the truth from a stranger at court." Something clicked in her mind. "I wonder if Mother and Father knew of Uncle Walter's craft. You know my father was Queen Elizabeth's principal secretary until his death."

When there remained a certain tension in Ian's behavior, her eyes narrowed. "I will have the entire truth, Laird Munro, not just a part."

"Your father…" When he paused mid-sentence, she stirred in the chair, and her fingers tensed on her lap. "Your father was also a spy, lass."

"Bloody hell." Elizabeth couldn't stop the words that escaped her. "This conversation keeps getting better and better. Is there no end to this sordid tale?"

"Ye wanted to know the truth. I am giving it to ye."

She shook her head to clear the cobwebs. "Yes, I'm sorry. I just can't believe…my father too?"

Ian stood and pulled her to her feet. He brushed his thumb lightly across her cheek. "Ye've heard more than enough for one eve. The sun will be up in a few hours, and ye need to rest."

"How can I possibly sleep now?"

He took her hand and guided her to the bed. "Lie down."

She was in no mood to argue. Heaven help her because she was completely numb. He leaned over her, covering her with a blanket and placing a gentle kiss on her forehead.

"Try to sleep, lass. I know my words come as a surprise, but everything always looks brighter in the morn. Trust me. We can talk later when your thoughts are clear." He blew out the candles and left the one beside the bed lit.

When he reached for the latch on the door, she called out, "Thank you for telling me the truth."

"I'd do anything for ye, lass."

"Uncle Walter did not have a carriage accident, Ian.

Someone is trying to kill all the members of the king's Privy Council."

❧

Ian hadn't slept at all. Although his room was currently a safe haven, he'd have to leave it and face Ruairi sooner or later. He only prayed that he'd reach his friend before Elizabeth. Not being able to delay the inevitable any longer, he walked into the hall and knocked on Ruairi's door. When Ruairi greeted him with a smile, Ian couldn't stay the trace of guilt he felt for telling Elizabeth her family's secrets.

"*Ciamar a tha thu?*" asked Ruairi. *How are you?*

Ian entered his friend's chamber and closed the door behind him. "*Tha gu math.*" *I am fine.*

"How was the theatre? I did nae receive word that anyone was killed. Am I to assume that Condell still lives?"

"For the moment…but I need to talk with ye about something else. Lady Elizabeth met two sisters at court—"

"The twins?" Ruairi sat on the bed to put his boots on.

"Aye. The lasses overheard their father discussing Ravenna, Grace, and Casterbrook. More than likely, the man did nae know his daughters were listening to his every word. One sister asked Elizabeth if the rumors were true."

Ruairi squeezed the bridge of his nose. "I'm afraid to ask, but which rumors would those be?"

"If Mildmay killed Casterbrook…"

"Damn."

"Aye."

"And what did Elizabeth say in response?"

Ian shrugged. "What could she say? She did nae know anything about her uncle and Casterbrook."

Ruairi stood. "Good. Let's make sure that she does nae find out. If the lass asks ye any questions, send her to me."

Ian turned away and ran his hand through his shortened hair. "'Tis too late."

"*Dè thuirt thu?*" *What did you say?*

He spun around and faced Ruairi. "*Tha mi duilich.*" *I am sorry.*

"Munro! What the hell did ye say to her? Why did ye nae tell her to ask me?"

Ian let out a heavy sigh. "'Twas nae for lack of trying, believe me. I lied to the lass about something else when I should nae have; therefore, she did nae trust my words when I told her that I loved her. Ye're my best friend, Ruairi, and Elizabeth knows that. Of course I would've known a piece of the tale. Furthermore, if the lass is one day going to be my wife, she needs to trust me. Ye, of all people, should know how difficult a task 'tis to deny a Walsingham. Ye live with four of them. The lasses are tenacious."

"What exactly did ye tell her?"

"She knows Mildmay and her father were spies for the Crown. And I told her that Casterbrook had ambitions of his own and used Grace as a pawn. She knows Fagan and Mildmay killed him for his treachery."

"And what of Ravenna?"

"I did nae tell her of your wife's involvement with the Crown."

"Well, I'm sure as hell nae going to be the one to tell her. Whatever ye do, donna answer any more of her questions. Ravenna will be the one to talk with her when we return from court."

Ian sighed. "There is more."

"And what is that?" Ruairi stretched his neck from side to side.

"Elizabeth is a smart lass. She knows her uncle was nae killed in a carriage accident."

"There is nay proof to believe otherwise."

"She's a Walsingham. The lass is nae going to leave well enough alone. Ye know that."

"Then 'tis up to us to make sure that she does."

⊷⊷

Elizabeth opened her chamber door, and Ruairi was standing in the hall with a fist raised in midair.

"I was just going to knock. I wanted to talk with ye before ye broke your fast."

She gestured him in, and he closed the door behind him. "Munro told me what happened last eve."

"Of course he did," she said dryly.

"Donna be cross with him. Do ye have any other questions? Ask them now because ye can nae be prodding anyone at court, lass."

"I'm having a difficult time understanding why my sisters never told me anything about Uncle Walter, Daniel, or my own father. I had to find out at court—of all places."

"We all have reasons to protect those we love, lass. 'Tis why your family has always kept ye shielded from the aristocracy. I would nae be too angry with your sisters. I'm certain Ravenna and Grace will talk with ye when we return from court."

She studied her brother-in-law intently and didn't want to miss his reaction when she asked the next question. "You are an intelligent man, Ruairi. My uncle's death was no accident." She didn't miss his hesitation.

"I can nae deny that other men of the council have been…targeted."

Her voice raised a notch. "Targeted? Don't you mean murdered?" When he attempted to grasp her shoulders, she pulled away.

"Lass, there is nay proof Mildmay was killed."

"Then we need to find it."

A chuckle escaped him. "And where would ye think to look, lass?"

"I don't know, but we can't let someone get away with murdering my uncle, spy or not. We have to do something. Perhaps when you meet with the king you can talk to him about—or maybe I can speak with the king."

"Elizabeth, how was the theatre?"

From her brother-in-law's abrupt redirection and the stern expression he held on his face, he was telling her that this particular conversation was over. "Are you truly going to ask me about the theatre right now?" When he gave her a dismissing look, she added, "*Henry VIII* was a lovely play. All the actors were superb."

"Condell?"

"Yes. He was a believable King Henry. I'm going to meet him at noon. He's going to show me Anne Boleyn's apartments above the gates."

Ruairi gave her a measured gaze. "I assume Munro is accompanying ye?"

"Yes."

"Elizabeth, ye are my sister-by-marriage, and Munro is like my brother. I know he told ye that he loves ye, and he said that ye told him the same."

"That's not exactly a secret, Ruairi."

"I'm pleased that he finally realizes how he feels about ye too, but mayhap 'tis nae the best of ideas to keep Condell close at hand. Both men are trying to woo ye, which can only end in disaster."

"What do you mean?"

"Ye are the first lass who has ever seen Munro for the man he truly is. He thinks because he is nae fair of face that nay lass would ever desire him."

She was tired of having the same conversation. "Why does everyone keep saying that he is not fair of face? I think Laird Munro is very handsome."

"Be that as it may, some may say Condell is nae lacking in looks."

She laughed to cover her annoyance. "Ruairi, just because Mister Condell has been blessed with a handsome visage does not make him any better of a man than Ian...er, Laird Munro."

"I'm only saying to be careful with Munro. In truth, I donna want to see either of ye hurt—or Condell."

❧

"My only hope is when Elizabeth finds out Ravenna was a spy for the king that she does nae have my wife's same reaction. Grace was relentless in trying to learn spy craft from Ravenna," said Fagan.

Ian swallowed what was left of his biscuit. "Aye, we know."

"Let's hope Ruairi curtails the lass's questions until we get back to Scadbury Manor. Ravenna and Grace will need to talk with her."

"Aye."

Fagan gave Ian a knowing grin. "Did ye manage to stay awake for the play?"

"'Twas a wee bit difficult, but I managed."

"And how was everything between ye and Elizabeth?"

"I donna know."

Fagan placed his cup down on the table. "What do ye mean ye donna know? Ye were there, were ye nae?"

"The lass did nae want to talk about me or Condell. She said she wanted time where naught else came to mind."

"Dinna fash yourself over that. Even though Elizabeth did nae want to talk, at least she still wanted to be with ye. Grace tells me to leave her the hell alone. God, I miss my wife. 'Tis nice nae to guess what a lass is thinking."

"Och, aye. Nay one ever has to render a guess with your wife."

"I do love that about her."

Elizabeth and Ruairi entered the dining hall, and Ian rose, pulling out the lass's chair.

"Thank you." She glanced at him as she sat, giving him a small smile.

"I heard Munro did nae snore too loudly at the play," said Fagan.

"He did well." Her eyes met Ian's, and then she lifted her hand and touched the ends of his cut locks. "This is the first time I've seen you with your hair down since you've cut it. It looks very becoming on you."

When her hand rested on his shoulder a moment too long, Ian heard himself swallow. He also realized everyone at the table was dead silent. He cast a quick look at Fagan, who stared at him with widened eyes, and Ruairi sat frozen with a biscuit at his lips. The moment was lost when Elizabeth pulled her hand away.

After everyone broke their fast and Elizabeth dressed for court, Ian managed to steal a private moment with her before she stepped into the waiting carriage. Gray clouds loomed overhead, and when a rumble of thunder echoed through the sky, he knew their moment would be just that.

"How are ye feeling this morn?"

"Weary, especially since I didn't sleep much after our talk."

He gave her a tender smile. "I want to make certain that ye know nae to ask questions at court about anything we've discussed, lass. Ye donna want your words falling on the wrong ears, and I donna want to see ye hurt."

"Yes, Ruairi lectured me about the same. Unlike Grace, I can keep my mouth closed." She looked up at the sky. "We probably want to make haste before the rain is upon us."

He brushed his thumb against her cheek, and she leaned her head against his hand. "Mayhap ye will give me the honor of a dance this eve."

"But you don't dance. I believe your exact words were 'not even under the threat of death.'"

"Aye, but I ne'er had the chance to have ye as my partner."

❧

Elizabeth waited for Mister Condell at the gatehouse as she'd promised. The intermittent drizzle of rain was heavy enough to spoil outside activities. As Ian leaned against the wall with his arms folded over his chest, she knew this was the last place he'd rather be, especially with Mister Condell.

"Would you look at that?" she asked. Ian walked over to her, and she gestured to the ceiling of the gatehouse.

"What am I looking at, lass?"

She grabbed his arm to turn him around and pointed with her finger. "There. Do you see it? Anne Boleyn's falcon badge is fashioned on a diamond-shaped carving. The letter of her name is entwined with King Henry's in lovers' knots. Can you see the 'A' for Anne and the 'H' for Henry?"

"Aye. I see it now."

"King Henry loved Anne, adored her even. I've heard the apartments that he'd built for her were very close to his private chambers. At one point in time, they couldn't bear to be separated from each other. I cannot understand how one moment two people can be so madly in love and then hating each other the next. It's rather sad."

"Lass, she was infamous for playing dangerous games at court and caught the attention of the king. Her fall from grace was inevitable."

"Perhaps, but that doesn't make their tale any less exciting."

"I couldn't agree more, Lady Elizabeth."

Elizabeth turned, and Mister Condell greeted her with a smile. "Mister Condell, it's a pleasure to see you again."

He gave her a slight bow. "Lady Elizabeth." He briefly tipped his head to Ian. "Laird Munro."

"Condell."

"The guard is coming to unlock the doors for us. Shall we proceed?"

When he extended his arm, Elizabeth hesitated, remembering Ruairi's words. Although she understood his concern about Mister Condell, she didn't want to be rude to the man. She placed her hand on his arm and turned to Ian. "Laird Munro, are you ready?"

He didn't look at her but glared at Mister Condell. "Aye." The way Ian answered her question made her think that he was ready all right—to do something to Mister Condell.

They made their way to the apartments as a guard unlocked the door. Mister Condell gestured Elizabeth and Ian inside.

"We are not permitted to touch anything, but you can look wherever you'd like."

Elizabeth couldn't believe she was standing in the same place where Anne Boleyn had lived. She wondered how many times King Henry had crossed that threshold to see his beloved—well, until the wind changed direction and he had her beheaded.

As she walked through Anne Boleyn's apartments, she noted the two sitting areas and a large stone fireplace, and again, the letters "A" and "H" carved into the mantel. She could only imagine the lavishness of these rooms during King Henry's reign.

"This area has not been touched for years," said Mister Condell. As if on cue, Ian let out a loud sneeze.

"Sutherland told me that I could find ye here,"

said Laird Fraser, walking into the room. He made no attempt to mask the look of disgust that crossed his face. "I did nae think the damn guard was ever going to let me pass. God's teeth! Ye'd think I was a vagrant trying to steal the precious wares. I've come to share good news. The MacLeod was granted his audience. It will nae be long now before we all are called before the king."

"Would you like to see the other rooms?" asked Mister Condell.

"Yes. That would be lovely." Elizabeth glanced at Ian, and he gave her an easy smile.

"Ye donna have to wait for me while I speak with the Fraser." He drew his attention to Mister Condell, and his expression darkened like a summer storm. As if the man's presence wasn't daunting enough, Ian placed his hand on the hilt of his sword in subtle warning. "The rooms are nae that large. I can come if I'm called."

Elizabeth coughed. "Yes, well, let's hope it doesn't come to that, shall we?"

She followed Mister Condell into another small sitting area, and the room opened into a bedchamber. Although the bed was covered in dust, the coverlet had hundreds of botanically accurate embroidered flowers. How fitting the petals were used to symbolize the love between Henry and Anne.

"I can't thank you enough for showing me these apartments, especially since not many men and women are granted access to such history."

Mister Condell gave her a roguish grin. "I cannot lie about my intentions, my lady. I'd show you anything you'd like to see just to have a chance to be with you again."

"Mister Condell, although I appreciate your words of kindness, I don't think it wise to accept more of your generosity."

He closed what little distance was left between them and lifted her chin with his fingers. As she stared at his handsome face, she felt nothing. Her heart belonged to only one man. She pulled away, giving Mister Condell an uneasy smile. Heaven help her. If she called for Ian, there would be a murder in Anne Boleyn's bedchamber.

"Lady Elizabeth, I'm willing to give you far more than words of kindness or my generosity. I give you me—my heart, my soul, and my love."

She cleared her throat. "Mister Condell, I—"

"Will. My name is Will. Please call me by my given name."

"Mister Condell, I cannot—"

Elizabeth's words were smothered by his lips in Anne Boleyn's chamber. His grip tightened, and she couldn't move. She could barely breathe to call out to Ian. When she finally managed to push him away, ready to give him a firm scolding, he glanced at the bedchamber door with a wicked smile.

Ian…

Seventeen

ELIZABETH STOOD WITHIN MISTER CONDELL'S EMBRACE knowing she'd never forget the expression on Ian's face as long as she lived and breathed. Her first feeling was fear for Mister Condell because Ian could've easily torn the man apart. She was shaking with trepidation but soon realized her assumptions were incorrect. That was not anger she saw in Ian's eyes—it was anguish.

She had opened her mouth to speak when Ian silenced her with his dark, angry expression. He whipped around, and his broad back thundered away.

Mister Condell chuckled. "That's one way to rid ourselves of your chaperone."

"Your kiss was not welcome."

A mischievous look came into his eyes. "Your body did not deny me."

"You held me so tightly that I couldn't even breathe, let alone deny you anything," she said vehemently.

"My apologies, Lady Elizabeth, but I must say that I'm quite taken aback by your words." He stepped around her. "This is a first for me. I've never known any woman to deter my favors."

"I'm sure not many women have," she said dryly, turning to face him. "Mister Condell, I enjoy talking with you about the history of King Henry, and I thoroughly loved the play, but there is nothing between us."

"And why is that, I wonder? We both love history. You're beautiful and intelligent. Very rarely does a man find both qualities in a woman."

"I'm afraid my heart belongs to another. It always has."

There was a heavy silence.

"Then he is a very lucky man, my lady." He gave her a slight bow. "Again, please accept my apologies. Let me make it up to you."

"I assure you. That's not necessary."

An apologetic look crossed his face. "Oh, but it is, my lady. In three days, I'll be giving my last performance as King Henry for the season before returning to Spain. There will even be a few surprises in the final act. Rumors are circulating there will be cannon fire. I'm sworn to secrecy, but you'll have to come and see for yourself."

"Mister Condell, I—"

"And *I* will only accept 'yes' as your answer. I've enjoyed your company, Lady Elizabeth. I do not want to part on unfavorable terms. Let me make amends." He gave her an easy smile. "I cannot return to Spain knowing I've tried to take something that was not offered. Come to the play and enjoy yourself one last time. That's the least I can do for my abhorrent behavior."

Part of this situation was her fault, and she felt guilty. Elizabeth blamed herself for not deterring his affections all along, which encouraged him to pursue her. As a result, the man had stolen a kiss. The way he was staring at her made her realize he wasn't going to relent until she accepted his peace offering. Besides, she could bring Ian along, and she needed to make haste to find him now.

"Very well."

His eyes lit up. "I will reserve the same seats for you, my lady."

She spun on her heel and walked with hurried purpose through the apartments. Even though she was leaving years of history behind, she didn't even take a second glance around. The past didn't matter. Henry and Anne's love had died, but there wasn't anything in the world that would stand in the way of the love she had for Ian. Nothing was more important than the present.

As soon as she made her way out the door, Elizabeth stopped dead in her tracks. The only man waiting was the guard.

"Have you seen Laird Munro?"

"The Highlander took his leave from the castle."

Her eyes widened. "What do you mean he took his leave? How do you know?"

The guard gestured behind her into the apartments. "I saw him leave the gates through the window."

Elizabeth wondered if poor Anne had felt the same way about Henry when the king turned his back on her.

⁂

Ian dismounted on a grassy knoll by the River Thames. At least the drizzle had stopped. He tied off his mount and stood at the water's edge, needing to be alone with his unpleasant thoughts. Although Elizabeth had spoken words of love, it didn't take her long before she threw herself into the arms of the bonny Condell.

How he'd wanted to believe with every fiber of his being that she was different from the rest of the lasses who avoided him like the plague. But now? His misery was like a steel weight. Why would he have ever taken the advice of Ruairi and Fagan?

He closed his eyes, his heart aching with pain. A flash of loneliness stabbed at him, and torment was eating him from the inside. He took deep breaths until he was strong enough to lift his head. The flowing river didn't even calm him. When thundering hoofbeats approached from behind, he didn't bother to turn around.

"What the hell do ye think ye're doing? *A bheil thu ceart gu leòr?*" *Are you all right?*

"Can ye nae even let a man brood alone in peace?"

Fagan tethered his mount. "I saw ye ride out the gates like the hounds of hell—or the bloody English—were nipping at your heels. Ruairi found Elizabeth alone, and I rode after ye. What happened?"

"I caught Elizabeth in the arms of Condell."

Fagan let out a heavy sigh and briefly closed his eyes. "Munro, the lass loves ye. There's probably a logical reason why ye thought ye saw what ye did."

"Och, aye, but I donna think there's any excuse the lass could give for her lips being locked with that bastard's the moment I turn my back!"

"They kissed?" Fagan paused, a puzzled expression crossing his face. "I can nae say for certain what happened, but I know well enough to recognize that Elizabeth did nae play a part in this. She loves *ye*, ye daft fool. Condell probably kissed *her*. Did she nae tell ye that? What did she say?"

"I donna know. I did nae ask her."

Fagan's tongue was heavy with sarcasm. "Munro, God knows ye are dangerous on the battlefield, but naught compares to ye being in love."

"*Na dean sin.*" *Don't do that.* "I am in nay mood to hear any more of your riddles."

"Then let me make my words clear. Ye're being an arse." When Ian's eyes darkened, Fagan took a step back. "I told Ruairi when he was being daft with Ravenna, and now I'm telling ye that ye're being an idiot with Elizabeth. Why are ye so quick to judge something ye know naught about? Get on your damn horse, ride back to court, and talk to the lass to find out what happened. Ye're going to look even more the fool when she tells ye Condell's actions were nae welcome. And let's nae mention the fact that ye took your leave. Ye left the lass in the arms of the actor believing the worst. Ye had nay faith or trust in Elizabeth. And because of your lack of self-assurance, ye turned your back on a man who was taking advantage of the woman ye love. What if Condell would've had his way with her?"

Fagan shook his head in disgust, and his voice was raised. "I pity ye, Munro. Because ye think nay lass would want ye because of your looks, that foolishness has blinded ye. Let me say this in a way ye'll understand. 'Tis nae your face, ye arse…'tis ye. Ye're losing the lass without even knowing it. I hope to hell 'tis nae too late to fix what ye've done. To be truthful, I donna know if Elizabeth will be so forgiving this time."

Ian stood motionless, and his body stiffened in shock. He was so wrapped up with seeing Elizabeth share a kiss with Condell, the thought had never crossed his mind she didn't desire to be in the man's arms in the first place. His face burned with the memory, realizing it was possible that he'd misunderstood the entire situation.

He stormed over to the tree and rammed his fist into the trunk. "*A mhic an Diabhail!*" *Son of the Devil!* Ian didn't attempt to mask his fit of rage. Fagan had seen him before at his worst. "She is ne'er going to forgive me. 'Twas bad enough that I've lied. I took my leave when I should've protected her! What the hell is wrong with me?"

Fagan walked to Ian's side, pulling a piece of material out of his sporran. "Ye're a man." He handed Ian the cloth. "Wipe the blood from your hand and come back to court. I have nay doubt ye've fired Elizabeth's ire something fierce. Fortunately for ye, I'm wed to Grace. I know how to prepare for battle, and ye've got a long one ahead of ye, my friend. This will be nay easy feat. If ye donna fix this the proper way, ye will lose her forever."

"Then what the hell are we waiting for?"

❧

When Ruairi had found Elizabeth wandering the halls of court alone, she wasn't surprised the first question he'd asked her was if something had befallen Laird

Munro. Ruairi would discover that Ian had abandoned her sooner or later, but she wasn't about to tell him what happened in the first place to make his best friend leave. After all, Ruairi was a brawny Highlander who carried a large broadsword. And she believed Mister Condell should live to see another day. She wouldn't have him meet his maker over a kiss—although men have been killed for less.

"And ye're nae certain why Munro took his leave from the castle?" asked Ruairi for the hundredth time.

"No." She knew perfectly well why Ian had left because her vision was still gloomily colored with the memory. She was seething with mounting rage, and the safest place for the man right now was out of her sight.

"Lady Elizabeth…"

When Elizabeth turned, the Tullibardine sisters greeted her with a smile. "Lady Margery and Lady Gillian, I don't believe you've met my brother-in-law. Pray allow me to introduce to you Laird Sutherland."

Lady Gillian—or it could've been Lady Margery—gave Ruairi a raking gaze from head to toe. "It's our pleasure to meet you, Laird Sutherland. I can see what they say is definitely true then."

"And what is that, my lady?" asked Ruairi.

Lady Gillian slapped her hands together in a giddy gesture. "Oh, I just adore your accent." She nudged her sister in the arm. "Don't you love his voice, Margery? It's very becoming." Lady Gillian gave Ruairi a wicked smile. "Highland men are so much… *larger* than most of our English men."

"Lady Gillian and Lady Margery, would you ladies

like to join me in the great hall? I didn't get a chance to eat the noon meal," said Elizabeth, trying to remove her brother-in-law from the clutches of the Tullibardine sisters.

"Laird Sutherland, will you join us?" asked Lady Gillian, her expression hopeful. "We'd love to have you."

"Nay. Thank ye, but I'm waiting for my captain. I'm sure ye'll be in pleasant company with Lady Elizabeth."

Lady Gillian rubbed her fingers on Ruairi's arm, and he stilled at the gesture. The way the woman behaved, Elizabeth wouldn't have been surprised if Lady Gillian tried to lift his kilt in the middle of the hall.

"I'm sorry to hear you won't be joining us." Lady Gillian gave Ruairi another frank and admiring look before she walked away with her sister. As Elizabeth turned, Ruairi grabbed her arm to stay her.

"Thank ye for that."

"I'll find you after the meal."

"Lass, be careful with them, especially the one who speaks like Grace."

Elizabeth was flanked at the table in the great hall with a Tullibardine sister on each side. As soon as she reached for a piece of bread, Lady Gillian cleared her throat.

"You're a lucky woman to have such a handsome brother-in-law, or I should say, your sister is a lucky woman to have Laird Sutherland as her husband."

"I'm certain my sister feels the same way," said Elizabeth.

"Don't mind Gillian," said Lady Margery. "She'll try to bed any man with a handsome visage, Scot or not."

Elizabeth choked on her bread and washed it down with a sip of mulled wine.

"You're just jealous you're not as beautiful as me, Margery."

Elizabeth gazed from left to right. "You do realize you are twins and look exactly the same."

"That doesn't stop my sister from thinking she has all the looks in the family," said Lady Margery.

Elizabeth thought it best to change the subject before the sisters started to feud in the middle of the great hall. "I went to the theatre yesterday to see the play."

Lady Gillian leaned toward Elizabeth and spoke in a conspiratorial whisper. "And how was the handsome Mister Condell?"

"He played a very convincing King Henry." Not wanting to talk about Mister Condell for obvious reasons, she added, "I also met Mistress Alexander while I was there. She's the woman who made the men in the play look like women. She did wonders with Queen Katherine. Don't you agree? I never would have known the queen was a man."

Lady Gillian laughed. "Yes. The queen did look like a woman, and rightfully so."

"The last performance is in three days. There are rumors that the actors have some surprises in store for the audience too, perhaps even cannon fire," said Elizabeth.

"A cannon…in the theatre?" asked Lady Margery. "Do you think that's true, Lady Elizabeth? How would they even manage such a daunting task without hitting the walls of the theatre or the people within it?"

"I'm not certain."

"We're going to attend the play with our father. He's joining some members of the Privy Council for the final performance," said Lady Gillian. "I find the second time I watch the actors that I catch everything I missed the first time. You should come, Lady Elizabeth. It's sure to be an exciting evening."

"I'm looking forward to returning home," said Lady Margery. "I think I've had enough excitement for a while." She lowered her voice and spoke in Elizabeth's ear. "At least there haven't been any more deaths. I've been very unsettled staying here in the palace and have been making certain our door is latched every night. But I don't know if that's even enough to keep us secure. We're under the same roof as the king's guard, yet men are killed in the light of day in places like the gardens. I wonder if anyone is truly safe."

"I don't think you have anything to worry about, Lady Margery. The man seems to be pursuing members of the Privy Council."

"That's part of the reason I'm afraid. My father is a member of the king's council."

Elizabeth paled.

❧

When Ruairi spotted Ian, he closed the distance between them, walking with long, purposeful strides. Without warning, he grabbed Ian by the tunic and shoved him against the wall. Neither paid any heed to the widened eyes watching them in the hall.

"I donna care if your damn arse was afire. Ye took your leave. Ye left Elizabeth unattended. If anything would have befallen her—"

"*Tha e ceart agad.*" *You've got it right.* Ian continued to speak in a solemn tone. "I should ne'er have left her. 'Twas a foolish mistake that will ne'er happen again." Even though he could've easily removed himself from Ruairi's grasp, he stood submissively before his friend, knowing he deserved whatever wrath was placed upon him.

Ruairi held Ian firmly to the wall. "Ye're right it will ne'er happen again. How can I give ye my blessing to woo my sister-by-marriage when your actions are undeserving of such a request?"

Fagan patted Ruairi on the shoulder. "*Fuirich mionaid. Gabh air do schocair.*" *Wait a minute. Take it easy.* "Let him go. Munro knows naught what he does. He acts like a fool in love."

Ruairi may have released his grip, but Ian wasn't able to escape the looks of death thrown his way. "Ye are my friend, Munro, but if ye ever place the lass in danger again, I will kill ye, and I will nae think twice about it."

Fagan pushed Ruairi back with one hand and held Ian with the other. "Now there is nay need to kill Munro. He returned to court to offer his apologies to Elizabeth."

"Why did he leave her in the first place?"

"Yes, Laird Munro. Why *did* you leave me in the first place?"

Ian whipped his head around as Elizabeth glared at him with burning, reproachful eyes. He couldn't stay the sourness in the pit of his stomach. Once again, he'd managed to hurt the lass, and he was entirely at fault. When she turned away without waiting for a reply, Fagan punched him in the arm.

"God's teeth, Munro! Donna just stand here like a dog in the rain. Go after the lass and make amends."

"Was I ever this way with Ravenna?" asked Ruairi.

"Ye're both idiots with the lasses."

"I hate ye both," said Ian.

He ran after Elizabeth through the garden. When he caught up to her, he grasped her arm and spun her around. He had not missed her flare of temper because she threw words like stones.

"How. Dare. You. I will never forget you—"

Before he realized what he was about, he pushed her between two bushes and pressed her back against the garden wall. His lips crashed down upon hers, and Ian silenced her with a brutal, punishing kiss. His mouth did not become softer as he kissed her, and his tongue explored the recesses of her mouth. He pulled her roughly to him in a firm embrace. He wanted her to know what she did to him. No female had ever made him lose such control.

At first, she tried to twist out of his hold. But then the air itself changed. Elizabeth gave in freely to the passion of his kiss.

～∞～

Liquid fire fueled Elizabeth's veins. Initially, she wriggled in Ian's arms, arching her body, fighting to become free. He didn't deserve her forgiveness for his careless actions. But he only gathered her closer, his firm hands slipping between her spine and the wall. Instinctively, she placed her fingers against the corded muscles of his chest, and that was her undoing.

His grip tightened, and the warmth of his arms was

so male, so bracing. She buried her hands in his thick hair and returned his kiss with reckless desire. Blood pounded in her brain, leapt from her heart, and made her knees tremble.

She drew herself closer, and her desire overrode all sense of reason. She could feel the thrill of his arousal against her, and the knowledge made her feel more wanton, knowing she was the cause. Ian's touch was purely divine.

Without warning, he pulled back. The smoldering flame she saw in his eyes startled her.

"*Tha gaol agam ort.*"

"Heaven help me. I love you too."

Eighteen

IAN HELD ELIZABETH'S HAND AS THEY SAT ON A BENCH in the garden. As she gazed at their entwined fingers, a troubled expression crossed her face. He knew a stolen kiss wouldn't erase his stupidity. He wasn't sure what to do next but needed to think of something. Looming silence was not working in his favor.

"When I saw ye in the arms of Condell, at first, I was furious. But then when I saw ye kiss, I felt betrayed."

"Why would you feel betrayed? Mister Condell held me so tightly against him that I couldn't even move, let alone breathe."

He felt his blood starting to boil and tried to calm his racing heart. "'Tis nae a simple task for me to admit the truth, especially about this, but we promised to have nay more lies between us." He hesitated, trying to gather the courage to speak the truth. "Condell is fair of face. When I saw your lips on his, I—"

"You assumed that I could be easily turned by a handsome face. You did not trust me, nor did you have enough faith in yourself to recognize that I did not return Mister Condell's favor. I love you, Ian, but

I cannot spend the rest of my life convincing you that I do. You turned your back on me. You knowingly left me in the arms of another man." She pulled her hand out of his grasp. "I was able to deter him, but do you know what would've happened to me if I hadn't been able?" Her eyes met his. "I was alone with Mister Condell in Anne Boleyn's bedchamber, and you *left* me."

Ian lowered his head.

"Whatever happened to your hand?"

"'Tis naught." His thoughts hammered him. How could he ever make amends when he turned his back on the woman he loved? Once again, he met her gaze, refusing to falter. "Elizabeth, ye are a beautiful, caring lass…woman. Any man would be lucky to have your love. I need ye to understand why I behave the way that I do."

He closed his eyes and prayed for strength. "Fagan and Ruairi have always had a way with the lasses, even when we were lads. When they fell in love with your sisters, they already knew how to treat a lass. I'm nae proud to admit that I donna share their experience. I've been with lasses before but ne'er for more than a night or two. I've ne'er loved a woman, and I've ne'er been gifted with one who loved me in return."

As he searched Elizabeth's face, she gestured for him to continue. "I know this sounds daft, but I donna know how to treat ye properly. How can I ask Ruairi for your hand in marriage when I donna know how to be with ye? I donna know what ye need in a husband because every time I do something, try to woo ye, everything runs awry."

Elizabeth graced him with a compassionate smile. "You try too hard. I've never asked more from you than you're willing to give. This is why I love you, Ian. I no longer see the burly Highland laird sitting before me, but a man who is honest and true. I need *you* to understand that I don't care about a handsome visage." A strange look must have crossed his face because she quickly added, "I want you to think of the most beautiful woman you've ever seen."

"I donna have to think. I'm looking at her."

She shook her head. "Listen to what I'm telling you. When you picture that pretty woman in your mind, does her image make you change the way you feel about me? Does your heart belong to her?"

"Of course nae."

"You've just had your first lesson in understanding yourself. Yes, Mister Condell is a beautiful man. But does his handsome face change the way I feel about you? Does my heart belong to him? No. You're the man who holds my heart. The only man who can ever make me alter my views of you is you. And if you stop acting like an arse, everything else between us will work itself out."

He chuckled in response.

"I want you to keep something else in mind. Have you ever wondered why my sisters and their husbands get along so well?"

"I donna know. I've pondered why Ruairi and Fagan would wed such wily lasses a time or two, especially English ones."

She let out a heavy sigh. "Lesson number two: you love an English woman. Stop talking about the English."

"Aye."

"The reason my sisters get along with their husbands is because they're friends. I don't need you to try and woo me. I want you to be yourself. When you took me to the library, the theatre, we jested between us, even though you slept most of the time. Stop thinking so much, and give me the best part of you... you. *Tha ort gaol agam.*"

"*Tha gaol agam ort.*" As Ian corrected Elizabeth's butchering of the Gaelic language, he smiled. "I think 'tis better if ye leave the Gaelic to me, lass."

"Aye," she repeated in the same tone he had used earlier.

"Now tell me what happened with Condell."

❧

Elizabeth shouldn't have forgiven Ian as hastily as she had, but she wasn't hurt, at least not physically, by Mister Condell. Granted, Ian's actions were all wrong, but once he explained the reasons why he'd thought the way he had, she had to excuse his poor behavior. He'd said the words himself. He'd never had any connection or lasting relationship with a woman. Was that truly his fault? Love was about forgiveness, and even though she'd certainly done a lot of that where Laird Munro was concerned, she recognized that she herself was far from perfect.

As she retold Ian what had occurred with Mister Condell, choosing her words carefully, he sat as still as a statue. She depicted an ease which she didn't necessarily feel. Now that he knew the truth, she didn't want him confronting the man.

"His arrogance is going to get him killed."

She flinched at the tone of Ian's voice. "Mister Condell should not meet the end of your sword for a single kiss."

"Howbeit he took what was nae offered."

"And as I recall, Laird Munro, so did you only moments ago against the garden wall."

A roguish grin spread across his face. "Your point is verra well taken, lass, but give me your word that ye'll stay away from Condell. Ye donna want to be encouraging his pursuits."

When Elizabeth tried to speak, her voice wavered. "There was one more detail that I had forgotten to mention." She chewed on her lower lip and stole a look at him.

"And what is that? Should I be afraid to ask?"

"You'll probably want to kill *me* once I tell you."

He rubbed his hand over his brow. "What did ye do?"

"Mister Condell apologized for his behavior and did not want to part on unfavorable terms. I promised him that you and I would attend the theatre again in three days."

"Elizabeth!" He sighed in exasperation.

"You, of all men, should realize that everyone makes mistakes. I was trying to go after you when you fled from the apartments, and he wouldn't let me leave until I agreed to his peace offering. Furthermore, this is his last performance playing King Henry for the season before returning to Spain." She squeezed Ian's hand. "The twins asked me to attend too. I can't go back on my word now."

"I suppose I can suffer through another performance if I have to. 'Tis the least I can do for my behavior."

"I was surprised to learn something else from Lady Margery today." When Ian shifted on the bench, she added, "Her father is a member of the Privy Council. Needless to say, she worries about her own safety and that of her father in the palace."

"I'm sure the king has increased the guards around the members of the council."

Elizabeth spotted Lord Kinghorne over Ian's shoulder escorting Lady Glamis through the gardens. The earl placed a supportive arm around his mother's back and held her tightly to his side. As they turned on the stone path, he reached down and grasped the woman's buttocks. If Elizabeth hadn't been paying attention to poor Lady Glamis, she wouldn't have believed it. She stiffened in shock.

"What is wrong?"

"I saw…"

"What did ye see?" Ian glanced over his shoulder.

"Lord Kinghorne in the garden with Lady Glamis."

"The woman is feeling better then."

"Apparently. You're not going to believe this, but the earl grabbed his mother in the buttocks."

"*Tha mi duilich. Dè thuirt thu?*" He shook his head. "I'm sorry. What did ye say?"

"Lord Kinghorne grasped his mother's behind."

Ian chuckled. "Lass, ye're sitting here with me. Ye can nae be sure what ye saw over there on the path. Let me assure ye that nay son would grab his mother in the buttocks. Ye're mistaken."

"I could've sworn that he did."

"Think about it, Elizabeth. Ye know Lady Glamis does nae get around that well. Mayhap she was about to fall, and Kinghorne's hand slipped when he was trying to support her."

"Munro, Elizabeth did nae kill ye after all. I'm glad to see it."

Elizabeth gave her brother-in-law a wry grin as he approached. "Fagan, why are you so cheerful?" The man was smiling from ear to ear.

"Lairds Ross, Fraser, and MacKay were just granted their audience with the king on the morrow. 'Tis only a matter of time before Munro and Ruairi are called. We will finally be able to take our leave from court and go home."

⁂

Second only to Elizabeth telling him that she loved him, those were the sweetest words Ian had ever heard. Even though he'd had enough of court and couldn't wait to return to Scotland, his mind was puzzled with new thoughts. Would the lass want to accompany him home as his bride? Then he remembered Elizabeth's words of wisdom. He would be her friend, and everything else between them would work itself out. Furthermore, thinking too much had gotten him into nothing but trouble.

He sat beside Elizabeth in the great hall to sup as Lairds Ross, Fraser, and MacKay were knee-deep in their cups. Ian couldn't say that he blamed them. The men would meet with the king on the morrow and then return home and not look back.

"The musicians will be playing again this evening,"

said Elizabeth. "I do remember you promising me a dance, Laird Munro." When she smiled, he felt like the clouds had parted and graced him with a sunny day.

"Och, aye. I remember, but donna say I did nae warn ye. I'm nae verra good."

She lowered her voice. "I'll tell you a little secret. I'm not very good at dancing either. I pretend to know what I'm doing."

"I donna think I could even accomplish that, lass."

"That's not true. I've seen you dance at Grace and Fagan's wedding when the bagpiper played."

He leaned closer. "Ye do realize that I had consumed more than my share of *uisge beatha* that eve."

"Perhaps, but at least tonight you should be lighter on your feet since most of your hair is gone."

He grunted. "I still donna know if I should've let Ruairi and Fagan talk me into cutting it. 'Twas part of who I was."

An amused look crossed her face. "If your hair was part of who you were, you do realize those tresses were unruly most of the time. What does that say about you, Laird Munro?"

When she placed her hand in an innocent gesture on his thigh, he was thankful certain parts of him remained hidden from view. Once they finished their meal, the men cleared the tables to make room to dance. Ian stood with the other lairds against the far wall with flasks of whisky in hand. There were so many bodies in attendance that the hall was stifling. As he wiped his brow, he wondered if the sweat was due to the heat in the room or because he was nervous to dance with Elizabeth. Perhaps if he had a few more swigs of whisky and the musicians played the bagpipes, he would feel more at ease. But it was too late now. Elizabeth was pulling him by the hand to the center of the floor.

"I donna think I've had enough to drink to do this, lass."

"And if I let you drink more, Laird Munro, you won't be able to dance."

He was unnerved when he glanced over his shoulder, and Ruairi and Fagan held up their flasks in mock salute. If those two knew what was good for them, they'd keep their mouths shut. Ian shook his head when he realized the crazy things men do for love.

When he bowed, Elizabeth curtsied in return. His hand touched hers in the air, and they turned in a circle.

"You're doing very well. You have yet to step on my feet."

"Give me time, lass. We've only just begun."

Elizabeth's hair was piled in curls on the top of her head. Her figure was slender and regal, and she moved with an easy grace. He found himself drowning in her emerald eyes and had no desire to be saved. She wore a black gown with hanging sleeves, and the embroidered petticoat under her skirts was lined in gray.

In his eyes, she was everything. There may have been a prettier dress or a bonnier woman at court, but there was only one woman he was drawn to—one woman who held his heart. No other woman would ever make him change the way he felt about Elizabeth. At that moment, he finally understood what she'd meant by her words.

When the musicians stopped, he simply stood there

and gazed upon her, proud that he'd only stepped on her foot once. He lifted his hand to her cheek and gently rubbed his thumb across it. "With ye by my side, lass, I can do anything."

"Ian, if you don't take me somewhere now in order for me to kiss you, we're both going to be in a heap of trouble in the middle of the great hall."

She didn't need to tell him twice. He clutched her hand, his only intent to race to the gardens to taste her sweet lips and hold her in his arms again. They'd almost made it to the door when Fagan called to him. He'd thought about paying his friend no heed, pretending not to hear him, but the last he needed was Fagan seeking them out among the blooms.

"Damn. Wait here, and donna move. I'll be right back."

A devilish look came into Elizabeth's eyes. "Do make haste, Laird Munro."

He walked with hurried purpose to Fagan. "What the hell do ye want?"

"Your dancing skills have greatly improved. How many times did ye step on the lass's foot?" asked Fagan with a grin.

"Once. What do ye want?"

"*Sguir.* I know what ye're doing." *Stop.*

Ian gave Fagan a measured gaze. "Then ye're wise nae to get in my way."

"Everyone has seen your display of affection for the lass in the middle of the floor. Be discreet. Ye donna want to ruin Elizabeth's reputation."

"Says the same man who ruined his wife before they were wed."

"Bastard."

"Aye."

"Just use caution, Munro. The last ye need is Ruairi wanting to run ye through. *Bi modhail.*" *Behave.*

He slapped Fagan on the shoulder and spied Ruairi against the far wall talking with the other lairds. "Dinna fash. I'll follow your example."

Ian turned, and he heard Fagan mumble under his breath, "That's what I'm afraid of."

As he made his way to where he'd left Elizabeth by the door, he had to step around a few men and women huddled in conversation. When he cleared the crowd, he gazed around the great hall. His eyes darted back and forth through the sea of people. She wasn't where he'd left her.

The lass was gone.

❧

"Lady Elizabeth, might I have a word?"

There was a pensive look in the shadow of Mister Condell's eyes. Perhaps it was simply Elizabeth's uneasiness toward the man, but she was suspicious about his motives. Why would he want to speak with her after their last encounter?

"Of course, Mister Condell."

"Not here. Let's go in the hall." He grabbed her by the arm and led her out.

When she tried to speak, her voice wavered. "Why couldn't we speak in the great hall? Is everything all right?"

He made his way down the hall into a quiet nook and then released her arm. As he stood in front of her, her back was pinned against the wall. This was probably not the best idea since she realized she had no means of escape.

"I've been thinking. Something has been troubling me, my lady, and I must know. Have I done something else to offend you?"

Elizabeth placed her hand to her throat as she became more uncomfortable by the minute. "No. Why do you ask?"

"We've shared our love of history. We've danced. I've sent you a flower and written you poetry. You came to see me in the play. Surely, you must know of my attempts to woo you. You had never mentioned your heart belonging to another, so yes, I must know if I've offended you in some way…before our kiss."

"Mister Condell, please accept my apologies if I've misled you. I've enjoyed our talks, the play, and seeing Anne Boleyn's chambers very much, but there isn't anything more between us."

He placed his hand above her shoulder on the stone wall. "So you've said. I saw you when you supped with Laird Munro. I watched him touch you after the dance. I can't imagine *that* Highlander is the man who holds your heart—yet, you let him touch you like a lover." His eyes darkened, and his fingers caressed her cheek.

"Mister Condell…"

"Do you know what I think?" His body moved closer. "Some women prefer the chase, the excitement of the hunt, the moment when the hunter stalks and finally captures his prey."

A warning voice whispered in her head. She needed

to get out of there. "Could you please step back, Mister Condell? I need to return. My chaperones will be looking for me." She instantly felt the hardness of his manhood—or lack thereof—rub up against her belly. He ground himself against her, and she closed her eyes tightly.

"Do you see what's become of me, Lady Elizabeth? Do you know what you do to me by denying me? No woman has ever refused to share my bed." He grabbed her chin and turned her head to face him. When his lips crashed down on hers, she felt bile rise in her throat.

She tried to push him away, but his weight had pinned her body against the wall with no room to move. "Please, stop! Please!"

He grabbed her breast hard over her gown, and she gasped in pain. Lowering her hand to her side, she fumbled for her dagger but couldn't reach it. When he attempted to lift her skirts, she cried out. She decided to take the only piece of advice Ravenna had given her as an infallible way to deter a man.

Elizabeth wedged her hand between them, and when she felt the hardness that pushed against her, she reached lower and grasped his manhood like a vise. Mister Condell dropped to his knees. She refused to yield, furious at her vulnerability. A steely Scottish accent startled her.

"Release his bollocks, lass." Ian's expression was thunderous.

As she released Mister Condell, he fell to the floor, and she stepped out of the way. Without warning, Ian pulled the man to his feet. He rammed his fist into

Mister Condell's face, and something cracked under the forceful blow. Blood gushed from the man's nose. One punch was all it took to defeat Mister Condell and knock him to the ground, but Ian wasn't satisfied. With one hand, he pulled the man from the floor and landed another blow right in the eye.

"*Mo mhallachd ort! An diobhail toirt leis thu!*" *My curse on you! The devil take you!* Ian wrapped his arm around Elizabeth. "Are ye all right?"

She nodded and could hear his labored breathing. "I am now."

"You broke my nose, and hit me in the eye! I have the final performance in three days." Mister Condell's hands cradled his nose as Ian chuckled.

"Mayhap ye can have Mistress Alexander fix your face, ye seedy bastard."

Nineteen

When Ian saw Condell's hands on Elizabeth, he felt murderous. Members of the king's Privy Council were not the only men who needed to fear for their lives at court. Ian's first thought was to unsheathe his weapon and behead the arse right in the middle of King James's court. But he didn't think removing Condell's bonny head from his shoulders in front of Elizabeth would've made her feel any better. Although, he would've felt due justice was served.

As he led Elizabeth away from the bleeding Condell, he spotted the Fraser and called out.

"Munro. Lady Elizabeth." Fraser glanced down the hall and then chuckled as Condell hobbled away. "Is that your handiwork?" For a moment, he had a puzzled look on his face. "Nay. The man would nae be alive if ye had a hand in that."

"Can ye seek Sutherland and Murray for me? I will stay here with Lady Elizabeth."

Fraser eyed Elizabeth. "Aye. Is everything all right, my lady?"

She gave a wooden nod. "Yes. Thank you, Laird

Fraser. I'm afraid that I've had more than enough excitement for one eve. I'm weary and ready to take my leave."

"Are nae we all? I'll be right back."

"What happened, lass?" asked Ian.

She spoke calmly. "Please. I don't want to talk about Mister Condell right now. Could we discuss this later?" She wrapped her arms around him, burying her head in his chest, and didn't seem concerned about who saw them embracing in the hall.

He rubbed his hand over her back and kissed the top of her head. "Aye. Ye're safe. Condell is ne'er going to touch ye again."

As Ruairi and Fagan approached and saw Ian holding Elizabeth in his arms, their expressions instantly changed, especially when Ian gave them a grave look in return. Ruairi rested his hand on Elizabeth's shoulder, and she gazed at him with tears in her eyes.

"*A bheil thu ceart gu leòr?*" *Are you all right?*

"I'd like to return to the inn. Please."

She pulled away from Ian and, not even waiting for Ruairi's response, walked away from the men. As Fagan followed her down the hall, Ruairi asked, "What the hell happened?"

"I donna know the tale, but Elizabeth was supposed to wait at the entrance of the great hall while I talked with Fagan. The next I knew, Condell had his hands all over the lass in a nook down the hall. When I came upon them, she had the bastard by the bollocks."

"Does he still live?"

"Why does everyone keep asking me that? I am nay fool. I can nae say that I did nae mess up his bonny face a wee bit, but aye, he lives for the moment."

"I'll talk to Elizabeth when we get back and find out what happened. Do ye think he touched the lass?"

Ian knew what Ruairi meant. "Nae that way, nay. But I know he forced himself on her and took liberties in ways that nay man should ever…" He had to pause and collect himself. "Ye do realize if we were in the Highlands I would've cut off the bastard's hands and handed him his cock before I killed him."

Ruairi slapped him on the shoulder. "Aye, and I would've helped ye."

"Let me be the one to talk with the lass."

"I am her chaperone."

"Aye, but I am the one who will be her husband."

❧

Refusing to let anyone ride with her, Elizabeth sat in the darkened carriage alone. All the men had offered to accompany her, but she didn't feel up to conversing. How could she have been such a fool not to see Mister Condell for who he truly was? Now she knew why Ravenna and Grace had warned her so many times before she'd left for court. Even though they'd told her never to accept a man's offer to walk in the gardens at night, Elizabeth never suspected anything untoward would have happened within the palace walls.

She closed her eyes and took a deep, calming breath. When the carriage stopped, she waited until the door opened and then took the coachman's hand to step down. A male voice spoke from behind her.

"I'll send Mistress Betts up to ye. Is there anything ye want or need me to bring ye?" asked Ian with concern.

"No, thank you. I just want to seek my bed." When

she stepped away, he wrapped his hand around her wrist and turned her to face him.

"Ye know that I'm here for ye if ye want to talk."

She gave him a tired smile. "I know. I'll see you in the morn."

"Sleep well, lass."

As soon as Mistress Betts left her chamber and closed the door, Elizabeth blew out the candle and embraced the darkness. Her cheeks ached from where she had rubbed her face raw, wanting nothing more than to remove every trace of that man from her body. She pulled up the blankets to her chin and closed her eyes.

The memory of Mister Condell's roaming hands sent a chill down her spine. No woman should be treated that way. Ian was such a strong and powerful man, yet she knew he would never physically harm her. She was sickened by Mister Condell's behavior, especially since she mulled over the evening's events. Ravenna had told her that men should never take from a woman what was never offered, even a kiss. Elizabeth hadn't realized at the time how right her sister was.

Shadows contorted under her door from the light in the hall. She was never going to sleep with only her misery for company. Perhaps she thought too hastily when she asked to be alone. As footsteps treaded past her door, she sprung from the bed. She cracked open the door, sticking her head out and peeking down the hall. Fagan was staring at her with a lifted brow.

"Are ye all right?"

She hid her body behind the door since she wore only her nightrail. "Yes, I was…er, seeing—"

"Waiting for Ian?" He gave her a knowing look, and she returned a sheepish grin.

"Yes."

"He will nae be long. He was coming right behind me." No sooner did Fagan say the last word then Ian turned into the hall. "*Oidhche mhath*, Elizabeth. Munro."

"Good night, Fagan," said Elizabeth.

As Ian stood before her, she let out a little nervous cough. She couldn't look him in the eye and bit her bottom lip. The door partially covered her body, and she was running her hand along the edge of the door.

"Do ye want me to come in, or are ye going to leave me in the hall?"

She spoke in a broken whisper. "I want you to come in." She donned her robe and then shut the door as Ian lit the bedside candle.

He turned and measured her for a moment. Without any words, he removed his scabbard from his belt and rested his sword against the wall. His eyes darkened with emotion, and when he extended his arms, she stepped into his warm embrace.

"I don't want to be alone."

He rubbed her back. "I thought as much, lass."

"Oh, Ian. I can't get that man out of my head. I told him to stop. I must have done something to make him think I'd toss my skirts. Was it the way I dressed? What did I do?"

He pulled back and held her face firmly with both hands. For a long moment, she looked at him. "*Sguir.*" *Stop.* "There is naught ye did, and there is nay excuse for Condell's actions. The bastard makes the rest of us look poorly. There are men like Condell in the world, Elizabeth, men who think they can take anything and that everything belongs to them. They're dangerous fools. For as long as I live and breathe, nay one will ever touch ye like that again. I give ye my solemn vow."

Tears fell down her cheeks, and he wiped them away with his thumb. "I give ye my body to protect ye, my heart to love ye, and my soul for all eternity. I am yours." He stepped over to the bed and pulled back the blankets. "Ye've had a long day and need to rest."

She closed the distance between them, and her fingers rested on his chest. "But I don't want you to go."

"I'm nae going anywhere. Come now, lass." Ian gestured to the bed, and as she nestled into the mattress, he covered her with the blankets. He bent over her, placing a kiss on the top of her head, and brushed the hair away from her face. When he lowered himself to the floor beside the bed, she sat up.

"What are you doing?"

"I told ye. I'm nae leaving. I'm sleeping on the floor."

"Ian, please don't sleep on the floor. Come lay beside me." When his eyes became sharp and assessing, she added, "Don't give me that look. I trust you. I desire to be in your arms and need to erase the evening from memory. I can lay with you on the floor if you'd like."

He rose and rubbed his hand over his brow. "Ye are nae going to sleep on the floor. I will come to your bed."

❦

Ian held Elizabeth in his arms, realizing she was

everything good and pure in this world. She made him a better man. He hadn't realized something was missing in his life until he found her, and she captured his heart.

She rested her head on his chest as her hand moved in tiny circular motions. "You make me feel safe." Raising herself on her elbow, she hovered over him, her long hair falling over him like a waterfall. As she ran her fingers through his hair and along his jaw, her voice became as soft as a caress. "I love you. You need to know that."

Her mouth gently pressed against his, and the touch of her lips set him aflame. Burying her face in his neck, she breathed a kiss there, and he wondered where this lovely enchantress had come from. Just when he thought she'd pull back, the lass reclaimed his lips, each time encouraging him to kiss deeper…harder.

When he could no longer hide his body's reaction to her, he stilled her. "I will nae deny that I am enjoying this immensely, but we must stop. I—"

His words were smothered on his mouth. When her body moved to partially cover his, he growled and rolled her onto her back. His lips recaptured hers, demanding this time, as she returned his kiss. He took her mouth with a savage intensity and couldn't get enough.

Lowering his hand, he unfastened her robe and was that much closer to touching her soft flesh. When she tugged on his tunic, he stilled, gazing into her eyes.

"I want to feel you, Ian. I want to be with you, only you."

He sat up and grasped behind him, pulling off his tunic one-handed. Elizabeth ran her fingers along the defined lines of his bare chest, reaching for him as though he was her lifeline from this world into the next. When she looked up with passion-glazed eyes, he slowly removed her robe and tossed it across the room.

His body covered hers, and he placed a kiss on her lips, jaw, and throat between each word. "I would ne'er ruin a lass, especially ye." He met her eyes. "I have ne'er known a lass quite like ye. Ye know me better than I know myself. I want naught more than to be with ye, claim ye as my own. I've ne'er wanted anything so badly in all my life. But if we do this, there will be nay turning back. Ye will be mine, and I will be yours. *Am pòs thu mi? Tha gràdh agam ort.*"

Her eyes lit up. "I'm afraid you'll have to speak English, my laird."

When Elizabeth addressed him as her laird, his entire being was filled with wanting and desire. "Will ye marry me? I love ye."

She closed her eyes tightly as a single tear ran down her cheek. She lifted her hand gently to his jaw and gave him a tender smile. "I want nothing more than to be your wife."

Their vow was sealed with a tender kiss.

It wasn't long before Ian was on fire. He had never been more aroused in his life. Elizabeth's innocent touches were driving him mad. His honorable intentions were forgotten, and all he could think of was tearing off her nightrail and thrusting inside her until the burning stopped.

His kisses became more demanding. He wanted her to know what she did to him. Never had he experienced this kind of urgency. She was so hot and willing. He could not get enough.

His tongue circled hers, probing in an anxious rhythm that mirrored his pulsing erection. Her soft whimpers only heated his desire. He slid his hands down to her waist and over her hips, molding every sweet curve closer to his body.

He tugged on her nightrail, enough to pull it past her shoulders, and his fingers encircled her breasts. The soft pink flesh was more than enough to fill his hands. He lifted her breast to his lips and flicked her nipple with his tongue.

"Elizabeth, ye taste so sweet," he murmured.

He cupped her mounds with his rough hands, and she groaned as he caressed their softness. He wanted to savor her sweetness.

Easing his hand under the hem of her nightrail, he slid up the center of her silky thigh. She moaned against his ear and was so damn responsive. His finger swept her sex…so wet. She was more than ready.

He teased her with his hand, and her hips arched against him. Her tiny whimpers increased in urgency as she grabbed his arms, sculpting his muscles. God's teeth! She was going to come apart in his hand.

When he felt her break apart, he pressed his finger against the sensitive part of her. His tongue delved into her mouth with the same rhythm as his finger pressing against her womanly heat.

She arched her back and cried out his name. He could not take his eyes off her. She was so tempting with her lips slightly parted and her passion-glazed eyes. Her desire and responsiveness drove him wild.

God how he needed to be inside her.

Ian lifted her arms and pulled off her nightrail as she lay bare beneath his sultry gaze. He removed his kilt and dropped it to the floor. When she lowered her gaze and her eyes widened, he drugged her with kisses. His roughened hand slid across her silken belly down to the swell of her hips, rekindling her passion.

"Ye are so verra bonny, Elizabeth."

He took her mouth with a savage force. Lowering his head, his tongue tantalized her hardened nipples. Instinctively, her body arched toward him. As he slipped his hands up her arms ever so slowly, she caressed the strong tendons in the back of his neck.

She gasped as he pressed his body against hers, the evidence of his desire rubbing against her belly. Moving his hands below her, he gripped her thighs, lifting her gently to straddle him. It was flesh against flesh, man against woman. He let out a tormented groan.

His hands skimmed her body, and she trailed tickling fingers up and down his arms. Passion pounded his blood, and he could sense the barely controlled power that coiled in his body.

With a single thrust, he made her his. She gasped in sweet agony and took him fully, her innocent touch sending him to even higher levels of ecstasy. He stilled, giving her body time to adjust, but it wasn't long before they found a gentle rhythm that bound their bodies as one.

The feel of her soft skin against his was exalting. He reached down between them and rubbed her sensitive spot. When she let out a cry of delight, he threw back his head and sought his own release.

For once in his life, he was filled with an amazing sense of completeness. They were as one and would be man and wife—forever bonded. As far as he was concerned, they already were.

∽

"Are ye all right? I tried to be careful."

Elizabeth nestled her bottom into his groin as he wrapped his arms around her. "Mmm… I am more than all right, Laird Munro."

She stroked her fingernails over the soft hairs on Ian's arm for quite some time. His breathing slowed, and when a little snort escaped him, she smiled. The man could fall asleep anywhere.

Ian had a pleasant way of distracting her from the evening's events. In fact, she wondered if he could distract her more often. Although her first time being with a man was uncomfortable, Ian was a tender lover. Speaking their vows was only a formality—there was nothing that would tear them apart. Who would've thought the young girl who adored this man would have her dreams come true? She was filled with a great sense of peace.

Elizabeth opened her eyes in the morning to Ian's bare, firm buttocks beside the bed. He donned his tunic and then wrapped his kilt around him. When he bent to pick up his boots, his eyes met hers, and she smiled.

"*Madainn mhath.*"

"Good morning to you, too. Isn't it still too early to rise?"

He sat on the edge of the bed and donned his boots. "Aye, but I'll take my leave before anyone wakes up. Can ye grant me a boon?"

"After last night, I'd grant you anything." She grinned when his face reddened.

"Can ye nae mention to Ruairi or Fagan that I asked for your hand?" When a worried expression crossed her face, he brushed his fingers across her cheek. "'Tis naught like that, lass. I have nae changed my mind. Ruairi knows that I've been trying to woo ye. I want to ask him properly for your hand."

"Of course." When he stood, she asked, "Could you please hand me my nightrail?"

He walked over and searched near the table, retrieving the cloth from under the chair. As he turned, he gave her a roguish grin as her nightrail hung between his fingers. "It seems to have made it across the room. Mayhap ye should come and get it, eh?"

Ian's eyes widened when she threw the blankets from the bed and stood before him as bare as the day she was born. His stare was bold and assessed her frankly. The way he looked at her...the meaning of his gaze was obvious. His nearness made her senses spin.

"Lift your arms, lass." He slowly lowered her nightrail over her arms until she was fully covered. "There is naught I would like more than to stay with ye all day abed, but I must take my leave."

He lowered his head to kiss her, and once again his expert touch sent shivers of desire racing through her. She pulled him close, feeling his hardness press against her. His mouth seared a path down her neck, her shoulders, and then he pulled back and brushed a gentle kiss across her forehead.

"I must go."

She walked him to the door, and he grabbed his sword that still rested against the wall. He lifted the latch on the door, and looking over his shoulder, he whispered, "*Tha gaol agam ort.*"

"And I love you."

She gently closed the door behind him. When she heard men out in the hall, she paused, recognizing one of the voices all too well.

"Munro, what the hell did ye do?" asked Fagan.

Twenty

Ian opened Fagan's door and shoved him back into his room. "Shut the hell up. Ye'll wake up Ruairi. Should ye nae still be abed? What are ye doing awake now anyway?"

"I could nae go back to sleep. Munro, what am I going to do with ye, eh?" Fagan sighed in exasperation. "I was hoping ye had enough sense to leave Elizabeth's chambers last eve, but clearly I was wr—"

"Donna even attempt to lecture me on taking my wife's virtue before we were wed," said Ian, interrupting vehemently. "As I recall, ye did the same with yours."

"And Ruairi knocked me on my arse for it. *Fuirich mionaid.*" *Wait a moment.* "Did ye say your *wife*?" A flash of humor crossed Fagan's face, and then he laughed in a deep, jovial way.

Ian only realized his slip of the tongue when the words had already escaped him. "Why am I plagued by friends who are such arses?"

"All I have to say is…'tis about damn time, Munro!" Fagan shook Ian's hand and slapped him on the back.

"Aye, well, keep your mouth shut. Elizabeth has

agreed to be mine and promised nae to say anything until I have a chance to ask Ruairi for her hand properly." His eyes narrowed. "Heed my words, Fagan. I know ye gossip more than the lasses. I donna want ye to breathe a word about this to anyone."

"Ye donna have to worry. 'Tis nay great secret I've been hoping ye'd find your way into each other's arms." A concerned look crossed his face. "How is the lass after last eve with Condell?"

"She'll be all right in time. Although, she asked me what she did wrong that made Condell think she'd toss her skirts. I donna understand why that's the first thing women think of when men misbehave. But I am thankful the lass knew enough to grasp the man by the bollocks to bring him to his knees before any more harm was done."

"Och, aye. Well, we can all thank Ravenna for that."

"In truth, it pains me to think about what would've happened to Elizabeth otherwise."

Fagan's eyes darkened with emotion. "I ne'er told ye this, but something similar happened to Grace many years ago."

Ian lifted a brow, and there was an uncomfortable silence. "Was she rap—"

"Nay. Even though it took her some time to erase the man from memory, she finally managed. I think men like us are put on this earth to protect those we love, and now that Elizabeth will be your wife, she'll have ye to shelter her from bastards like Condell."

"I could nae have said the words better myself. I'm weary. I'll meet ye below stairs in an hour."

"I imagine the lass is feeling much the same." When

Fagan gave him a knowing look, Ian punched him in the arm.

"Arse." Ian reached for the latch on the door.

"Aye. Munro…"

Ian glanced over his shoulder.

"I'm happy for ye both. I'm glad ye let Elizabeth into your heart." Fagan paused. "She wanted to be there for a long time."

❦

"Lady Elizabeth, the men are bringing up a tub for you to bathe," said Mistress Betts through the door.

Elizabeth sat up, trying to clear the haze. "Just a moment."

As she lifted the blankets and placed her feet on the floor, she noticed a spot of blood on the bed. She felt a rush of panic, knowing she wasn't due for her monthly courses. But she didn't have time to think about that now. Hastily, she donned her robe and flipped back the blankets into their rightful position. With one last look around her room to make certain everything was in order, she smoothed her unruly tresses and opened the door.

"Laird Munro said you wanted a bath this morn, my lady," said Mistress Betts.

"Umm…yes. I'm sorry. I overslept."

"That's quite all right. The men are bringing up a tub, and the hot water will be ready soon." Mistress Betts walked over to the table. "Let me push this and the chairs against the wall, and I'll make room for you."

"Don't trouble yourself. Here. Let me help you with that." Elizabeth lifted the other end of the table, and then they moved the two chairs flush against the wall.

Two men brought the tub through the door, and even though it was smaller than most, it was a tight fit, especially because there wasn't a lot of open space to walk around in her room anyway. As soon as the men departed, three young boys dumped buckets of steaming water into the tub.

Mistress Betts smiled. "Do you need me to assist you?"

"I'm able to manage. Thank you."

"I'm sorry. I forgot something." Mistress Betts walked out into the hall and returned with towels, placing them on the table beside the tub. "There's a rag to wash and a couple drying cloths. There's also a small piece of soap. I'm sorry that I don't have anything to offer you, my lady."

"This is more than enough."

"I'll be back in a few moments with a tray, and then I'll help you dress."

"You take such good care of me, Mistress Betts."

"And it is my pleasure, my lady."

The door closed, and Elizabeth opened the lid to her trunk. She rifled underneath her dresses until she found her pouch of lavender. Her fingers made quivering motions in the water as she sprinkled the contents into the tub. She tied up the small bag, and once she secured it in her trunk, she removed her robe and nightrail.

Grabbing the side of the tub for support, she climbed in, letting the warm water soothe her aching body. She let out a heavy sigh of pleasure, and a smile crossed her face when she thought of Ian. Although she was tender and sore, she enjoyed being with him. She closed her eyes, musing on private memories, and her lips tingled in remembrance of his touch.

When he'd removed his kilt and she'd caught a glimpse of his jutting manhood, he had pleasantly distracted her before allowing panic to set in. She was glad he did because she'd wondered how in the world they'd even be able to complete the act. Ian was a large man so she shouldn't have been surprised the rest of him would follow suit. She still had no idea how she'd managed to accept him fully. But she'd never forget how respectful and caring he was with her, the way every man should treat a woman.

The steam and smell of lavender calmed her. She felt at peace. There was a quiet knock, and Mistress Betts entered with the tray of food.

"There's no need to rush. Enjoy your bath, my lady."

Mistress Betts placed the tray on the table beside the bed, and before Elizabeth could stop her, the woman lifted the blankets in an attempt to straighten what Elizabeth had done in haste earlier to cover the blood.

When Mistress Betts stilled and a puzzled gaze crossed her face, Elizabeth's mind raced. "I...er, what I mean to—"

"You don't have to say anything, my lady." Mistress Betts grabbed all the blankets from the bed and gathered them into a ball. "I'll wash these myself. And what happened is no one's business but yours and a certain laird's." Her eyes were kind and understanding, and then she turned and lifted the latch on the door. "I'll take these below stairs and bring you some fresh blankets." Before she could respond, the door closed again.

Elizabeth didn't think Mistress Betts would tell anyone about her indiscretion, but she felt ill at ease the woman knew Ian had shared her bed last night. Furthermore, she favored Mistress Betts. She didn't want the woman thinking she was a harlot.

Pulling herself from the tub, Elizabeth grabbed a drying cloth from the table and stepped out of the water. Once she was dry, she donned her nightrail and robe and then sat on the bed to break her fast. There was a single knock, and Mistress Betts returned with an armful of blankets.

"We have enough room over here for you to dress, if that suits you, and I can have the men remove the tub after you leave for court," said Mistress Betts.

"That would be fine." Elizabeth paused. "I must admit that I'm feeling rather humiliated, but I do want you to know… Laird Munro and I are betrothed."

Mistress Betts smiled. "It was only a matter of time, my lady. I'm glad to hear it, but you don't need to offer me an explanation."

"Yes, well, it's important that you don't think poorly of me."

"Lady Elizabeth, I could never think poorly of you. Now let's get you dressed for court."

❧

"Are ye certain ye donna want me to talk with Elizabeth?" asked Ruairi, walking with Ian to the stable.

"I talked with her late last eve. She was a wee bit shaken, but she's all right. Ye do remember she is a Walsingham and comes from a long line of tough stock. But I do give thanks to your wife for showing the lass how to bring a man to his knees."

"At least Ravenna did nae show Elizabeth how to kill a man because then we'd have one hell of a mess to explain."

"There is that."

The sun was shining, and a cool breeze lifted the edge of Ian's kilt. As they watched the stable hands saddling their horses, Ian felt like a lad about to ask his father for a big favor. He wiped his sweaty palms on his kilt, folded his arms over his chest, and then placed his hands at his sides.

"I told ye before that I loved Elizabeth."

Ruairi glanced at Ian and spoke hesitantly. "Aye, ye did."

"I'm asking ye now for her hand in marriage. I want her to be my wife."

"Ye want that responsibility?" Ruairi's eyes grew openly amused. "I mean to say that ye were uncertain she'd have ye when Condell was fighting for the lass's affections."

"I've ne'er been surer of anything in my life," said Ian with conviction.

"After last eve, I donna think ye have to worry about Condell winning Elizabeth's favor anytime soon. But is that why ye're asking me for her hand now?"

"Nay. I've been an idiot for too long."

"Good. I wanted to make certain ye were nae just asking me because ye were afraid of losing the lass to another man." His friend smiled from ear to ear. "Ye've made my day, Munro. Although I will miss Lady Elizabeth being on Sutherland lands, I thank ye for taking a Walsingham out from under my roof. With Ravenna, wee Mary, Katherine, another bairn on the way, and especially Grace, I need all the help I can get. Poor Torquil needs a brother soon. My home is completely overrun by women."

"I could have told ye that. Do I have your blessing to take Elizabeth as my wife?"

"Aye, if the lass will have ye. I can nae see Ravenna having any disagreement with that either."

"*Mòran taing.*" *Thank you very much.*

Ruairi studied Ian intently. "When will ye ask her?"

"When the time is right."

"The sun is finally shining upon us. Do ye think we'll be granted our audience with the king?" asked a male voice.

Ruairi and Ian turned as Fagan greeted them with a smile.

"Being that the Ross, Fraser, and MacKay arrived three days before us, that is my hope. I'm ready to take my leave and wash my hands of this place. I want to take my wife and my clan home where they belong," said Ruairi. "And speaking of wives, it seems Munro will be taking one home too."

Fagan placed his hand over his heart, and his jaw dropped. "Munro will be taking someone to wife? Who might that be?"

"I hate ye both," said Ian.

"Come now, Munro. What would ye do without us?" asked Fagan.

"Do ye want me to answer that?"

❧

Elizabeth wasn't proud to admit that she'd made the men late for court. Even though none had complained, she felt guilty. A jousting tournament had already begun. As they made their way to the bleachers, a warm hand rested against the small of her back, and a lovely Scottish accent whispered in her ear.

"I did nae think it possible, but ye are glowing this morn."

She looked at Ian and smiled. "I believe I have you to thank for that, Laird Munro."

"How are ye feeling? Are ye all right?"

When she realized what he'd meant, she smiled. "I'm fine, but I do thank you for the bath."

"'Twas the least I could do."

They took their seats in the stands, and Elizabeth watched two men prepare for the tournament across the field from one another.

Jousting armor was being securely fastened on each man as grooms cared for the large destriers. The horses wore caparisons displaying their rider's heraldry as well as chamfrons to shield their heads. Barding was also being placed into position to protect the bodies of the horses. She was pleased so many precautions were taken to shield the riders and their mounts from harm.

As she looked closer, Lord Kinghorne was escorting Lady Glamis away from the riders. The woman must've been thrilled to meet the competitors, and for a moment, Elizabeth's faith was restored in the earl because of his kindness toward his elderly mother. Ian was right. Elizabeth couldn't have been sure of what she had seen.

"Lady Elizabeth! Lady Elizabeth!"

When she turned and gazed over her shoulder, Lady Margery was waving her hands madly in the air. She sat with her sister three rows behind Elizabeth. Leaning forward in the stands, Lady Margery rested her hand on the man in front of her in order to talk with Elizabeth.

"Please beg my pardon." Lady Margery offered the man an apologetic smile. "Lady Elizabeth, do be sure to cheer for the man on the right. He's my father's friend and a member of the council. Jousting has been Lord Dormer's pastime for years."

"I will, Lady Margery." Elizabeth turned around and leaned closer to Ian. "Did you ever joust?"

"I've ne'er had a desire to maim my enemies. I prefer their deaths to be quick with a blow from my sword." When a soft gasp escaped her, he added, "I'm only jesting with ye. I've ne'er jousted."

A hushed silence fell over the crowd as the competitors mounted their horses, and both men moved into position. The men kicked their mounts, thundering toward each other at breakneck speed. One of the lances shattered on his opponent's shield, and Lord Dormer was unhorsed, falling hard to the ground with a heavy thump. Shouts erupted from the bleachers, and the winner held up his lance in victory.

Elizabeth gazed at the fallen man who still did not move. "Ian, is he all right?"

"Aye, the breath was probably knocked out of him. Give him a moment."

Lord Dormer's opponent handed his lance to a groom and dismounted. He removed his helmet as he walked with haste to Lord Dormer's side. The man dropped his headgear and fell to his knees. He was shouting for assistance to remove Lord Dormer's armor, and then Elizabeth could've sworn she heard the man cry out.

As men gathered, encircling Lord Dormer, Elizabeth couldn't see anything. She glanced behind her at Lady Margery and Lady Gillian, and their expressions mirrored her own. Elizabeth felt Ian grasp her arm with the intent to lead her away from the unfolding scene.

"No. Please, Ian. I have to stay and find out if he's all right."

He released his grip, but she took his hand and held it tightly. When a handful of men stepped back, Lord Dormer's armor had been removed. His clothing was soaked in blood. What frightened her more was that she could see a pool of blood from where she sat in the bleachers.

"I don't understand. I thought the lances had blunt tips. How could Lord Dormer be bleeding?"

No sooner did she ask the question when one of the grooms grabbed the lance that had unseated Lord Dormer. As men studied the tip, Lord Dormer's opponent shouted as the king's guard raced toward him.

"That is not my lance! Someone replaced mine with a pointed tip! It wasn't me!"

"Hang him! He's been killing members of the Privy Council!" shouted someone from the stands.

"Off with his head!" screamed a man from behind her.

Elizabeth sat in awe as the man was dragged away by the king's guard, and Lord Dormer's lifeless body was carried off the field.

Twenty-one

IAN WANTED TO TAKE ELIZABETH FAR AWAY FROM THE bowels of court. Not only was he unsettled that she'd witnessed a man being killed in the light of day, but what irked him even more was that there was nothing he could do. Last evening Condell was an arse, and this morn, someone was murdered before her eyes. He couldn't shelter her. He couldn't erase what she'd seen. And he couldn't take her home.

As Ruairi, Fagan, Ian, and Elizabeth reached the entrance to the great hall, Laird Fraser walked toward them with an annoyed expression.

"I swear the king's only purpose is to torture the Highland lairds."

"Fagan, would ye take Elizabeth inside?" asked Ian.

"Aye. Come now, lass." Fagan wrapped his arm around her shoulders, and the men followed them into the great hall. Ian gestured the Fraser and Ruairi against the far wall.

"What do ye mean? Tell me ye had your audience," said Ruairi.

"Och, aye. We met with the king...for less than

five minutes. He asked us the same questions he always does about crops and rents, but he wanted to know how many men I had at my command. The MacKay thinks the king is considering a costly war with Spain."

"There's been a peace treaty for years," said Ian.

The Fraser's eyes darted around the hall, and then he leaned against the wall, lowering his voice. "'Tis nay secret the Crown is in debt. As ye can see for yourself—" He gestured with his hand. "The king spares nay expense. Since he dismissed parliament and has nay parliamentary subsidies, the entire realm has nay coin with which to bargain. It will nae be long before they donna have a pot to piss in."

Before the Fraser continued, he glanced around the hall to make certain no one overheard. "There are whispers the king has been making futile attempts to negotiate policies with Spain. But Spain does nae want war. The country declared they would nae interfere with King James's rule in Ireland if he was willing to curtail English attacks in Spanish waters. But ye know the damn English, always wanting to take what is nae theirs. The Ross heard the king has resorted to selling earldoms to gather coin for his cause."

"I can nae see how anything would become of it, even selling earldoms," said Ruairi. "Ye can nae support a war with coin ye donna have."

The Fraser shrugged. "Nevertheless, the king is nae alone with his thoughts. Och, aye. He dismantled parliament for nae agreeing with his views, but there are men who yet share his opinion like his damn Privy Council. But that problem may work itself out."

"Sooner than ye may think. Did ye hear another

man, a member of the council, was killed at the joust-ing tournament just now?" asked Ian.

The Fraser smiled. "As I said, the problem may yet work itself out."

"Are ye traveling back to Scotland on the morrow?" asked Ruairi.

"Nay, we take our leave now. I donna want to spend one more waking moment in this hell with the English."

"I can nae say that I blame ye," said Ian.

"Ah, there's the Ross and the MacKay now." The Fraser's eyes lit up. "I am going home."

"*Turas math dhut*," said Ian. *Have a good journey.*

When the man walked away, Ian sighed. "I know the king's guard has been watching over members of the council, but I ne'er would've anticipated a jousting tournament ending in such disaster."

"Every day I am thankful my wife did nae accom-pany us to court. I donna think I'd be able to stop her from investigating the murders and finding out the man responsible. At least we donna have to worry about Elizabeth being a spy for the Crown."

&

"Who could have done such a horrible thing? Who could have replaced Lord Dormer's lance with a sharp tip?" asked Lady Gillian.

"Shhh…lower your voice, Gillian," said Lady Margery.

Elizabeth glanced at Fagan sitting at the other end of the table waiting for Ian and Ruairi. If he'd heard Lady Gillian's question, he didn't acknowl-edge it.

"They seized the wrong man. Any fool can see

that. Something is not right. Why would he kill Lord Dormer in front of a crowd with hundreds of eyes upon him?"

The way Lady Gillian asked the question Elizabeth didn't think she wanted an answer.

Lady Gillian's accusatory voice stabbed the air. "It had to have been one of the grooms. They were the only men who could've switched the lances. Margery and I were there early and didn't see anyone except the men in the competition and their grooms."

"But what could a groom possibly gain by murdering a lord from the king's council?" asked Elizabeth. "I can't think of anything, can you?"

While Lady Gillian mulled over the question, Lady Margery said, "No one knows why men do what they do. Some will do anything to advance their position for political gain." She paused, deep in thought. "At least Father has guards around him night and day. And we can be assured that he will *not* be participating in a jousting tournament."

Elizabeth gave Lady Margery a compassionate smile. "I'm certain your father is very well protected. You don't have anything to worry about." Elizabeth wished that was true. The only thing she knew for certain was the man responsible for killing members of the council must have also murdered her uncle.

"Let's think of something else. There's been enough darkness for today. Have you seen Mister Condell lately?" asked Lady Gillian.

Elizabeth tried to mask her uneasy expression. "No, I haven't."

"I've heard he will not be performing as King Henry

for the final performance in two days. More's the pity, if you ask me. He made a debonair king and was the perfect match for the role."

"I haven't heard that," said Lady Margery. "Did they say *why*?"

Elizabeth took a sip of mulled wine.

"I think he had an accident with his horse. His face was bruised and his nose was broken."

Elizabeth choked on her drink, and Lady Gillian patted her on the back. "Are you all right, Lady Elizabeth?"

"Yes, thank you."

"I suppose another actor will assume his role, but I don't think anyone will compare to the handsome Mister Condell. Lady Elizabeth, we'd love you to accompany us to the play as our guest," said Lady Gillian. "I'm sure *Henry VIII* will not be the same without Mister Condell, but your company would be most welcome. To be honest, I can't imagine sitting with my father and listening to his tedious conversations with the council. I swear, sometimes they barely stop to breathe."

"Yes, won't you join us, Lady Elizabeth? We'd love to have you. We're leaving court the day after the play and traveling home to the country. I'm afraid we won't have much longer together," said Lady Margery.

Ian walked into the great hall with Ruairi, and Elizabeth stood, smoothing her skirts. "Pray excuse me."

"Lady Elizabeth, are you sure you don't want to ask Laird Sutherland to join us?" asked Lady Gillian coyly.

"Gillian, he's wed," said Lady Margery in a scolding tone.

"Yes, but that's never stopped me before."

Elizabeth walked away before Lady Gillian thought of something else to ensnare Ruairi into her lair. Elizabeth took her seat beside Ruairi and across from Ian at the table.

"Was everything all right with Laird Fraser? He seemed distraught."

Ruairi chuckled. "He was because he traveled all this way to court. When finally granted his audience, he met with the king for less than five minutes." He lowered his voice. "The lairds all know the king does this. It happens every year. He tries to make us heel because he thinks we are barbarians."

She tried to wipe the smile from her face. "Well, you all *are* a bit unruly."

"Did I hear Grace?" asked Fagan, gazing around the hall. "Did ye hear anything, Munro?"

"Nay. I was too busy being unruly." Ian glanced over Elizabeth's shoulder. "I almost did nae recognize Kinghorne without his mother."

Something clicked in her mind. Lady Gillian and Lady Margery said they were at the tournament early. Elizabeth remembered the sisters mentioning they didn't see anyone except the men in the competition and their grooms. But Elizabeth realized that she had seen someone else.

Lord Kinghorne.

❧

"Laird Munro, would you like to escort me for a walk in the garden?"

Ian finished what was left of his mulled wine and smiled. "Aye, I would." He stood, and when he rounded the table, Ruairi grabbed his arm to stay him. A devilish look came into his friend's eyes.

"Good luck, Munro."

As soon as they walked away, Elizabeth took his arm. "What was that about?"

"I'll tell ye in the garden."

They walked through the halls and out into the fresh air. The scent of roses wafted in the wind as he ambled along the path with Elizabeth. When he reached down and removed his *sgian dubh* from his sock, Elizabeth's eyes widened.

"What are you doing with that?"

He stopped in front of a rosebush, and his eyes darted back and forth. "Ye keep watch."

"Keep watch? For what may I ask?" He turned around and handed her two red roses. "Ian, although I appreciate the gesture, the gardeners will have your head if they find out you've cut the flowers from the palace grounds. Let's not forget your little attack on the rosebush when you beheaded the blooms at the other end of the gardens."

He placed his *sgian dubh* back in his sock. "Then 'tis best if we donna get caught. Let's keep moving."

As he walked through the gardens with Elizabeth, he wondered if she'd want him to bring her flowers once they were wed. At that moment, he realized he'd give her anything she asked.

"The Tullibardine sisters are worried for their father. You don't think Lord Dormer's killer was his opponent, do you?"

"Nay."

"Lady Gillian thinks one of the grooms replaced the lance with a sharp point."

"I donna think a groom would try such a feat."

A curious expression crossed Elizabeth's face. "The sisters were at the tournament early and only saw the men in the competition and their grooms."

Ian remained silent, not willing to offer encouragement.

Elizabeth stopped. "But I saw someone else near the grooms and lances at the tournament. The sisters did not."

"Who?"

"Lord Kinghorne. He was with his mother."

He gave her an appeasing smile. "Lass, Kinghorne is ne'er anywhere without his mother."

"Yes, but what if he's using his frail mother as a cover to—"

"Kill the members of the council? Elizabeth..." Although Ian didn't say anything more, his face spoke.

"Well, when you say it like that, it does sound rather absurd."

He took her by the elbow and led her to a bench. "I know ye're unsettled over what happened this morning so let me offer ye a distraction."

"Here, Laird Munro? In the light of day? Even though I wouldn't mind repeating what happened between us, I think everyone in the garden would be quite surprised, unless that was your intention."

Seeing the amusement in her eyes, he laughed. "That was nae exactly what I had in mind right now, but I have something to tell ye."

"What is it?"

"I talked with Ruairi this morn and asked for your hand."

She gasped. "You did?"

"Ye seem surprised."

"I didn't think you'd ask so quickly."

A shadow of alarm touched Ian's face. "Ye have nae changed your mind, have ye?"

She gave him a gentle smile. "Of course not. So what did my brother-in-law have to say?"

"He gave me his blessing but said the decision was yours. Nevertheless, I have a confession. Now that I've had a chance to think about it, I donna like the way, or where, I asked ye."

He stood, and as he lowered himself on bended knee before her, she blurted out, "What are you doing?"

"What does it look like I'm doing?" He grasped her hand and gazed into her eyes, refusing to falter. "Lady Elizabeth, I have been a fool. Ye saw something in me that I could nae see in myself. I have to warn ye. Loving me will nae be easy. I ask for your patience and understanding, but know that I'll ne'er again leave your side because I have been away from you for far too long. I am nae good with flowery words, but I offer ye all that I have. I give ye me, and ye'll have my love until I draw my verra last breath."

He cleared his throat. "Elizabeth, would ye bestow upon me the greatest honor of becoming my wife? *Am pòs thu mi? Tha gràdh agam ort.*"

She sat forward on the bench, and her hand caressed his jaw. "Yes, Ian. I will marry you, and I love you too." Elizabeth pulled him to his feet and gave him a raking gaze. "If you don't take me somewhere that I can kiss you, I'm going to have you in the middle of the garden."

❧

Ian pulled Elizabeth by the hand as they walked with
hurried purpose through the garden. They stepped
between two bushes and continued until they reached
the garden wall. Ian's fingers took her arm with
gentle authority and turned her to face him. His hand
brushed the hair back from her neck as he studied her
intently. His nearness was overpowering. At the base
of her throat, a pulse beat and swelled as though her
heart had risen from its usual place.

"Thank ye."

"For what, may I ask?" she asked.

"Agreeing to be mine."

She smiled. "I was always yours, Ian."

He lowered his head, and the touch of his lips sent
the pit of her stomach into a wild swirl. When he
moved to plant a kiss in the hollow of her neck, she
felt her knees weaken.

His lips recaptured hers, more demanding this time,
and she shuddered. She pulled him close, running her
fingers through his shoulder-length hair.

Placing his hands behind her head, Ian deepened
the kiss. Instinctively, soft mewling sounds escaped.
Rubbing his hands down her back, he pulled her
bottom close, letting out a guttural moan as they
made contact.

Elizabeth needed more. She rubbed her hands over
his chest, feeling the strong, defined muscles that she
knew lay beneath his tunic.

He smothered her lips with mastery, and the gentle
touch of his fingers sent currents of desire through
her. Trailing kisses down her neck, Ian slowly raised

his hand to cover her breast. She melted into him and arched her back into his grasp.

She had never felt this...hot. She was burning for him.

When he forced open her mouth with his thrusting tongue, she savored every delicious moment. Her thoughts spun, her emotions whirled and skidded, and her body moved toward him instinctively. Her response was so powerful that for a long moment, she felt as if she were floating.

He slowly inched back. "I love ye more than words can say."

Elizabeth had a burning desire for another kiss. Her betrothed needed to stop...talking. She pulled his head closer, and he gave her the kind of kiss her tired soul could melt into. He slipped his hands up her arms, ever so slowly, while she caressed the back of his neck.

He pressed her even closer, and she could feel his desire hardening against her belly. Blood surged from her fingertips to her toes with a giddy sense of pleasure. An undeniable magnetism was growing between them.

Ian pulled back and placed his forehead to hers. "We need to stop because verra soon I will be unable, and ye will nay longer think of me as a gentleman." His voice was low and alluring.

An unwelcome blush crept onto Elizabeth's cheeks as she tried to swallow the lump that lingered in her throat. She was conscious of Ian's scrutiny. The man must think his betrothed some type of harlot for kissing him so wantonly in broad daylight.

Twenty-two

IAN GLANCED DOWN AT HIS KILT AND THEN PLACED HIS hand on the garden wall. Elizabeth had no idea it took every ounce of his being to stop because he wanted nothing more than to toss her skirts and take her like an animal. He took a deep breath and willed himself to calm his ardor.

"Let's wait here a moment or two longer," said Ian, trying to think of anything other than Elizabeth's soft flesh and burying himself in her womanly heat.

"What's the matter? You look…pained."

He chuckled. "That's a good word for it." He glanced down at his tented kilt, and her eyes widened.

"Oh, I'm sorry."

"Why are ye apologizing? Ye can see that I'm mad with need for ye."

She placed her fingers over her lips as if he had told her a secret. If he weren't watching her, he wouldn't have believed it. Her expression became hungry and lustful. Lowering her hand, she extended her arm a few inches from his manhood. "May I touch you?"

Ian spoke through gritted teeth. "For God's sake lass, are ye trying to unman me?"

"Well, perhaps you'll let me touch you later then." When her eyes raked over him with a passionate gaze, he spoke in a low tone.

"Be verra careful, Elizabeth. Your innocent words are enough to fire a man's blood. Furthermore, now that we're betrothed, I think it would be proper nae to share a bed again until we're wed."

Her gentle laugh tinkled through the air. "Surely you're jesting." When he didn't respond, she folded her arms over her chest. "You cannot offer me a gift such as that and then tell me we'll wait until we're wed. That will be *months*. Besides, you have taken my virtue, Laird Munro. I'm afraid I'm ruined for any other man." She paused, surely thinking of more words to win the argument. "What difference does it make if you share my bed now or wait until after we're wed? You've already bedded me, and we're still going to be wed."

"Nevertheless, ye are a lady. I should nae be wanting to ravish ye in the bushes in the middle of the garden at the English court."

"You wanted to ravish me?" As if she realized what she'd said, she waved her hands in a dismissive gesture. "Never mind my words."

Pulling her close, he kissed the top of her head and then patted her bottom. "When ye think about what I've said, ye'll see reason." When he turned to walk out of the bushes, he heard her mumble under her breath.

"We'll have to see about that."

Elizabeth smoothed her hair because she had a feeling her locks were tousled. She didn't need to look as though Ian had ravished her in the bushes—although, the thought did make her smile. At the same time, she stole a glance below his waist, and everything was back in its rightful position.

"Now I understand why Grace and Ravenna told me to never accept a man's invitation to walk alone in the gardens, especially at night."

"Your sisters were giving ye fair warning all right, but they were referring to Englishmen and Spaniards, nae Scotsmen." He pounded his chest with his fist. "We are honorable men and would ne'er take advantage of a lass—well, an unwilling lass anyway."

Joy bubbled in her laugh and shone in her eyes. "Is this what I have to look forward to?"

"What do ye mean?"

"Is this what I can expect from you—this jesting? If so, I'm counting the days until we can start our life together as husband and wife."

He placed his hand on her shoulder in a tender gesture. "I should wish every day to bring a smile to your face."

Elizabeth jumped when her brother-in-law called out.

"Munro, was your walk everything ye'd hoped it would be?" asked Ruairi as he and Fagan made their way toward them.

Ian smiled, and when he did, he looked ten years younger. "Why donna ye ask my betrothed?"

Ruairi embraced Elizabeth. "I am happy for ye,

lass. Congratulations on your betrothal. I'm sure your sisters will be happy for ye too."

"Thank you."

"Hell, it took ye two long enough," said Fagan. "But I'm glad it was worth the wait—and trouble. Ye are both glowing, even the fierce Munro. And now, I believe he's turning red."

"Arse."

"Aye."

Out of the corner of her eye, Elizabeth spotted Lady Glamis sitting on a bench alone. "Pray excuse me a moment. I want to see how Lady Glamis fares."

"We'll wait for ye here, lass," said Ian.

As Elizabeth made her way to Lady Glamis, the poor woman sat hunched over on the bench in her green dress, the large hat on her head shielding her face from the sun. Elizabeth sat beside her and gently touched Lady Glamis's shoulder.

"Lady Glamis, it's lovely to see you. I'm glad you're out enjoying this fine weather."

"Yes, Lady Elizabeth. One never knows how much time is left in this world. I tell myself every day that if I'm able to open my eyes in the morn, it's a good day." The woman could barely lift her head, and her legs were shaking.

"I saw you earlier at the jousting tournament. It was an unfortunate turn of events. Poor Lord Dormer, I can only imagine what his family must be feeling."

"What a horrible tragedy. At least they arrested the man responsible. He deserves what he gets for doing such a thing, especially in front of all those people."

There was a brief silence, and Elizabeth treaded carefully. "I was surprised Lord Kinghorne escorted you to see the riders and their mounts this morn."

"Why would that surprise you, my dear? Patrick is a good son. He loves his mother."

"Of course he does. Was Lord Kinghorne acquainted with Lord Dormer?" All of a sudden, Lady Glamis's shaking legs stopped moving, and an eerie feeling swept over Elizabeth. When the air stilled, she felt uneasy, as if a spell had been cast upon her. "I would offer my condolences on the loss of his friend."

"My son was not acquainted with Lord Dormer."

"I'm so glad to hear it."

When Lady Glamis's legs began to quiver again, Elizabeth knew her imagination was getting the best of her. But she needed to make certain her suspicions about the earl were nothing more than foolishness. She gently prodded for the answers.

"Did Lord Kinghorne ever leave your side this morn at the tournament? I wouldn't have wished anything to happen to you."

"Lady Elizabeth, how lovely it is to see you on such a gorgeous day. Thank you for keeping Mother entertained in my absence."

Elizabeth stood and gave Lord Kinghorne a small curtsy. "My lord, it was my pleasure. I didn't wish for her to be alone in the garden."

"Yes, well, come along, Mother." He assisted the woman to her feet. "You've had a busy day and should lie down."

"Do not rush me, Patrick."

"Take your time, Mother."

"Lady Glamis, it was a pleasure to see you again." Elizabeth glanced at the earl. "My lord."

❧

Patrick Lyon, Earl of Kinghorne, gazed at the slender back of Lady Elizabeth as she walked away. He was no fool and knew to keep a watch on her. After all, her sister and her uncle had been spies for the Crown. The last he needed was to add a meddling Walsingham into the mix. But being that Mildmay was no longer a problem, and Lady Elizabeth's sister hadn't accompanied her to court, he assumed it could have been worse.

"What the hell was that about?" he asked.

"She knows, Patrick."

A shiver ran down his spine. "That's not possible. I was very careful."

"She saw us this morning at the tournament."

He shrugged. "That means nothing. I was able to change the tip of the lance in less than a minute. If anyone had seen me, I'd now be the one in the dungeon."

"Lady Elizabeth is suspicious. She asked if you had ever left my side during the tournament."

He gave her a measured look. "And what did you say?"

"I didn't say anything. You interrupted us. I'm tired of cleaning up your messes, Patrick. It's about time you clean up your own. I'm leaving this one for you. Do you think you can do that, or will you leave this up to your mother again?"

His face lit up. "I'll take care of Lady Elizabeth. And you know that I'd do anything for you."

❦

Ruairi, Fagan, Ian, and Elizabeth were standing in the hall as a male voice spoke from behind them. Instinctively, Ian rested his hand on the hilt of his sword.

"Laird Sutherland?"

As the king's secretary stood before them, Ian felt as if the clouds had parted and the sun was finally in sight. He prayed the man came to deliver the news they'd all been waiting to hear since the day they'd arrived at the English court.

"The king will meet with you at noon the day after tomorrow." He glanced at Ian. "And you as well, Laird Munro."

"Is there any chance we can be granted an audience before then?" asked Ruairi. "My wife is with child."

"I'm sorry, Laird Sutherland. That's the only time the king is available. His time is precious, and there are other pressing matters that require his immediate attention."

As soon as the king's secretary departed, Ruairi shrugged. "Ye can nae blame a man for trying."

"I'll be sure and tell Ravenna you tried your best to return to her and Mary," said Elizabeth. "In two days, we'll be going home. You should all be thrilled there is an end in sight."

"Ye have nay idea, lass," said Fagan.

Ian placed his hand at Elizabeth's back. "Are ye ready to go to the library? I could use a nap."

When she placed her elbow into his gut, Fagan laughed. "See what ye have to look forward to, Munro? Ye better get used to that. Our women donna hesitate to put us in our place, and rightfully so."

"As long as that place is by Elizabeth's side, I donna mind."

Fagan managed a choking laugh. "Munro, I could nae have said that better myself. And ye say ye're nae good with flowery words. Ye learn verra quickly. Be patient with him, Elizabeth. Remember all the kind words he says to ye now because I have nay doubt he'll make ye angry for plenty of days to come."

"I have a feeling his words are true, lass. But until then, I could use a respite. Are ye ready to go to the library?" asked Ian.

"We'll meet ye for sup," said Ruairi. "Good sleep, Munro."

As Ian escorted Elizabeth to the library, he noticed even his walk had a sudden cheeriness. In two days, he'd be done with this madness and would take Elizabeth home. The thought gave him great pleasure, and he couldn't wait to start their life together.

"What do ye think your sisters are going to say when they hear the news about us?"

She looked at him and smiled. "Ravenna will be happy for us, Grace will wonder if I've gone mad, and as long as Torquil is by Kat's side, she couldn't care less."

He chuckled. "Kat and Torquil used to chase each other— well, I think 'twas more like your sister giving chase to Torquil. They seem to have grown verra fond of one another." Ian treaded carefully. "They nay longer look at each other as though they're brother and sister." When he gave her a knowing look, she lowered her gaze.

"They're not bound by blood, and Katherine has

grown up in the same home as Torquil. I wouldn't be surprised if what you say is true."

As soon as they entered the library, Ian sought his soft chair. There were two men sitting at the long, wooden table with their noses buried in books. He couldn't say he wanted to do the same.

Her laugh reverberated through the room. "You weren't jesting."

"Nay. I can see why ye enjoy the library. 'Tis nice and quiet. Wake me when ye're ready to take your leave."

Ian closed his eyes, listening as the two men closed their books and replaced them on the shelf. The legs of a chair scraped against the floor, and their voices disappeared after a door closed. He could hear Elizabeth's footsteps as she wandered from book to book. When complete silence spread over the library, Ian fell into a deep slumber.

❧

Elizabeth could die in this spot as a happy woman. She'd always had a love for reading and would ask Ian if his home had a library. Since she hadn't set foot on Munro lands for years, she couldn't remember. If he didn't, perhaps Ruairi would let her borrow some of his books to take along.

A door closed on the second floor. She didn't pay it any heed until a familiar male voice echoed through the library.

"What the bloody hell happened to your face?"

"The damn Highlander is what happened. Shhh... lower your voice."

Elizabeth darted behind the steps to shield herself. She glanced at Ian, who still slumbered in the chair hidden from view from the second floor. Footsteps came midway down the stairs and stopped.

"Hello?"

She dared not breathe. When Mister Condell retreated up the stairs, she released the breath she held.

"There's no one here."

What was Mister Condell doing with Lord Kinghorne? The men spoke in hushed tones.

"My sister told me what happened, and you know she's not happy. You were supposed to be careful," said Mister Condell in a Spanish accent. "And now the chit is asking questions."

"I was careful. If anyone suspected me, the king's guard would have taken me into custody by now."

Elizabeth's blood pounded in her ears.

"*She* suspects you." Mister Condell let out a sinister growl. "I thought when I killed Mildmay that would've cleared our path of obstacles, but the last we need is another Walsingham where she doesn't belong. At least her spying sister didn't accompany her to court. You know how much damage she's caused in the past."

There was a heavy silence before Mister Condell continued. "I will not have my country at war with the English. That is a costly endeavor no one can afford. When the king dismissed parliament, luck was in our favor. But I don't want to leave anything else to chance. Everything is in order, and we will not fail. Within a sennight, the king will be lost without his faithful council to guide him. Heed my warning, Kinghorne, and do not contact me again. Do you understand?"

"Yes."

The door closed, and Elizabeth paused, needing to make certain both men had departed.

"Elizabeth, what are ye doing?" asked Ian. He sat up and ran his fingers through his hair.

Her eyes widened in panic, and she placed her finger over her lips to silence him. When she pointed to the second floor, Ian stood. She had no idea if Lord Kinghorne had taken his leave with Mister Condell, or if he still lurked above. Not knowing made her tremble with fear.

She lifted her skirts, unsheathing her dagger, as she gestured for Ian to remove his sword. As soon as she placed one foot on the steps, he pushed her back.

"Ye stay here, and donna move," he whispered. "Do ye understand?" When she gave him a look of agreement, he climbed the stairs without her and gazed around at the top. "Lass, there is nay one here."

"Oh, thank heavens." Her breathing was labored. "I can't believe what I just heard! Mister Condell and Lord Kinghorne are going to kill the men in the king's circle."

Ian descended the stairs and sheathed his weapon. "Lass, what are ye talking about?"

"Did you know that Ravenna or Grace—one of them—is a spy?" When an expression crossed his face that wasn't one of surprise, she added, "You knew. You're supposed to be my husband. Is there ever going to be a time when I can trust you?"

"'Twas nae my place to tell ye. Ruairi was to have—"

"Ruairi knew? Of course. Ravenna's the spy. Why should I even be surprised?" she asked dryly. She lifted her skirts and secured her blade under her dress. "Not only did I find out at court that my uncle and father were spies, but then I learn my uncle had killed my sister's betrothed. If that wasn't bad enough, now I discover that Mister Condell murdered my uncle. And let's not forget the fact that Ravenna *is* a spy."

Elizabeth knew she must have sounded like a lunatic, but she was so beside herself that she couldn't think straight. "Is there anything else you'd like to tell me, Laird Munro? Perhaps something about Grace? Oh, and let's not forget about Katherine. Is Kat a spy too?"

"Elizabeth, calm down."

"That's very easy for you to say," she snapped. "You didn't find out that *you* come from a family of spies."

He reached out and rubbed her arm. "Ravenna has been retired from service for years, ever since she wed Ruairi. I'm willing to talk with ye about this, but right now, I have to ask ye to repeat what ye said."

She cast him a disgusted look. "Which part?"

"Condell. Why would ye say that he murdered your uncle?"

"Because I heard him confess when he and Lord Kinghorne were plotting to kill the rest of the council."

Twenty-three

IAN, FAGAN, AND RUAIRI COULDN'T BELIEVE WHAT Elizabeth had told them as they stood in Ruairi's room at the inn. Ian knew he despised that damn Condell for a reason. Now that he thought on the matter, he wasn't too fond of Kinghorne either.

Although Condell was from Spain, Kinghorne was an Englishman who wasn't loyal to England. Any man who would betray his own country had no morals. And that was another reason Ian was proud to be a Scot. Of course Highlanders fought and warred with neighboring clans, but every Scot had one thing in common.

They hated the English.

"What are we going to do?" asked Elizabeth. She sat at the table and tapped her fingers on her thigh, her face clouding with uneasiness.

Ruairi pulled out the other chair and sat beside her. "*We?* Ye are going to do naught."

"That…that…bastard killed my uncle! Are you going to tell me my sister would've sat idle while the actor and the earl were plotting to kill more members of the council?"

"Being that ye're Grace's sister, I can nae say I'm surprised to hear ye curse, but having had similar conversations with my own wife, I'm telling ye this now. Ye are going to do naught," said Fagan. "Ye are nae going to win this battle with us, lass. Ye have three Highlanders standing in your way."

She looked at him imploringly. "Please, Ian."

He frowned. "My answer is still nay, lass. Condell and Kinghorne have killed men and nae thought twice about it. What makes ye think they will nae kill ye?"

"We have to do something. The task falls on our shoulders. We can't let anyone else be hurt. We—or someone—must stop them."

Ian grabbed Elizabeth's arm and pulled her to her feet. "Seek your bed. Ruairi, Fagan, and I will discuss what we'll do. This is nay place for ye to be, lass."

She placed her hands on her hips and scowled. "No place for me to be? You were telling me only a few hours ago my place was by your side. Perhaps you should sleep on the matter and mull over your thoughts." Elizabeth swung open the door and shut it in their faces.

Ian sighed. "Do ye think I should go after her?"

"Nay," said Ruairi and Fagan at the same time.

"Let her cool her ire," said Fagan. "The lass reminds me so much of Grace. If ye try to talk with her now, ye will lose your head or worse."

"I suppose ye're right. Do ye have any ideas about Condell and Kinghorne?"

Ruairi dragged the table over by the bed, and Fagan moved the two chairs. Lifting the lid to his trunk, Ruairi pulled out his flask. "Let's have a wee dram and devise something clever."

Elizabeth couldn't sleep. How could she when her uncle's murderer was walking around without a care in the world? She punched the lumps out of her pillow as she pictured Mister Condell's face. The thought of that man's touch made her stomach sour.

There was a light tap on the door. "Elizabeth…"

Perhaps Ian had come to apologize for shooing her off. If he was going to be her husband, he should. They were supposed to be as one. She lifted the latch to find him standing there, and her senses were immediately engulfed with the smell of sweet whisky on his breath.

"I saw the light under your door. Can ye nae sleep?"

"No."

"May I come in?"

She gestured him in and closed the door behind him. In no mood to be concerned about propriety, she climbed back in bed, covering herself with a blanket. "Are you going to sit, or are you going to stand there and stare?"

He chuckled. "I was going to stare at ye for a while, but I'll sit." He sat on the bed and sighed. "I know ye only want to help, but I can nae let ye place yourself in danger, lass."

"So why are you here, my laird? You and my brothers-in-law made it perfectly clear that I'm to do nothing." When he was about to speak, she asked, "How would you feel if someone you loved was murdered and you knew who the killer was? Uncle Walter was like a father to me. How can I do nothing?" Her voice sounded unnatural. "I want Mister Condell to pay for what he's done."

"And he will. I swear on my honor if ye give me *your* word that ye will nae put yourself in harm's way."

She hesitated, thinking how she could persuade him to change his mind.

"Elizabeth…" When she still didn't answer, Ian said her name again.

"I heard you. I'm not happy with this, but I give you my word."

He gave her a roguish grin. "I also came for another reason."

"And what is that, may I ask?"

"I've come to ravish ye."

A giggle escaped her. "Laird Munro, you're evidently into your cups and don't know what you're saying. What happened to us not sharing a bed until after we're wed, eh?"

He looked deep in thought. "I realized your words made a lot of sense, especially when I sought my own bed and found it without ye in it." Before she knew what he was about, he had removed his boots, pulled off his tunic with one hand, and…

Laird Munro was naked.

His brawny chest was covered with tawny hair, and at that moment, she could no longer argue. Elizabeth silently cursed, realizing she was weak. She longed to touch him.

He lay down beside her with his arm resting casually on his bent leg, looking as though he was a gift from God. He arched his eyebrows mischievously and cast an irresistible grin.

Elizabeth's mouth was suddenly dry. "Although

I am quite flattered by your efforts, there are more pressing matters that we need to discuss."

He gave her a smile that sent her pulse racing. "Lass, we can speak about anything ye want on the morrow. But this eve, ye are mine." His eyes were full of promises, and then he winked at her.

Perhaps the man was right, and this was what they both needed.

Ian pulled back the blankets and tugged on her nightrail. "I think one of us is wearing too much clothing."

She stilled his hand. "Stop."

"Is it too soon? I'll cease. Does your body ache?"

"Does my…no. I just don't want you to think of me as some type of harlot."

He rolled onto his side, his expression holding a savage inner fire. "A harlot? Ye're going to be my wife." Desire pooled in his eyes, and his maleness became increasingly evident.

Slowly, he raised his hand and fingered a lock of her hair. "Ye are beautiful."

Elizabeth couldn't speak. She could only gaze into Ian's eyes. She loved this side of him—the kindness, the desire, and the passion. This was the man she had grown so fond of and who had captured her heart from the beginning.

She threw herself into his arms, and he brought his lips down to hers. Her calm was shattered by the hunger of his kisses. His firm mouth demanded a response, one that she was more than willing to give. She was shocked at her own delight in his touch.

His lips seared a path down her neck, her shoulders.

She laced her fingers in his hair, pulling him close. His gentle touch sent currents of desire through her.

She felt the thrill of his arousal, and when he moved his thigh between her legs, the glorious heat nearly caused her to swoon. He pulled back slightly and ran his exploring fingers over her curves. Her skin tingled wherever he touched her, and shivers of pleasure slid up her arms and down her spine.

Elizabeth placed her hand on his rock-hard chest and brushed the tawny hairs. His gaze slowly dropped from her eyes to her shoulders to her breasts. Her nightrail crept up to her thighs as she moved closer to him. He pulled the fabric upward over her belly, her chest. His tongue caressed her sensitive nipples, her breasts surging from his touch. He continued to tantalize the buds, which had swollen to the fullest.

When Ian's strong hand seared a path down her abdomen and to her leg, she thought she would come undone. He explored her thighs and then moved up.

He paused to kiss her, whispering his love for each part of her body. The stroking of his fingers sent pleasure jolts through her. Completely aroused now, she drew herself closer.

His body moved partially to uncover hers. "I want to see all of ye."

She wiggled her way out of her nightrail and tossed it to the floor. As he lay her back down, she moaned softly. Her breasts tingled against his hard chest.

"Do ye still wish to touch me?" he asked, his voice low and alluring.

"Yes."

He took her hand and guided it to himself. Her

fingers encircled him, and he moved his body against her. When he reached between her thighs, opening her legs and then inserting his finger, she gasped in sweet agony.

"Ye are so wet for me."

Her desire for him overrode all sense of reason. He recognized her need and entered her in a single thrust, sending a jolt of pleasure straight through her. It was a raw act of possession. Sweat beaded on his forehead, and his chest heaved. She surrendered to his masterful seduction, her eager response matching his.

When they were roused to the peak of desire, he pulled back and gazed into her eyes. With another heavy thrust, she arched her back and couldn't control the outcry of delight and the feeling of satisfaction Ian left within her as he spilled his seed.

Elizabeth looked up, and her heart lurched madly. When he collapsed on top of her, she could feel his heart pounding against her own. He rolled onto his side as she lay panting. They shared a smile, and both burst out laughing because his breath was as labored as hers.

"God's teeth, lass, are ye trying to kill me?"

She giggled in response and ran her fingernails up and down his arm. "That was very enjoyable."

"For me as well." He gathered her into his arms and held her snugly against him.

Elizabeth had never dreamed Ian's hands would be so warm, so tender. She was astonished at the fulfillment she felt. She allowed her thoughts to emerge from their hidden depths, and looking back, she knew Ian was never the battle-hardened warrior everyone made him out to be.

She lay in the drowsy warmth of her bed, thinking of the days to come.

❧

Ian and Ruairi stood in front of the large, wooden doors to the king's private study, knowing at least one member of the king's inner circle wasn't happy with them. After insisting they needed to speak with King James on a matter of grave importance, they had finally managed to convince the king's secretary to grant them an audience.

"Are ye sure about this?" asked Ian.

"If anything is in our favor, 'tis that Ravenna is my wife and her uncle was Mildmay. For now, that's all we have."

"Aye, but for some reason, that does nae make me feel any better."

The king's secretary opened the door. "The king will see you now."

Ian and Ruairi entered the room and passed a large window on the left that overlooked the king's private gardens. Ian stole a quick glance, and there were so many colored blooms that the ground looked like a rainbow of flowers. When he noticed the fine paintings displayed on the walls, he whispered to Ruairi, "Did ye take notice of the walls? They look like yours, naught but scenes of death and battle."

"The king has good taste. I'm sure he would appreciate my tapestries."

As they approached King James, he was sitting behind a large desk in front of a stone fireplace. His brown hair was combed back, and a large chain hung around his shoulders over his silk doublet. There was a tall man, about as old as Ian, gazing over the king's shoulder at something on the desk. When both men looked up, Ian and Ruairi gave their liege a low bow.

"Your Majesty."

"Rise. I heard you mention my paintings. Do you favor Mantegna?"

"My apologies, but I donna know of whom you speak," said Ruairi.

The king stood and walked over to one of the canvases. "These paintings are a series of nine called the *Triumphs of Caesar*. This one depicts a military procession celebrating the victory of Julius Caesar in the Gallic Wars. They're my favorite collection." He resumed his position behind the desk and gestured for Ian and Ruairi to sit. "This is Lord Tullibardine."

"My lord, I believe your daughters are acquainted with my sister-in-law," said Ruairi.

"Ah, yes. They've told me about Lady Elizabeth." The man rounded the desk and sat in a chair beside Ruairi.

"My apologies we couldn't meet sooner, gentlemen. I'm sure you're aware there are more pressing matters that require my attention," said the king in a scolding tone. "Nevertheless, Mildmay was my trusted friend. If Lady Elizabeth wants for anything, be sure to let my man know."

"Thank ye, Your Majesty," said Ruairi.

"My secretary tells me that you couldn't wait for an audience on the morrow because of a matter of *grave* importance. What can I do for you Laird Sutherland and Laird Munro?" asked the king in a dry tone.

Ruairi shifted in the chair. "We have information regarding members of the Privy Council."

"Go on." The king leaned forward, placing his elbows on the desk. "You have my undivided attention."

The way he said the words made Ian wonder if he talked to all his subjects that way or just the Highland lairds. It was no secret the Scots were nothing more than savages by the king's standards.

"There are two men responsible for murdering the men of your council and Lord Mildmay."

"Are you going to make me ask you, Laird Sutherland, or are you going to tell me?"

"Condell and Lord Kinghorne."

There was a heavy silence, and then the king sat back in his chair and tapped his fingers on the desk. "Mister Condell? The actor playing Henry VIII at the Globe Theatre?" He cast a speculative gaze at Lord Tullibardine and then chuckled. "I find that highly unlikely. He has been my guest."

"He said ye favored his performances and had given him leave to certain parts of the palace," said Ian.

"Yes, he was walking the same path, so to speak, as King Henry for his role at the theatre." He sat forward. "And Lord Kinghorne you say?"

"Aye. He murdered Lord Dormer," said Ruairi.

"Laird Sutherland," said the king in a patronizing tone. "My personal guard has the man who murdered Lord Dormer in custody. There were hundreds of eyewitnesses."

"Ye have the wrong man." When Ian realized he blurted out the words, he added, "Lord Kinghorne admitted he switched out the lance, Your Majesty."

"And to whom did he give this confession of guilt to, Laird Munro? You?"

Ian was starting to lose patience. Evidently, the king didn't believe a word he or Ruairi said.

"My sister-in-law, Lady Elizabeth, overheard both men."

When King James gave them an amused grin, Ian willed himself not to reach across the desk and smack his liege.

"So neither of you heard Mister Condell or Lord Kinghorne give this confession, you're taking the word of a mere woman, and you're accusing a peer of the realm of a heinous crime."

"Ye had nay trouble listening to the words of my wife, a mere woman," Ruairi snapped.

Ian placed the heel of his boot into his friend's foot as the king's eyes darkened.

"Because you care for Mildmay's nieces, Lady Ravenna's sisters, I'll pretend I didn't hear your words. But I suggest you tread carefully, Laird Sutherland. These accusations are quite serious, and you have no tangible evidence to support your claim. Tell me, gentlemen. Did Mister Condell or Lord Kinghorne give an explanation why they're killing members of my council?"

"Lady Elizabeth heard Condell admit that he killed her uncle, Mildmay. He also knew about my wife being a spy for the Crown."

The king's eyes narrowed with suspicion.

Ruairi continued. "Condell said he does nae want Spain to war with England because it would be costly for both sides. He went further to say that ye have nay parliamentary support and that your Privy Council consists of the only men left who support your efforts for war with Spain. He told Kinghorne that within a sennight, ye will be lost without your faithful council to guide ye. Ye will have nay support."

Ian cleared his throat. "Your Majesty, ye are verra well protected. The men can nae reach ye to cause ye harm, but if they kill your advisors, the men who guide ye, what impact would that have on the realm? As Lady Elizabeth recalled the words of Condell and Lord Kinghorne, the men are somehow going to attack the council in whole."

"Guards watch over the members of the council as we speak. And I will not take the word of some Highlan—er, someone without tangible proof, before I accuse Lord Kinghorne and Mister Condell of a crime against the Crown."

"Your Majesty," said Lord Tullibardine, "I don't know if the words these men speak are the truth, but most council members are attending the final performance of *Henry VIII* on the morrow at the Globe. I believe Lady Elizabeth has been asked to accompany my daughters. Perhaps we shouldn't attend."

When the king studied Ian and Ruairi intently, Ian had a feeling whatever was coming next out of the king's mouth wasn't going to be good. "If what you say is true, there needs to be proof. What better way to expose Mister Condell and Lord Kinghorne's machinations and bring their true character to light? No. Let members of the council attend the play. We don't want to alert anyone that you've voiced your suspicions to me. If the men are responsible, give them the noose to hang themselves. Laird Sutherland and Laird Munro, you will accompany Lady Elizabeth to the play. I'll speak with the captain of my guard later and devise my next move. Good day to you."

Twenty-four

RUAIRI AND IAN RODE WITH ELIZABETH IN THE COACH to the theatre. She couldn't believe the king hadn't believed them. Because she was a woman, and Ruairi and Ian were Highlanders, they couldn't be trusted. For heaven's sake, Uncle Walter had been the king's friend for years, and Ravenna had been a spy for *his* realm.

When the carriage stopped, she took Ian's hand and stepped down. She hoped the king was taking necessary precautions to see to their safety. There weren't guards around the theatre—well, at least none that she could see.

The grounds surrounding the building were bustling with men and women, like the first time she'd attended the play. Merchants were selling their wares of breads, cheeses, pastries, and pies, and men were cooking sweet-smelling meat on a spit. Nothing appeared out of the ordinary.

"I'm glad Fagan's nae here with us now. He'd be over there eating the entire time," said Ian.

"There is that," replied Ruairi. "He's around. He'll keep watch and have our backs."

"I don't know why I'm so nervous," said Elizabeth, her hands shaking.

Ian placed his hand at the small of her back. "'Tis nae every day ye get to take your sister's place as a spy for the Crown. But remember…"

"I know. I'm just an observer. I suppose that I'll observe while you slumber in the chair."

"I donna think I'll have any trouble staying awake this time." He gestured to the door of the theatre. "They're beginning to let people in."

Seats filled up quickly as Ruairi, Ian, and Elizabeth made their way to their seats. Members of the Privy Council sat in the two playhouse boxes on each side of the stage. When Lady Margery and Lady Gillian waved from the balcony, Elizabeth smiled. She wished she would've had the opportunity to warn them, but their father would keep them safe.

The trumpet sounded to signal the start of the play.

"Do you see anything yet?" Elizabeth asked softly.

"Lass, we just sat," Ian whispered. "If ye're going to ask me that question every few moments, 'tis going to be a long night."

"Of course."

The play opened again with the Duke of Norfolk, Buckingham, and Lord Abergavenny discussing the power of Cardinal Wolsey. King Henry wouldn't be introduced until the second scene, and she wondered if Mister Condell dared to show his injured face.

Gazing around the theatre, everyone's eyes remained fixed on the actors. Elizabeth didn't notice anything or anyone out of place. When the second scene arrived, she realized Lady Gillian was right. Another actor was playing King Henry. Elizabeth studied the playhouse box on the left, and when that grew tiresome, she gazed at the one on the right. She'd watch the play and then switch her attention back to the members of the council.

Scanning the crowd, she started to ponder if she'd lost her mind. She hadn't seen Mister Condell or Lord Kinghorne, and the play was almost over. Although she was grateful that nothing untoward had befallen the members of the council, now it would be that much harder to prove that Mister Condell and Lord Kinghorne were behind the attacks.

As the final act approached, a cannon was rolled onto the stage. This must have been the surprise for the audience that Mister Condell had told her about. Apparently, the rumors were true. After the last word was spoken, cannon fire shot through the air and she jumped, but then it hit the thatched roof, setting it on fire.

Panic swept through the crowd as men and women made their way hastily to the door. Ruairi and Fagan flew to their feet and escorted Elizabeth to the front of the theatre. Men were pounding the door and women were screaming. Smoke billowed into the air. The door wouldn't open, and the fire was spreading quickly, making its way down the walls of the theatre.

Ian handed her a cloth from his sporran. "Place this over your mouth."

She glanced at the council members. A handful of men were pushing on the second-story playhouse door, which wouldn't open, and that's the moment when Elizabeth realized they'd all been locked inside to die. That was Mister Condell's grand scheme.

Kill them all.

Even with the strength of Ruairi and Fagan, the men couldn't break down the door. It must have been barricaded from the outside. A large man ran past her and knocked her to the ground. Smoke filled her lungs, and she couldn't catch her breath. Elizabeth sat up, her eyes burning and tearing. She could barely see. Strong arms lifted her and carried her onto the stage.

"There is a hidden door somewhere under here. I saw it the last time," Ian yelled. "*An cuidich thu mi?*" *Will you help me?* Ian placed her down on the stage, and Ruairi searched for the secret door.

"*Tha e a-bhos an seo!*" *It's over here!*

Ruairi lifted the latch and climbed down as Ian grabbed Elizabeth, lowering her into the floor. The smoke wasn't as thick where they were, but she felt as though she was suffocating. Her chest burned. Even the men were coughing.

Candles lit their way, as some actors had used the passage earlier for the performance. They walked a short distance until they found another door on the right. She prayed the darned thing wasn't locked or barricaded.

Ruairi swung open the door. Costumes, gowns, masks, and shoes hung on the wall and lay throughout the room. Ruairi quickly found another exit that led outside, but then Elizabeth froze.

"Wait!"

"Lass, there is nay time. We have to get out," said Ian.

"Look at this! Do you recognize it?" She held up the material.

"'Tis a gown."

She coughed and tried to find her voice. "Not just any gown. It's Lady Glamis's gown." She dropped the dress on the floor and picked up another gown that was green. "And this is what she wore in the garden." Her expression darkened. "Dear God." She pointed to the wall, and Ian's eyes widened.

"Is that…hair?"

"That's why Lord Kinghorne grabbed his mother's arse! His mother is Mistress Alexander! She's Mister Condell's sister!"

By the time Ian pulled her from the room and out the door, the Globe Theatre was engulfed in flames. There were a large number of men and women sitting on the grass, the only sounds crying and coughing. She prayed everyone got out safely.

"Elizabeth, are ye…all right?" Ian's voice was rough, and he could barely speak.

She nodded. "Ruairi?"

Her brother-in-law held up his hand and coughed again.

"'Tis done," said Fagan. He poured water onto a cloth and handed it to Elizabeth.

"Did everyone…get…out?" she asked, coughing between each word.

"Aye, lass. The king's guard knocked down the barricades and caught Condell, Kinghorne, and a woman as they fled the theatre after the doors were blocked."

"The woman…is…Lady Glamis," said Elizabeth.

Fagan's jaw dropped. "Did ye say what I think ye said? The woman they captured was young. How is that even possible? She was in costume?"

Elizabeth bobbed her head. She had to look pitiful sitting there in the grass with her blackened face. She leaned into Ian, who smelled of smoke.

"Have ye had enough…of court?" he choked out.

"Will you take me home now?"

The man smiled from ear to ear.

❧

Elizabeth tapped her foot nervously, and Ian took her hand. "There is naught to fear."

"Why would the king ask to see me too?"

The king's secretary opened the door. "The king will see you now."

Ian, Elizabeth, and Ruairi entered the king's study and passed the garden window. When Ian stole a quick glance at Elizabeth, she was gazing at scenes of death and battle on the walls. As they approached King James, he was sitting behind his large desk. They gave their liege a low bow, and Elizabeth curtsied.

"Your Majesty."

"Rise. Please, please rise," he said in a jovial tone. The king stood and walked around his desk. He approached Elizabeth and grasped her hands. "Lady Elizabeth, I hear that I have you to thank. Because of you, members of my council still live. I'm certain your actions have made your uncle and your sister very proud."

"Thank you, Your Majesty."

The king released her hands and gestured for them to sit, once again resuming his place behind the desk. "Mildmay was a good man, and as you already know, Lady Ravenna is no longer in my employ. I could use someone with your family's talents to work for the Crown." The king sat forward, "I could use someone like you, Lady Elizabeth, if you're interested in such a task."

"Nay." Ian stiffened, and the king lifted a brow.

"Pardon, Laird Munro?"

Elizabeth placed her hand on Ian's arm, probably to prevent him from jumping out of the chair. "What Laird Munro is trying to say is that my family has served you well, Your Majesty. I am honored that you would offer me such a place among your court. But Lady Ravenna is again with child, and my place is beside my husband. I am betrothed to Laird Munro."

"Is this true, Laird Sutherland?"

"Aye, Your Majesty."

The king paused and tapped his finger on his desk. For a moment, silence enveloped the room. Ian had never been so afraid in his life. King James had the power to shatter his hopes and dreams, his life with Elizabeth, with a single command. Furthermore, their liege could force Elizabeth to do his bidding whether she was willing or not. He could place her life in danger.

"I have to admit that answer was not what I'd expected to hear. But as you stated, your family has served me well. I want to repay you for your service to the Crown and saving my council. Is there anything I can do?"

"No, Your Majesty. We'd just like to return home."

The king cast a wry grin. "Lady Elizabeth, when your king grants you favor, you accept. I'll wed the two of you before you leave court. Would that please you?"

Elizabeth gasped, and Ian released the breath he held.

❦

Elizabeth once again sat in the coach and should have been able to fall asleep, but she couldn't. She was awake, too excited and nervous to slumber. Having experienced all that court had to offer, she was eager to return home as Lady Elizabeth Munro.

She fingered the jeweled necklace King James had bestowed on her as a wedding gift, and her mood was suddenly buoyant when they drew closer to London Bridge. She was halfway home. But when they reached the bridge, her jaw dropped.

Closing her eyes, she tried to banish the memory of Mister Condell and Lord Kinghorne's heads impaled on long spikes as a warning to all those who conspired against the realm. Thinking of poor Uncle Walter, Elizabeth forced herself to open her eyes. As far as she was concerned, justice was served. Her uncle's murderer was dead. Now she was certain why this part of the bridge was named Traitors' Gate.

No one told her what had happened to Mistress Alexander, and Elizabeth thought it was in her best interest not to ask. She gazed out the carriage for the hundredth time, watching pieces of wood floating in the strong currents of the River Thames.

When they finally crossed the drawbridge to Scadbury Manor, the sight pleased her. A smile even crossed her face when she realized whatever place she decided to call home didn't matter, as long as Ian was by her side.

They were immediately greeted by the chaos she was proud to call family, and Elizabeth hadn't realized how much she'd missed them. She embraced her sisters, little Mary, and then Torquil.

"How is Aunt Mary? Please tell me she is well."

Ravenna smiled. "I'm so happy you're all home safe. And yes, Aunt Mary is doing much better. Of course, we all miss Uncle Walter, but I think she'll be all right in the days to come. We missed you at Apethorpe Hall." Her sister's gaze lowered, and then she touched Elizabeth's necklace. "Where did you get that?"

"His Majesty."

When strong arms embraced Elizabeth from behind, Ravenna's eyes widened, Kat's jaw dropped, and Grace cursed.

Fagan gave his wife a peck on the lips. "God, I missed ye, Grace."

"Fagan, what is this about? What has happened?" asked Grace with a look of concern.

Elizabeth grabbed Ian's hand as he stepped beside her. She gazed at her family of spies and smiled. "I'd introduce you, but I think you already know my husband."

For the first time in her life, Elizabeth's sisters were rendered speechless, even Grace.

Epilogue

AFTER CURSING OUT HER SISTERS THE ENTIRE JOURNEY to Scotland for withholding family secrets, Elizabeth was proudly keeping a secret of her own. She was with child. Of course Ian knew, but she didn't want to tell her family until she was further along. For now, she was content having this special bond just between them.

As she sat in the great hall of her new home, she never thought she'd be the lady of a castle, especially not Lady Elizabeth Munro. Ever since Ian withheld the truth from her about Ravenna, he'd been honest to a fault about everything else. The poor man had even confessed he'd told her family she wasn't feeling well so that he didn't have to see them again so soon.

"What are ye thinking? Ye have that look on your face a lot lately," said Ian.

"That's happiness you see, Laird Munro. I'm glad to be away from court. I'm proud to be your wife. And I really enjoy the quiet. I never realized how loud my sisters could be."

He laughed. "Now ye know why I avoided Ruairi's

lands like the plague when the Walsingham sisters invaded…moved there." He pulled her onto his lap. "I do have a single regret though."

"And what is that, my laird?"

"I took too long to realize what a special woman ye are. I missed time, Elizabeth, and I have every intention of making up for it." He placed his hands lovingly on her stomach. "There will ne'er be a day that I miss telling ye and our bairn how much ye mean to me. Ye have given me the greatest of gifts, lass. Your love. *Tha gaol agam ort.*"

"I'll always love you too, Ian."

Fall in Love with the Ultimate Bad Boy
from Victoria Roberts's Award-winning
Bad Boys of the Highlands series

X Marks the Scot

Royal Court, England, 1604

"GET UP, YE WHORESON."

Praying he was still in an ale-induced state and only dreaming, Declan MacGregor of Glenorchy slowly opened his eyes as he felt the prick of cold steel against his throat. A man with graying hair at his temples stood a hairbreadth away from the bed, dagger in hand.

A muscle ticked in the man's jaw. "Get up," he said through clenched teeth.

The blonde in the bed next to Declan—what was her name?—gasped and tugged up the blanket to cover her exposed breasts. Her eyes widened in fear.

"Ye defiled my daughter," the stranger growled.

Declan raised his hands in mock surrender. "I assure ye that I didnae." He stole a sideways glance at the woman and silently pleaded for his latest conquest to come to his aid.

"Papa?" The fair-skinned beauty sat up on the bed. "What are ye doing here?"

Glancing at his daughter, the man spoke in clipped tones. "This whoreson had ye and will wed ye."

"Now just a bloody minute. I…"

Whipping his head back around, the enraged father glared at Declan, repositioning the dagger—much *lower*. Feeling the contact of the blade, Declan took a sharp intake of breath while the woman sprang from the bed as though it was afire. Hastily, she grabbed her clothing and started to don her attire.

He silently chuckled, realizing the irony of the moment. What would Ciaran think? Declan had chosen to remain at court to escape his older brother's scrutiny, now only to be thrown deeper into hot water. In fact, it was scalding.

The fair-colored lass rolled her eyes at her father. "Really, Papa, ye must cease your attempts at matchmaking. I donna wish to wed him."

She pulled on her father's dagger-held hand, thankfully removing the blade from the most favorite part of Declan's anatomy. He breathed a sigh of relief when he reached down and felt that his most prized possession was still intact.

What the hell had he gotten himself into? The gods knew he had needs, but if he wasn't more selective of the women he bedded, the fairer sex would surely be the death of him.

He needed to escape.

Declan threw back the blankets, stood, and quickly tossed his trews into the air with his foot. While father and daughter were huddled in deep conversation, he donned his trews, pulled on his tunic, grabbed his boots, and simply walked out—unnoticed and unscathed.

When would he learn that ale always led him into trouble? The last he wanted to think of was Ciaran's constant ramblings about how he was destroying his life, but perhaps there was a string of truth to his brother's admonishments. Not wanting to contemplate that revelation, Declan proceeded out the door for a breath of fresh air.

"MacGregor!" Sir Robert Catesby called, waving him over.

In the fortnight Declan had attended court, he had met Sir Robert Catesby and Thomas Percy several times. Upon his approach, both Englishmen smiled in greeting.

Declan nodded. "Catesby. Percy."

"We head to shoot targets," said Catesby, holding up his bow. "Would you like to join us?"

The corners of Declan's lips lifted into a teasing smile. "The first time I bested ye wasnae enough? Ye are actually coming back for more?"

Catesby slapped him on the shoulder. "Perhaps it was purely luck the first time around, eh?"

"Come with us. I challenge you to a match, and we'll see if you can equal my skill with a bow," said Percy with a sly grin.

Declan refrained from commenting that Percy barely had any skill with a bow. At least the man did not challenge him to swordplay, for Declan knew he would be sorely lacking in that. Praise the saints for small favors.

His brothers had often tried to engage Declan to practice swordplay with the men, but he knew he could never match their prowess. So why even attempt it? Ciaran and Aiden were quite skilled, whereas he was only a third son. Besides, he was interested in more manly pursuits, such as raising things of a personal nature for the lasses. The bow, on the other hand, was another matter entirely. Declan had mastered archery as soon as he was old enough to shoot. He never really practiced it—the bow was something that came naturally to him, a gift from the gods.

A bit of sport was exactly what he needed after this morning's spectacle. Engaging in some healthy competition might do him some good, cleanse his spirit, so to speak.

He nodded in agreement. "If ye are up for the challenge, it would be my pleasure to have ye *attempt* to best me again."

"That's the spirit," said Percy.

The men made their way to the targets. The sun was shining and the winds were relatively calm, a great day for shooting. When they arrived at the area, a handful of men were gathered and the boards were already in place. When Declan turned, he felt like he had been punched in the gut.

Lady Liadain Campbell stood in the distance and brushed an errant curl away from her face. Her hair was the black of a starless night and hung down her back. Her high, exotic cheekbones displayed both delicacy and strength. Her lips were full and rounded over even teeth. The flush on her pale cheeks was like sunset on snow. She looked ethereal in the sunlight. Enchanting—well, that's what he had thought the first time he held his dagger to her throat.

Percy cleared his throat. "What say you,

MacGregor? Let's have some practice shots before we compete."

Declan laughed, reaching for the bow that Percy held. "'Tis fine with me, Percy. Ye need all the practice ye can get." Declan adjusted the arrow and took aim. He studied the board and shot, the whizzing arrow flying out of his fingers. His eyes never left the mark.

Dead center.

"Well done, MacGregor! Come now, Percy. Do not let me down, young chap," said Catesby, handing Percy his bow.

Percy adjusted the arrow. He raised the bow and took aim. His eyes narrowed and the lines on his forehead contracted. At the last moment, his elbow moved and he shot—to the left. Very far to the left.

Catesby shook his head. "Well, clearly not your best shot, man."

Declan stepped forward. "Percy, ye study too much on the board. Think ye are one with the mark and just shoot. Donna hesitate. Try again." Handing Percy another arrow, Declan stepped to the side. Percy raised his arm and Declan readjusted his stance. The arrow soared through the air and landed only a few inches away from the center, but closer than Percy's prior attempt. "Ye breathed. Ye would have done much better had ye nae breathed until the arrow was released."

Percy's eyes widened in amazement and he chuckled. "Thank you, MacGregor. Truly. What a difference that even made. I will try not to breathe next time."

Declan gave Percy a knowing look. "Do ye still wish to challenge me?"

"I never back down from a challenge." Something unspoken clearly passed between Percy and Catesby before they masked their expressions.

Catesby was reaching out to hand Declan the arrows when Declan spotted the swish of a skirt out of the corner of his eye.

The daft woman leisurely walked along the edge of the forest. He stifled a sigh, trying not to let his displeasure show. Quickly making his apologies to Catesby and Percy, Declan followed the lass with purposeful strides. Where did she think she was going without an escort? He had lost count of how many times he'd lectured her about that.

Lady Liadain Campbell—healer, half sister to the late Archibald Campbell, seventh Earl of Argyll—was nothing but a thistle in his arse. He strived to be patient with her—after all, Ciaran had recently slain her brother, the bloody Campbell, the right hand of the king.

When the Campbell had disobeyed King James's orders and abducted members of the MacGregor family, Ciaran had been left with no other alternative. The Campbell chose his fate the moment he touched the MacGregor clan. Declan supported his brother completely in that regard. His nephew's screams of terror still plagued his thoughts. Since Ciaran still nursed a shoulder injury, he'd ordered Declan to attend court on his behalf to explain the circumstances. To Declan's relief, Liadain Campbell had not only affirmed her brother's treachery, but the king exonerated Ciaran.

Now she was a ward of the court, which meant there was no suitable male presence to watch over her.

And with a clan debt to be paid, he could not abandon her to all the courtly vultures. He at least owed her that much. Although he had no problem watching over her from a distance, a very far distance, times like these drove him mad.

Someone had to keep a watchful eye on the wily minx.

He increased his pace. The faster he could get to her, the better. He lost sight of her somewhere in the dense forest. Where did she wander off to now? He finally spotted her, chopping branches with her dagger.

Declan thundered toward her, his temper barely controlled. "What the hell do ye think ye are doing?" he bellowed. "Didnae I tell ye nae to—"

The obstinate woman lifted her chin, meeting his icy gaze straight on. "*Ye* arenae my husband, MacGregor. Ye have nay right to tell me what I can or cannae do!" she spat. She tossed her hair across her shoulders in a gesture of defiance.

He stepped toward her and reached out to clutch her arm.

She held something close to her chest and tugged away from him. "Careful, ye fool. I donna want them broken."

He looked at her puzzled. "What is that? Sticks?" he asked, pointing to her bundle.

The lass responded sharply, "They arenae just any sticks, ye daft man. This is willow bark for healing."

Declan smirked in response. "Willow bark? And they donna have enough for ye at court?"

She brushed past him and increased her gait. "I donna expect ye to understand."

He grudgingly trailed behind her. "I donna *want* to understand. Ye need to cease wandering off by yourself. Do ye hear me?" He quickened his pace to catch up with her.

"Of course I can hear ye. Ye are bellowing at me," she called over her shoulder.

He grabbed her shoulders and spun her around. His eyes narrowed and he studied her with curiosity. Was she completely daft? Did she have no idea of the dangers that could befall a woman without an escort? He remembered a time not long ago when he had sprung out of the brush and startled her. He could have killed her. Did she not learn a lesson?

Apparently not.

She stiffened at his silent challenge, and her emerald eyes were sharp and assessing.

Declan chuckled at her demeanor. "Tell me, healer. What if a man found ye out here alone?" he asked, giving her body a raking gaze. "What would ye do since ye have nay escort?"

Every generous curve of her body bespoke defiance. "I came this far without your assistance and I donna need it now." Turning on her heel, she started walking back without him—again.

Who was he to argue with a stubborn Campbell? She could bloody well walk back on her own.

Still, his conscience hammered away at him. "Wait, healer." His voice softened, losing its steely edge. He ran up beside her and extended his arms. He did not think she would accept his offer and she obviously weighed her response.

Looking down at her bundle, she sighed. "I donna

want the willow bark broken. It needs to be chopped. I donna like it snapped."

Damned twigs.

"Here. I will carry it for ye and promise to be careful."

Reluctantly, she released the bark into his care and they continued to walk silently. Declan was grateful for the quiet because if he heard her sharp tongue again, he might just take her back into the trees and show her what could befall a woman who was caught out here alone.

Acknowledgments

A very special "thank you" goes out to the following people:

To my clan, for bearing with me on deadlines and not following through with their threat to bury their wife and mother out behind the shed because she was making them crazy. *Psst! If I disappear, you know where to look!*

To Mary Grace, always.

To Cass Wright and his dear departed Grammy, Hiley Burnham Wilber, for sharing your secret of how to shame the devil.

To my street team Bad Girls of the Highlands, I love you girls!

To my readers, for your posts, emails, and pictures, and for being so incredibly supportive. Thank you for sharing my love of Scotland.